MARGARET MANCHESTER

The Dress in the Window

VINE HOUSE

For Leslie and Annette Manchester

Acknowledgments

I want to thank my dear husband, Alec Manchester, for his unwavering patience, understanding, and support while I was writing this novel. He has been a sounding board when necessary and provided feedback throughout the process. I could not have completed it without his assistance.

I am very grateful to my team of readers, which comprises my husband, Alec, my father-in-law, Leslie Manchester, my sisters, Linda Brown and Dawn Morgan, and my long-time friend, Jacky Hutchinson, for reading and providing feedback on this book from the first draft to the final copy before publication.

Finally, I would like to thank my readers for buying my books and providing feedback on them, as well as for their kind words and encouragement. It is greatly appreciated.

1

Chapter 1

Tow Law, County Durham
April, 1881

When she heard the back door open, Rose Lawson turned and saw her father, Sam, his face and clothes blackened with coal dust, arriving home after his shift at the mine.

'By! That's a cold wind out there,' he said, rubbing his hands together and holding them in front of the coal fire to warm them. 'But at least it's not raining today.'

'I hope you're hungry,' said Rose, stirring a pan of chicken broth. 'I've made too much again. I'm still not used to cooking for just the three of us.'

'I'll be as fat as butter if you keep feeding me up like this,' said Sam, chuckling as he removed his jacket and cap and washed his hands and face. Sitting at the kitchen table, he asked, 'Where's your mother got to?'

'She'll be back in a minute,' said Rose. 'She's just fetching the washing in.'

Jane Lawson came into the house, her arms full of clothing

that she'd dried on the washing line in the garden, and dumped them all on the table.

'I don't know why I bother! Really, I don't,' said Jane, shaking her head from side to side. 'They're covered in soot. The air's thick with it from that damned ironworks and everybody's chimneys. I never had this problem at Edmundbyers. The air was clean and fresh up there, not like in this filthy place. They could do with another wash, really, but what's the point? They'll just end up mucky again.'

'Sit down, Mother,' said Rose. 'I'll fold the clothes and I'll iron them after we've had our teas.'

'You're a good lass,' said Jane, sitting opposite her husband at the table. 'You'll never guess what's been going on next door. The nerve of that woman!'

'That woman is your Goddaughter,' said Sam.

'Not any more she's not!' said Jane. 'How can she be my Goddaughter when she up and left our church and joined them Catholics?'

'The Catholic folk aren't that different from us,' said Sam. 'I work with some of the lads down the pit and they're good grafters, I'll give them that.'

'Mary, who used to work with me in the bakery, was Irish,' said Rose. 'She was a good laugh and she had a heart of gold. She'd do anything for anyone.'

'You two!' said Jane, 'You're always defending them. Will you let me carry on with what I was telling you?' When she saw that she had the attention of both her husband and daughter, she said, 'That woman next door has taken in two more of them. Two young fellas, by all accounts.'

'If Hannah McKenna is taking in more lodgers,' said Sam, 'it's because she needs the money. Her husband died, leaving her with two little lads to bring up on her own, and she's had no help from you or her family. What else is she supposed to do?'

'It doesn't look good, though, does it?' said Jane, looking from her husband to her daughter. 'Five men living in the same house as a young widow. What will people think? Eh?'

Neither of them replied to Jane's question.

As she folded the laundry, Rose's mind was on her mother. She couldn't understand why she'd turned against the Catholic families in Tow Law—they'd done nothing to her, as far as she was aware. People had come to the town in their droves to fill the jobs at the ironworks and the coal mines in recent years. Many of them were Catholics. Some had come directly from Ireland, but most were of Irish descent, their parents or grandparents having moved to England decades earlier during the Great Hunger in Ireland.

The Catholics kept themselves to themselves. They had their own church and a separate school in the town and even drank in different pubs. Of all the pubs in Tow Law, and there were many, O'Riley's was the liveliest. Whenever Rose had walked past the place, she'd seen crowds of men drinking, heard fiddle music and laughter from inside the building, and everyone appeared to be having a good time.

Occasionally, there were fights outside O'Riley's, planned or otherwise, and her mother objected to that because she hated violence of any kind. But fighting wasn't just a Catholic trait—fights also occurred at other pubs from time to time.

Rose folded the last shirt, added it to the pile on a chair, and then turned her attention back to the stove.

'I'm famished. Is that food ready yet, hinny?' asked her father.

'Aye, it's ready,' said Rose, placing a loaf of crusty bread and a knife in the centre of the table. Then, she filled three bowls with thick, steaming broth.

Sam cut an extra-thick slice from the loaf, dipped it in his bowl, and took a large bite.

'Mmm—that's good!' he said, his mouth still full.

While they ate, Rose remembered that years ago, her eldest sister, Lily, had taken a liking to an Irish boy, and the young couple had gone out for a walk together one Sunday afternoon. When her mother found out about it, she'd almost had a fit. Lily had heard the worst of her mother's acerbic tongue that day, and she'd not been allowed out of the house for a month. By this time, the young lad had found another sweetheart, and Lily was heartbroken. Thankfully, everything had worked out well for Lily in the end. John Patterson, the butcher's son, asked her out shortly afterwards, and they were married within the year. Rose smiled to herself at the memory of their wedding day.

After their meal, Rose cleared the table and washed the dishes. Her father wrapped up well and went to the back garden to dig manure into his vegetable patch, and she watched him from the small kitchen window.

Her mother might not have been happy when the family moved to Tow Law, she thought, but her father had settled in well. From the moment he'd been offered the terraced house when he came to the town for work, he had loved the garden. He spent an hour or so every evening tending it after his tea, whatever the weather, in spring, summer and autumn. There was no point in the winter months because nothing would grow then, with short, dark days, hard overnight frosts and severe snowfalls. After her father had done what needed to be done in his garden, he usually went for a pint at the pub on the corner of the street. He was never late home, and he never drank to excess, unlike many men in the town, and he was always in his bed early because he started work at six in the morning.

Then, Rose ironed the washing her mother had brought in earlier, which was spotted with soot.

Dirty or not, Rose preferred living in the town. From what she remembered of the small village where she'd been born, the family never had quite enough food, and she remembered being hungry at times.

Rose had always worn hand-me-down clothes from her three older sisters. She had rarely worn anything new as she was growing up, and she wondered if that was why she loved new clothes now.

There was little to do in the village and hardly anyone to talk to. Dances and social events had been a rare occurrence. If she'd stayed there, Rose reckoned she would be working as a house servant by now because that was the only job for lasses in the countryside.

The town was a much better place for a young woman. There were many more shops and opportunities. Rose had been delighted to get a job at the bakery on the High Street, and she loved working behind the shop counter, serving the customers, and hearing all their gossip. Many more people lived there— she'd heard a rumour that there were over five thousand after they filled in the census earlier that month—and they had come to the town from all manner of places. As well as the Irish folk, several Scottish families and even a few Welsh lived there. The English incomers came from all corners of the country. Rose loved hearing the customers speaking in different accents when they entered the shop.

'Will you do some quilting with me tonight?' shouted Jane from the front room.

'Aye, I'll go and bring mine down.'

Rose went upstairs and carefully removed the package from a cupboard in her bedroom. It was odd to think of it as her bedroom as it had always been the girls' bedroom, but her sisters no longer lived there. They were all married now and had homes of their own.

Rose looked down at the quilt she held in her arms and hoped she would finish it by the time she was to marry. She sighed softly. She was sure she'd have plenty of time to complete it because she didn't have anyone in mind yet.

She sat by the window in the front room with her mother and sewed the delicate-coloured patches of cloth together, taking advantage of the light from the gas lamp on the street outside. They concentrated so hard on the stitching that little conversation passed between them, and Rose was grateful for that. She loved her mother, but lately, she'd become quite quarrelsome. Rose knew it was because, deep down, her mother was unhappy with her lot. She hadn't been happy since the family moved from Edmondbyers ten years ago, and ever since, she had picked fault with everyone and everything in Tow Law.

Before she went to bed that night, Rose wrapped a shawl around her shoulders and went outside to the netty at the bottom of the garden. When she tried to open the wooden door, she was shocked to find it was fastened shut. Her mother was putting her sewing away inside the house, and her father had already gone to bed. So, who could be using their netty?

She knocked on the door and asked, 'Who's in there?'

'I won't be a minute,' said a man with a soft lilting accent.

Rose didn't recognise the voice. A few seconds later, the door opened, and a tall, dark-haired young man stood before her.

'I'm sorry,' he said. 'There was a queue next door, and I couldn't wait. I've hardly seen anyone using this one, and I didn't think anyone would notice if I hopped over the wall.'

'What a cheek!' said Rose. 'You could have at least had the decency to ask if you could use our netty before you went in.'

'I'm sorry if I've upset you, miss,' said the stranger. 'We seem to have got off on the wrong foot here. I'm Daniel Kelly. I'm lodging with Mrs McKenna next door.'

He held out his hand.

Rose was still annoyed that this lad had used their netty without permission but thought it would be rude not to introduce herself after he had given his name.

'I'm Rose Lawson, and I live here with my parents,' she said begrudgingly, shaking his hand. 'You're lucky it wasn't my mother who caught you out here. She'd have chased you back over that wall with her broom.' Seeing the laughter in his eyes, she said, 'And I'm not joking!'

'Goodnight, Rose,' said Daniel, smiling at her. Then he lithely jumped over the stone wall into the next garden and soon disappeared from sight.

'Goodnight,' she whispered, although she guessed he was too far away to hear her.

'Who are you talking to?' asked her mother, walking down the path to where Rose stood looking into thin air.

'Nobody,' said Rose. 'You can go in first if you want. I don't mind waiting out here. It's a nice night.'

'It's a nice night,' repeated Jane. 'No, it's not. It's freezing out here! I can't believe you haven't been in yet. You've been out here long enough. What have you been doing all this time?'

Jane looked at her daughter suspiciously before darting into the small stone building and closing the door behind her.

Rose thought she heard Daniel chuckle in the garden next door. Was she imagining it, or was he still nearby?

If he'd overheard their conversation just now, he'd know she hadn't been exaggerating about her mother. She thought he'd do well to keep out of Jane Lawson's way.

2

Chapter 2

Tow Law, County Durham
April, 1881

Daniel Kelly climbed up the wooden staircase in Mrs McKenna's house and entered the room he shared with four other Irishmen, including his cousin, Jimmy McNally.

After saying goodnight to Jimmy, Daniel lay down on his bed and recalled the events that had brought him to this windy town on the top of a remote English hill, where the prettiest young lass he'd ever seen just happened to live—and in the house next door. How lucky could he get?

Back in Ireland, his cousin had been his best friend for as long as he could remember. They had done everything together as boys—from helping out on their fathers' neighbouring farms to getting into trouble. Not being a pair of lads to do anything half-heartedly, they had excelled at both.

From a young age, they'd visited Mr O'Dowd's house in the village for boxing lessons. Mr O'Dowd had been one of the best boxers in the country in his younger days and was happy to coach any lad who showed a keen interest and a bit of aptitude out of the goodness of his heart, which was just as well as their parents would never have been able to pay for the lessons.

Daniel had often heard his father complain about the rent rises year after year on their small farm. Then, one day, totally out of the blue, his father said, 'Daniel, I'm very sorry about it, but I can't afford to keep you on here any longer.'

Daniel had worked on his father's farm for next to nothing, just his bed and board and a little pocket money, and didn't initially understand what his father meant by it.

'But I don't take a wage,' he said.

'Aye, that may be as it is,' said his father sadly, 'but you're a grown man now you've turned twenty-one and you're going to have to find your own way in this world.'

Daniel realised that his father's profits from the farm had dwindled so much that he couldn't afford for his eldest son to stay in the family home any longer.

'Your brothers will take on your chores,' said his father by way of explanation as to how he would manage without him.

Daniel stared at his father, his mouth open, shocked at his words. His father was throwing him out of the family home. Despite the hard work he put into the farm every day of the week, he had become a burden to the family. He was just one more mouth to feed.

'Aye, I understand. I won't stay where I'm not wanted,' said Daniel, and then he went to find his cousin.

Daniel and Jimmy discussed the matter at length and considered taking on a bit of land for themselves. They didn't have high aspirations. They were content to share a small farm, the house, and the costs, but when the young men worked out the costs, they were far too high by Daniel's reckoning. He couldn't fathom how they could produce enough crops or raise enough animals to pay the rent money, never mind having any spare to take on wives and raise families in the future.

He'd heard the government were to investigate the problem of excessive rents in Ireland, but he didn't hold out much hope that they would fix it. Had they ever done much for Ireland except to cause trouble?

That was when and why he and Jimmy McNally decided to leave their homes in Galway and go to England.

Moving to England was something they had talked about many times when they were young lads. The thought of leaving behind everybody they knew and everything familiar to them and travelling to a new country had felt adventurous, exciting and brave.

So many people from Ireland did exactly that during the potato famines that had plagued Ireland decades earlier. His mother and father were always telling tales about the people who had left Ireland to start new lives in England and America and the horrors of starvation they had witnessed by staying behind. Luckily, both of his parents had survived the ordeal, which is more than could be said for some of their brothers and sisters, and they'd gone on to get married and have children, or else he would never have been born into this world. He was glad for that, at least.

His mother had shed a few tears and hugged him the morning he left the tiny thatched cottage that housed his parents and eight siblings and the four acres of land surrounding it that had kept them all fed. His father had shaken his hand and wished him all the luck in the world, and there were tears in his old man's eyes, too, when he said it.

Daniel didn't think he needed luck. He was leaving home and

starting a new life, and he was optimistic and confident that everything would work out well. He was young, fit, healthy, and a bloody hard worker—the odds were stacked in his favour as far as he could see.

Jimmy and Daniel walked to the port of Cork, accepting lifts on carts when offered, and there they climbed aboard a ship to Liverpool. Then, they travelled by rail to the north-east of England because they'd heard the best wages in the country were to be had in the coal mines there.

They arrived at Tow Law that morning, found a reasonably priced lodging house, and were offered work at the first pit they visited, which was Inkerman Colliery. They were due to start working there first thing in the morning.

Daniel was excited about his prospects and what his new life might entail. He was eager to find out. He smiled as he turned onto his side and drifted asleep, dreaming of the pretty girl next door.

3

Chapter 3

Tow Law, County Durham
April, 1881

The following day, Rose finished her shift at the bakery and walked along the High Street on her way home from work. The dark clouds moved quickly across the sky, threatening more rain, and she pulled her woollen shawl tighter around her body to keep her warm.

A window display caught her eye as she passed the dress-maker's shop. In the window was a red satin dress with a stunning white lace trim around the neckline and a beautiful full skirt with a bustle, and Rose fell in love with it as soon as she saw it.

She stood at the edge of the road admiring the dress, dream-ing of where she would wear it when she heard someone call her name. Turning around, she saw two young men walking up the other side of the road, one of whom was the lad she'd met outside the netty the night before. How embarrassing!

They crossed over the road, dodging a pony pulling a trap

and several large puddles, and approached her.

'Good afternoon to you,' said Daniel, removing his hat. 'This is my cousin, Jimmy McNally. He's staying at Mrs McKenna's as well, so he's another next-door neighbour of yours.'

'Hello, Jimmy,' said Rose, smiling at the small, lean man standing before her. She thought he looked more like a boy than a man and wondered how old he was.

'Have you come to Tow Law for work?' she asked.

'Aye,' replied Jimmy. 'We started at the Inkerman pit this morning. We've just got back and cleaned up, and now we're having a look around the town until our dinner's ready.'

Rose noticed Daniel looking at the red dress in the shop window.

'Lovely dress,' he said. 'There's no price tag on it. I bet it costs as much as a coal miner earns in a year.'

'Never mind,' said Rose. 'It wouldn't suit you anyway. It's not your colour.'

Briefly, she saw the shock on his face as she turned away and walked home.

Why had she been so rude to him? Daniel Kelly, it seemed, brought out the worst in her. She might say something like that to her sister or a friend in jest but not to a man she hardly knew.

She chided herself for gawping at the dress, too. Daniel had hit a nerve when he'd mentioned the cost. There was no way she could ever afford it, and even if she could, she didn't have anywhere to wear it. It was much too good to wear at home and far too fancy for church. It was a dress for a lady from a grand house to wear for special occasions, such as entertaining dinner guests or attending charity events. It was never meant for the likes of her.

Heavy rain began to fall around her. She lifted her skirt and ran the short distance home, not caring that it was considered unseemly for a nineteen-year-old woman to run in the street.

Later that evening, her father returned from the pub, took off his hat, and stood in front of the fireplace to warm his backside. Steam rose from his damp clothes.

'You'll not believe what I've just seen,' he said to Rose and Jane, who were sat by the window quilting. 'I wouldn't have believed it if I hadn't seen it with my own eyes.'

'What was it?' asked Jane, lowering her sewing and looking at her husband, her interest piqued.

'There was quite a commotion outside of O'Riley's earlier, so me and a few of the fellas went over the road to see what was going on. There was this young lad—he looked no more than fifteen but he claimed he was eighteen—anyway, he squared himself up to Bill Wheatley, and with just one punch, he knocked Bill to the ground.'

'Well, I never!' said Jane. 'How on earth did he manage that? Bill's a huge fella.'

'Apparently, the young lad trained as a boxer in Ireland before he came over here.'

'That sounds about right,' said Jane scornfully. 'They breed them to fight over there. It's no wonder there's so much trouble around here these days. We're surrounded by them.'

'It was Bill's fault,' said Sam. 'He kept teasing the lad 'cos he looked too young to be out drinking. He'll not make that mistake again. Watching them two tonight reminded me of that bible story about David and Goliath—you should never underestimate the underdog because sometimes they might surprise you.'

Smiling to himself, Sam went upstairs to bed.

Rose was glad the rain had stopped by the time she went out to the netty that night. As she walked up the garden path, she heard Daniel's voice from the other side of the wall.

'I just wanted to let you know that I've never worn a dress in my life,' he said, 'and I have no intention of ever doing so, but that red dress would look stunning on you, Rose.'

Rose smiled. She looked into Mrs McKenna's garden but couldn't see Daniel anywhere. 'Where are you?' she asked.

Daniel had been sitting behind the wall, waiting to hear her footsteps. He stood up and leaned against the wall, looking very relaxed, and smiled charmingly at her.

'Here I am!' he said as though she'd conjured him up from thin air.

'I'm sorry about what I said earlier,' she said. 'It was very rude of me. I don't know why I said it.'

'I do,' he said. 'You loved that dress. I could tell by the way you were looking at it. And when I opened my big mouth and mentioned the cost, it ruined your dream of ever wearing it. I'm sorry I stole your dream away from you, Rose.'

Rose looked down at the wet flagstone path. What he had said was right. She had been upset when he'd mentioned the cost of the dress, which was far more than she would ever be able to afford.

'You're forgiven,' she said graciously.

'And so are you,' he replied with a smile.

Jane opened the door and said, 'Is there somebody out there, Rose? I thought I heard voices.'

Rose looked towards the wall, but Daniel had disappeared.

'No, Mother. It's just me.'

'Who were you talking to?' she asked, knitting her eyebrows.

'Just that black cat that sometimes comes into the garden,'

said Rose, and she heard Daniel try to suppress his laughter behind the wall.

'Don't let your father know that damned animal has been about again,' said her mother. 'He can't stand cats doing their business in his vegetable plot. He'll be buying oranges by the dozen and putting the peel out there to keep the bloomin' things away.'

After visiting the netty, Rose returned to the house and went to bed. Lying in the darkness, she wondered what it was about Daniel that raised her interest and, at times, her hackles.

She guessed Daniel was a year or two older than herself. His hair was dark, and his eyes were a vivid shade of blue, and they twinkled when he talked. His voice, with its soft Irish accent, made her want to listen to him for longer each time they met, and she was disappointed every time they parted. She realized that she was attracted to him and sighed loudly.

Daniel was Irish, which meant he would be Catholic, so that was that. Her mother would never stand for it. Nothing more could come of their budding relationship.

4

Chapter 4

Tow Law, County Durham
April, 1881

The following night, as Rose went out into the garden to use the netty at bedtime, she saw Daniel on the other side of the wall, and her heartbeat quickened.

Was he waiting for her again, or was she imagining it? He could just be waiting to use the netty next door.

'Good evening, Rose,' he said, with the soft accent she had grown to love. 'How are you today?'

'Hello, Daniel,' she said. 'I'm fine, thank you. And you?'

'Better for seeing your pretty face,' he said, grinning at her.

She was pleased it was dark, so he couldn't see her blush at his compliment. To hide her embarrassment, she said, 'Aye, well. That's a fine thing to say when it's dark out here. You can hardly make out who I am, never mind what I look like.'

'I've seen you plenty of times to know that you're the most beautiful girl I've ever set eyes on,' he said. He leaned over the wall and surprised her when he kissed her cheek. 'I was hoping to see you tonight,' he said, his eyes twinkling. 'I wondered if you would like to go for a walk with me on Sunday afternoon.'

'I'm sorry, I can't. I have other plans on Sunday,' she said, her voice faltering slightly at the lie. There was no way that her mother would allow her to walk out with Daniel, and there was no way she could explain that to him. She couldn't say her mother hated all Catholics, without exception and with no valid reason. What on earth would he think?

Daniel's smile disappeared.

'I'm sorry to have troubled you,' he said. 'It's just I thought... well, never mind. Good night, Rose.'

Rose felt a sadness descend over her as she watched him return to the lodging house. He must have thought she wasn't interested in him when she turned down his offer to spend time with him at the weekend, but that wasn't true.

She wondered what he'd been about to say when he'd stopped short. 'It's just I thought...you liked me, too?' He would have been correct if that was what he'd been about to say. She liked him and would have loved to spend Sunday afternoon in his company—looking into those beautiful eyes and listening to his voice.

She put her finger on her cheek where his lips had touched her and sat down on the ground with her back to the garden wall. A tear ran down her cheek.

Jane came to the door and shouted, 'Is everything alright, Rose? You've been in there a long time.'

'Yes, Mother,' Rose called back. 'I won't be much longer.'

Rose was serving in the bakery the following afternoon when she saw Daniel and Jimmy walking by the shop window. Daniel stepped back, looked through the glass, and waved at her. She realised he must have seen her out of the corner of his eye as he passed the shop.

The shop door opened, and the two men entered and walked over to the counter.

'Can I help you?' said Rose, smiling at them.

'I hope so,' said Daniel. 'I don't suppose you've changed your mind about Sunday afternoon, have you?'

'I'm sorry, Daniel,' said Rose. 'I can't on Sunday.'

Daniel's face fell. 'You can't blame a man for trying,' he said. 'Well, in that case, we'll take three meat pies—no, make that four, please. Our Jimmy is training for a fight.'

'Was it you who floored Bill Wheatley, Jimmy?' asked Rose, remembering the story her father had told her and her mother.

'Aye, it was,' said Jimmy proudly. 'But he asked for it, mind you.'

'Jimmy might be small,' said Daniel, 'but he's one of the best boxers I've ever seen. He's three years younger than me, and I've not been able to beat him since he turned thirteen.'

'Do you fight as well?' Rose asked Daniel.

'Aye, me and our Jimmy trained together for years,' he said.

Rose was slightly disappointed by his answer. It made little difference to what she thought of him. Perhaps she even admired that he could defend himself if need be, but it was one more reason why her mother would never accept Daniel as her suitor. Not only was he an Irish Catholic, but he was also a trained fighter.

Why had she fallen for this man?

5

Chapter 5

Sunday morning was dry and bright, and a gentle breeze blew through the streets of Tow Law as Rose and her parents walked to the Anglican Church of St. Philip and St. James. They met her sisters and their families there, who all lived in and around the town.

Lily, her eldest sister, stood by her husband, John Patterson, the butcher. He'd taken over his father's business the previous year when his father's eyesight failed. Their two little girls chattered to each other secretively, and their young son clung to his mother's coat. Lily was expecting their fourth child soon.

Violet was the second sister in the family. She held an infant son in her arms and scolded her husband, Jim Ridley, a coal miner, for lifting their elder son onto his shoulders and larking about when they were about to go to church. Rose had never got along with Violet, who was like her mother in nature, constantly complaining and making a fuss about nothing.

Daisy was the closest sister to Rose in age, and they had always been the best of friends. She and her husband, Bobby Young, also a coal miner, were expecting their first child in about four months.

Rose wondered who had decided to name the sisters after flowers, and she guessed it would have been her mother. When they were small, her mother loved taking them on walks around the village of Edmundbyers, pointing out flowers, trees, wild animals, and birds and teaching them their names.

Her mother was a country woman at heart. When the family moved to Tow Law, she stopped taking her daughters out for walks, even though there were plenty of countryside walks on the outskirts of the town. She appeared to lose interest in everything except for her family and home.

Looking around the church, Rose hoped to spot Daniel and Jimmy in the congregation, but they were not there, confirming her fears. If they were not attending the Anglican church service, they must have gone to the Roman Catholic church.

As they left the building, Daisy said, 'Bobby's had a hard week this week. He was daft enough to take on some extra shifts, and he's been working day and night. He can hardly keep his eyes open. No doubt he'll have a nap after dinner.'

Bobby yawned and shook his head.

'I'll be going back to bed after my dinner,' he said.

'Aye, I thought so,' said Daisy. Turning to Rose, she asked, 'Would you like to go for a walk this afternoon?'

'Yes, I'd love to,' said Rose, looking at the blue sky and smiling. 'I'll call round your place after we've eaten.'

After a long chat, the families parted company, and Rose and her parents returned home. Rose changed out of her church clothes and then prepared dinner. Her mother had put the beef in the oven to roast before going to church, so it was ready by the time they returned. Her father carried in some fresh potatoes, carrots and cabbage from his garden, and Rose cleaned, chopped and boiled them. Then, she thickened the meat juices to make a delicious gravy.

The family sat around the table to eat their Sunday dinner, and Rose noticed her mother kept looking at her during the meal.

'What is it?' asked Rose. 'Is there something wrong?

'You tell me,' said her mother. 'You've been very quiet lately.'

'Everything's fine,' said Rose.

'If you say so,' said Jane shrewdly.

Rose felt uncomfortable under her mother's scrutiny. As soon as she finished eating, she asked her father for permission to leave the table, which he granted without looking up from his plate.

Relieved, she went upstairs to fix her hair. Looking in the mirror, she wondered if her mother knew she liked Daniel from next door but dismissed the idea as fanciful. Her mother couldn't possibly read her mind.

Rose left the house and walked to the other side of town, where Daisy and Bobby lived in a small terraced cottage in the middle of a long row. She knocked at the door, and Daisy answered with her finger pressed against her lips.

'Shush! Bobby is asleep,' said Daisy, closing the door gently behind her. 'He should get all the sleep he can now because once this little one joins us,' she placed her hand on her swollen belly, 'he'll not get much.'

'I don't think it works like that,' said Rose, laughing.

They strolled through the town towards Hedleyhope Fell, where they liked to walk because the air was always fresh. They were often lucky enough to spot hares, rabbits, deer, and birds of prey, too—their love of nature had passed down from their mother.

'I know it's only six months since you got married,' said Rose, 'but I've missed you since you left home.'

'Aw! I've missed you an' all,' said Daisy, hugging her younger sister. 'It must be strange for you to live at home with Mother and Father when the rest of us have moved out.'

'Aye, it is,' said Rose sadly. 'Can I ask you something, Daisy? When you started seeing Bobby, do you think Mother knew?'

'She had an inkling that something was going on,' said Daisy. 'She asked me so many times that I ended up telling her all about him. Luckily for me, she liked Bobby's family and was all for us getting married. Why do you ask?'

Rose wondered if she should confide in her sister. They had been very close when they lived together, but she had hardly seen Daisy since she'd moved into her new home.

'You have a fancy man, don't you?' asked Daisy, beaming at her sister.

Rose felt her cheeks flush. She hated her blonde hair and pale skin; she could never keep a secret or tell a lie without her face giving her away.

'Who is he?' asked Daisy.

'Nobody,' said Rose. Then relenting, she added, 'It's just a lad who moved in next door.'

'Have you spoken with him?' asked Daisy.

'Yes, a few times.'

'He must be interested in you,' she said. 'He wouldn't be

spending time with you if he wasn't interested.'

Rose wondered at Daisy's words. Daniel had crossed the street to introduce his cousin and waited in the garden several times to speak with her on an evening. He had even kissed her cheek and asked her out. She supposed he must be interested in her and smiled wistfully.

When the last houses were behind them, and the wild fell spread out in front, Rose suddenly felt free. She wanted to let down her hair so the wind could blow through it, take off her boots and run through the grass like the hares.

She wondered if her sister felt the same way. Rose looked across at Daisy and thought that if she did, she didn't give any hint of it. She looked every bit the respectable young woman out for an afternoon stroll.

Further along the fell, Rose spotted two men up ahead, walking towards them, and she felt heat rise in her cheeks once more. She was sure it was Daniel and Jimmy, and their paths would cross in just a few minutes. Would they stop and speak to her? If they did, she would have to introduce them to Daisy—just after she'd confessed to liking the lad next door. She wished she had never mentioned him to her sister.

Her throat felt dry, and she cleared it before the men reached them.

'Hello, Rose,' said Daniel, stopping beside them. 'It's a beautiful day for a walk, isn't it?'

'Yes, it's lovely,' she replied. 'Daniel, this is my sister, Daisy...Mrs Daisy Young. Daisy, this is Daniel Kelly and his cousin Jimmy McNally. They live next door to us.'

'It's very nice to meet you, Mrs Young,' said Daniel, bowing his head slightly.

'And you too, Mr Kelly,' said Daisy, grinning at him.

Jimmy held out his hand to Daisy, and she shook it, and then the men continued on their way back towards the town.

'By! That little fella has a strong grip,' said Daisy, stretching her gloved hand.

'He's a boxer,' said Rose.

'You'd never think it looking at him,' said Daisy. 'I guess it was the other one you were talking about?'

'Aye, that was him,' said Rose.

'I could tell by the way he looked at you,' said Daisy. 'He's a handsome fella, but he's Irish. Mother would never allow it. Do you remember what she was like when our Lily went out with Michael Byrne that day?'

'I remember it well,' said Rose sadly.

Every time Rose saw Daniel, she liked him more and more. He was good-looking, gentle and easy-going, and his voice made her feel weak at the knees. Perhaps it was knowing that she could never have him that made her feel that way about him, like her longing for the dress in the window; she knew she could never have that, either.

'I'm sorry, Rose,' said Daisy. 'I didn't mean to upset you.'

'I know,' said Rose. 'It's just that this is the first time I've felt like this about anyone.'

Taking Rose's arm, Daisy pulled her sister to a stop.

'Take a good look around you, Rose. This town is full of fellas who have come here for work. Some of them are single, and some of them aren't Catholic. There's bound to be one amongst them who's right for you.'

'Thank you, Daisy,' said Rose, hoping her sister was right, but she doubted she'd like any of them as much as she liked Daniel.

The sisters hugged, and they turned around to walk home.

6

Chapter 6

Tow Law, County Durham
May, 1881

Rose and her mother played Whist until her father returned from having his pint at the pub on the corner of the street.

'Good evening, ladies,' he said when he entered the house. He stood beside the fireplace with his elbow resting on the mantelshelf. 'Do you remember that young fella I was telling you about? The one who knocked Bill Wheatley down the other night.'

'Aye,' said Jane. 'What's he been up to now?'

'Nothing yet,' said Bill, raising his eyebrows. 'But he's going to fight on Saturday night at O'Riley's. He's up against a fella from Crook. After what I saw that other night, I'll be going over to watch him, and I'm tempted to put some money on him to win.'

'What a waste of good money!' said Jane, almost spitting out the words. 'I'm sure you could find something better to spend it on.'

'I'll double my money, that's what I'll do,' said Sam. 'Then, I'll have twice as much to spend on something better. Eh? Did you know the boxer fella lives next door?'

'No, but it doesn't surprise me,' said Jane bitterly. 'Half of Ireland lives next door.'

'I've seen him at the bakery,' said Rose. 'He seems like a canny lad.'

'Don't you be getting any ideas about him,' said her mother.

Rose rolled her eyes, which made her mother scowl.

She knew she wouldn't be allowed to watch the fight, so she didn't bother to ask. She also knew that if Jimmy were there, Daniel would be, too, but as much as she wanted to see him again, she had to put all thoughts of him to the back of her mind. Her heart sank.

Rose cleared away the playing cards, and Jane went outside to use the netty first that night. Her mother had only been outside briefly when Rose heard her shouting. She ran to the door, opened it and ran up the path to where her mother stood gazing into the next garden, clearly upset and shaken.

'What's wrong?' asked Rose, putting her hand on her mother's arm.

'What's wrong!' said Jane. 'I'll tell you what's wrong. There was a man in that garden talking to me as if he...as if he was my...my lover. Speaking like that to a woman of my age. I told him if he ever spoke to me like that again, I'd set the polis on him. The dirty Irish bugger.'

'Mother!' said Rose, taking a step back. 'You can't say that.'

'Oh, yes, I can,' she said. 'And I will...because that's what he is. Just wait until your father hears about this.'

Jane returned to the house to tell her husband about her encounter with an Irishman.

After Rose closed the netty door and headed back towards the house, she heard footsteps in the garden next door.

'Is that you, Rose?' a familiar voice asked.

'Aye, it is,' she whispered.

'Thank God for that,' said Daniel, leaning against the wall and sighing dramatically. 'You weren't kidding about your mother, were you? I thought she was going to come over here and beat me to death.'

'What on earth did you say to her?' asked Rose.

'I asked her what a pretty woman like her was doing outside alone at night and that it might give a fella ideas.' He wriggled his eyebrows suggestively, and his eyes twinkled. 'I must say in my defence that I thought she was you.'

Rose chuckled. As well as all the other qualities that she admired in him, Daniel was funny.

He leapt over the wall and stood close to her, lowering his face toward hers. She tilted her head upwards and felt his lips gently touch hers.

'Good night, sweetheart,' he whispered in her ear.

'Goodnight, Daniel.'

He jumped over the wall, smiled at her, and watched her return to her house.

Rose had trouble sleeping that night. As she tossed and turned in bed, she wondered why Daniel had been so charming and why he had kissed her goodnight and called her sweetheart.

When she'd turned down his offer of a walk, he had thought she wasn't interested in him. So, what had changed?

Then, it struck her. Daniel had seen her walking with Daisy on Sunday afternoon. He must have thought she had arranged the walk before she'd received his invitation to spend Sunday with him, and she'd declined his offer. Then, her rejection would not be of him but of that time.

Now, it seemed Daniel believed she still liked him or perhaps more than liked him.

7

Chapter 7

Tow Law, County Durham
May, 1881

Rose worked in the bakery on Saturday, serving customers at the counter. There was a lot of talk about the boxing match which would take place that evening between Jimmy and a well-known fighter from Crook.

Late in the afternoon, Jimmy and Daniel came into the shop and received a round of applause from the other customers, which surprised Rose. Jimmy hadn't been in the town for very long, and already, the townsfolk regarded him as their hero. She imagined that the story of Jimmy flooring Bill Wheatley would have travelled widely—it was such an unlikely tale—and would have earned Jimmy a lot of support.

When the men reached the front of the queue, Daniel took off his cap and asked, 'Have you heard that our Jimmy's fighting tonight?'

'I've hardly heard about anything else,' said Rose. 'Everybody's talking about it.'

'Will you come and watch?' asked Jimmy.

'I'd love to, Jimmy,' said Rose, 'but I'm afraid my mother wouldn't allow it.'

She saw the disappointment on Daniel's face.

'My father will be there, though,' she said. 'He told me he was going to put some money on you to win.'

'Thanks! That's good of him,' said Jimmy. 'It's a shame you can't come though. Our Daniel was hoping you'd be there.'

Daniel nudged his cousin with his elbow, and Jimmy laughed loudly.

'He's right,' said Daniel, nodding his head. 'I did hope to see you later.'

Rose blushed thinking about the nights they'd met in the garden and the gentle kiss they'd shared.

'I'll see what I can do,' she said.

He grinned at her, his eyes twinkling, before ordering more meat pies for Jimmy and leaving the shop.

Why had she said that and raised Daniel's hopes? That was an easy question to answer. It was because she wanted to see him, too. But how could she get out of the house without her mother knowing? She hardly took her eyes off her, and her hearing was uncanny. But Rose knew that somehow she must try.

When her father returned from work that evening, Rose ate dinner with her parents.

'The men at work were talking about nothing but the fight tonight,' said Sam. 'There's going to a huge crowd outside O'Riley's later. Me and Joe are going over there early to get a good spot to watch from.'

'Men and fighting,' said Jane, shaking her head. 'I don't know why they do it. This is supposed to be a civilised world that we live in.'

'It's a bit of fun, Jane,' said her husband. 'God knows, we need some fun around here. What life would we have if we spent six days a week working down the pit and the other one at church? We need something to look forward to—like a good football match or a fight.'

'But grown men punching each other,' said Jane, 'drawing blood, knocking each other out, and everyone standing around enjoying the spectacle, it's barbaric—like bear baiting and cock fighting and fox hunting. I don't see what there is to enjoy in any of it—watching men and animals suffer unnecessarily.'

Sam looked at his wife and shook his head sadly.

Sport was a subject that her parents would never agree on. Rose knew her father enjoyed all those things, as most men did, and he couldn't understand his wife's point of view. Her mother was against all those things, but then again, her mother didn't seem to enjoy anything any more.

Her father drained his mug of tea, rose from the table, and left the house.

'Are you going to bring your quilt down tonight?' asked Jane.

'Not tonight,' said Rose. 'I'm feeling tired, I think I might have an early night.'

'Are you poorly?' her mother asked, leaning over the table to touch her brow. 'You don't have a temperature.'

'No, I'm just tired. It was busy at work today.'

'Alright, love,' said Jane. 'If you're going to bed, I think I'll pop round to see Betty. She keeps inviting me over there to play cards with her, and she'll likely be on her own tonight. No doubt her men will be at that fight an' all.'

Rose struggled to suppress a smile. If her mother was going out, she could sneak out of the house without her knowing.

'That's a good idea,' said Rose, trying not to sound too enthusiastic and raise her mother's suspicions. 'I'm sure Betty will enjoy a bit of company.'

As she climbed the stairs, Rose frowned. Her father would be at the fight. How could she go to O'Riley's and not be seen by him?

She lay on her bed until she heard her mother close the front door, and then she got up and searched for a blanket. She found an old, grey one in the linen press. In her room, she placed it over her head, tucked in her hair and wrapped it around her body. She looked in the mirror and hardly recognised herself. She looked like a poor woman, down on her luck, who didn't have a decent coat or shawl to wear. She was sure her father wouldn't notice her in the crowd. People like that were invisible.

Rose crept down the stairs, checked to ensure her mother had gone out, and then left by the front door. She walked down the street with her head lowered so her face couldn't be seen and crossed the road to O'Riley's pub. There was already a good number of people there. She spotted her father with his friends and turned her face away. She couldn't see Daniel or Jimmy anywhere, so she waited at the back of the crowd, watching the bookies take bets on the men.

It wasn't long before Jimmy came out of the pub to a massive round of applause and cheers from the crowd. Daniel walked proudly by his side. A large man followed them. His opponent from Crook, Rose guessed. The reaction to him was mixed. Some men cheered, and others booed.

Already, the atmosphere was tense.

The fight was about to start. Daniel said something to Jimmy and then moved to the edge of the crowd.

Rose pushed past a few people to reach him and touched his arm. He looked around briefly but didn't acknowledge her. He hadn't recognised her in her disguise. She giggled and touched his arm again, leaving her hand there this time.

When he turned to her, it took him a second to figure out who she was, and then he laughed.

'Thanks for coming,' he said. 'What did you do to your mother? Give her a sleeping draught?'

'No! Of course not,' said Rose. 'She went out to visit a friend.'

'Well, I'm glad you've come.'

The landlord, Mr O'Riley, introduced the two fighters to the crowd.

Daniel put his arm around Rose's shoulder and gently pulled her towards him.

The two boxers stood facing each other, their fists raised, their bare knuckles gleaming in the lamplight. Rose hadn't noticed how large Jimmy's hands were before. They looked out of proportion to his lean body.

Jimmy moved lightly on his feet and danced around his opponent, throwing a few half-hearted punches in his direction.

The larger man turned on the spot to face Jimmy, never letting him out of sight. His fist moved towards Jimmy's chin, but Jimmy dodged it and resumed his dance.

Then, Jimmy's fist moved like a lightning strike and caught the large man's cheek. Jimmy had moved so quickly that his opponent hadn't expected the hit. The man stepped back with a look of surprise but quickly righted himself. There was a small cut on his cheek, and blood trickled down his face. Before then, the man appeared composed, but now he looked angry as he turned to face Jimmy again.

'Come on, Jimmy!' shouted Daniel. 'Finish him off!'

Jimmy continued to move around his opponent, taunting him to throw a punch. When the man's fist moved towards Jimmy's head, Jimmy lunged to the side and avoided it with ease, and before the man had time to compose himself, Jimmy lashed out, his knuckles connecting with the man's jaw, and the man from Crook fell heavily to the ground.

The crowd roared with delight, whistling, clapping and cheering for Jimmy. Their champion had won!

Daniel drew Rose into his arms and kissed her lips. She had no idea that a kiss could make her feel so good. Her knees felt weak, and she was pleased that Daniel was holding her; otherwise, she might have fallen to the ground. When he released her, they smiled lovingly at one another.

'I should go,' said Rose. 'I need to get home before my parents get back.'

'Thanks for coming,' said Daniel. 'It was lovely to see you without a wall between us.'

Reluctantly, Rose turned away from him and rushed up the street towards her house. As she approached, she saw a light in the front room window. Someone must be home already. Her heart thumped loudly in her chest. Panicking, she rushed to the end of the row of terraced houses, ran around the back, and climbed over the wall into their garden. She opened and closed the netty door, removed the blanket from her shoulders, casually draped it over her arm, and went into the house by the back door.

'Where have you been?' shouted her mother.

'To the netty,' said Rose.

'Oh, no, you haven't,' said Jane. 'Betty wasn't in so I came straight home. With you not feeling well, I went to your room to see how you were, but your bed was empty. I checked the

36

netty an' all and you weren't there either. Now, are you going to tell me the truth, young lady? Where have you been?'

Her mother had caught Rose red-handed. Sweat beaded on her brow, and she wiped her clammy hands on the blanket.

'I went to watch the fight,' she said boldly. 'I didn't tell you because I knew you wouldn't approve.'

'You what?' said her mother. 'A boxing match is no place for a young woman, Rose. How could you? Did you go on your own?'

'Yes,' said Rose. 'But I knew I'd be safe because Father said he was going to be there.'

'Did he know about this?' asked her mother, raising her eyebrows.

'No, I didn't tell him I was going and I don't think he saw me.'

Rose hung her head in shame.

'I can't believe that you have done something so deceitful,' said her mother. 'We brought you up better than that. After the service tomorrow morning, I want you to tell Reverend Hardy what you've done and listen to what he has to say, and I'm sure he'll have a lot to say to a wayward young woman like you. He might just be a young man, but he's wise for his years is Reverend Hardy.'

Jane went upstairs without wishing her daughter good night. Rose couldn't remember her mother ever doing that before, which made her realise how upset she must be.

What would her mother have been like if she'd known she'd gone there to meet Daniel and that she'd wantonly allowed him to kiss her in front of a crowd? She knew many people who had been there that evening and desperately hoped that none of them had recognised her.

Rose felt terrible for upsetting her mother.

Daniel had tempted her to go to the fight that night. She wouldn't have been interested in going if he hadn't been there. Maybe he was a bad influence, and perhaps her mother was right about the Irish and the Catholics. They did seem to bring trouble with them.

Rose had hardly ever been in trouble before. As the youngest girl in the family, her older sisters had taken the blame for many of the things she'd done as a child, and she suspected her parents were more lenient with her because she was the baby of the family.

She recalled Daisy's words about finding another man—a more suitable man—and she vowed to begin her search the very next day.

There had to be someone out there who would be suitable for her and of whom her parents would approve. All she needed was a good Protestant man with an income large enough to support her. A handsome one with sparking blue eyes who could make her laugh would be a bonus.

Perhaps she could narrow her search by checking out the men who went to the church alone. They were likely to be single, and she could be confident they weren't Catholic.

8

Chapter 8

Tow Law, County Durham
May, 1881

On Sunday morning, Rose paid more attention to her hair and attire than usual. She wanted to look her best for the church service in case she found the single man she sought.

Rose and her parents arrived early, as usual, and chatted with her sisters and their families in the cool morning sun on the lane outside the church. She paid little attention to the multiple conversations taking place, being too busy watching for men arriving without a wife and children alongside them. She watched a few wander into the church and ruled them out one by one for various reasons. Was she being too picky?

As Rose and her family began to move toward the church gates, a horse and rider came into view. The horse was a tall, elegant chestnut, and sitting astride was a well-dressed man with dark brown hair and a neatly trimmed beard. He looked like a gentleman.

'Who's that?' Rose asked her father.

'Dunno,' said Sam. 'I haven't seen him before.'

She followed her family into the church, and aware that the gentleman was behind her, she turned around and smiled at him. She was surprised when he returned her smile and tipped his hat at her. She noticed that his eyes were a bluish-grey colour and quite pleasant to look at, but they didn't twinkle the way Daniel's did.

During the service, her eyes were drawn to the man several times. She guessed he would be in his mid to late twenties— quite a few years older than herself. His face was rather ordinary. He wasn't what she would call handsome, but he was far from ugly. She admired his tailored clothes and the beautiful horse he had ridden and wondered who he was and about his lifestyle. How very different it must be from her own, she thought.

She imagined he would live in a large house with a house-keeper, a cook and maids, and he'd have a beautiful flower garden outside with a gardener to tend it. As he had a horse, he must also have stables and presumably a stable lad to care for it. In her mind, she built up an idyllic picture of the place where he lived and saw herself entering that scene with him.

If she were his wife in that beautiful house, she would wear the red satin dress at home, maybe for a special dinner or to entertain guests.

The more she thought about it, the more she liked the idea of moving up in the world by marrying a man of means and, thereby, having an easier life.

Could she, the daughter of a humble coal miner, marry a man like him?

Rose thought about her three sisters. Lily lived in a small apartment above the butcher's shop and the others in tiny, rented houses in crowded areas of the town. They didn't want for much. Their husbands' wages were enough to feed and clothe their families, but they spent their days washing, cooking, cleaning and caring for children. They always seemed to be pregnant or nursing an infant. Was that the life she wanted for herself?

Sadly, she thought about Daniel. That would be the life she could expect if she married him, and not only that, she would be shunned by her family for marrying a Catholic, like Hannah McKenna from next door had been.

When the service ended, Rose decided she would try her best to attract this man's attention. He was everything she was looking for in a potential husband, and she thought she would never know if there was a future for them together if she didn't at least try.

Rose stood up and turned towards the door when she felt a firm hand on her shoulder.

'Have you forgotten what I said last night, young lady?' asked her mother. 'You'll wait until Reverend Hardy's finished and then you'll tell him what you did.'

Rose sat back down in the pew and hung her head in shame. She felt like a young child being scolded for misbehaving. She was nineteen years old and shouldn't have to creep around behind her mother's back or explain herself to the vicar, but to keep the peace, she waited until everyone had left the church, including her parents, and approached Reverend Hardy.

'Miss Lawson,' he said. 'Is there something troubling you?'

'I'm sorry to bother you, Reverend,' said Rose. 'My mother said I should come and see you.'

'Oh! Well, in that case, we'd better sit down.' He led the way to the front pew, and they sat side by side. Turning to her, he said, 'So, what appears to be the problem?'

'My mother!' said Rose.

She thought she saw a slight smile on the vicar's lips.

'I'm sorry,' she said. 'I know I should be grateful for everything she's done for me. It's just sometimes she's so unreasonable.'

'Is it unreasonable for a mother to worry about her daughter sneaking out alone at night?' asked Reverend Hardy. 'Or for her to be concerned about who her daughter is associating with?'

'You know?' asked Rose, the heat rising in her cheeks.

'Yes, I saw you outside O'Riley's last night,' he said with a rueful smile. 'At your age, I know you want more freedom, and you want to see young men, but you must understand, as difficult as you think your mother is being, she's only concerned for your safety—and perhaps your honour.'

Rose blushed even more at his words.

'The answer is to be honest with her, Rose,' he said. 'Tell her when you're going out, tell her who you're going out with, and tell her when you'll be home. If you can't do that, ask yourself why. If your mother doesn't approve of what you're doing, then perhaps you shouldn't be doing it.'

'Thank you, Reverend,' said Rose sincerely, regretful that she had worried her mother.

That night, when Rose went out into the garden to use the netty, Daniel was waiting for her.

'Hello, Rose,' he said in his lovely lilting accent. 'That kiss last night—'

'That kiss last night should never have happened,' said Rose.

'What do you mean it should never have happened?' asked

Daniel. 'I loved it, and you loved it, too. I won't believe you if you say you didn't.'

Rose looked away. She couldn't deny that she had enjoyed kissing him.

Daniel hopped over the wall and whispered, 'What's with the change of heart, Rose? Did you get into bother last night?'

'Aye, my mother got home before me.'

'I'm sorry,' he said, hugging her. Rather than releasing her from his hold, his lips found hers, and he kissed her tenderly— and she returned his kiss.

'No matter what you tell me, Rose,' he said, 'I know how you feel about me. Your body gives you away.'

Rose knew he was right. Not only had she kissed him back, but her body was pressed tightly up against his; he held her so close that she could feel his breath on her face.

'I love you, Rose Lawson,' he whispered, 'and I think you love me.'

He gradually released his hold and moved away slowly, his eyes looking lovingly into hers.

Rose was left standing by the wall, shocked by his words.

Daniel loved her. Did she love him, too?

9

Chapter 9

The Lawsons sat around the table for their evening meal. Rose was proud of the special roast chicken dinner she had prepared for her father's birthday. They only had roast chicken on his birthday and at Christmas.

Sam carved the meat and placed it on their plates with the potatoes and vegetables Rose had already served. They passed a gravy boat around the table and poured it liberally over the food.

'It smells delicious,' said her father. 'Thank you.'

'You're welcome,' she said. 'And happy birthday!'

'We should have a glass of sherry to celebrate,' said Jane. 'I don't mind a glass of sherry.'

She went to the sideboard and took out a bottle and three small glasses, which she filled and brought to the table.

'Thanks, love,' said Sam, taking a sip. 'Now, Rose, that fella you asked about at church yesterday, he started work at our pit this morning.'

Rose was disappointed he was a coal miner when she'd been convinced he was a gentleman. 'He didn't look like a miner,' she said.

'He's not a miner, hinny. He's the new manager of Black Prince Colliery,' said Sam, stabbing a roast potato with his fork.

'The manager!' said Rose. 'What's he called?'

'Mr William Ashworth,' said her father. 'He's come here all the way from Scotland.'

'Nothing wrong with the Scots,' said Jane, who had already finished her glass of sherry. 'They're fine people, the Scots.'

Rose was in a quandary. For most of the day, she had been thinking about Daniel after his declaration of love the previous night, and she'd come to realise that she did love him, too. If only he weren't Irish and Catholic and a boxer, she would look no further.

But he was.

At church, Rose had selected this man, William Ashworth, as a potential suitor. She was sure that her parents would approve of him. As a mine manager, he held a high position in the town and earned a good salary. He was Scottish—apparently, her mother liked the Scots—and he attended their church. How could they not approve of him?

As Rose couldn't court the man her heart desired, she concluded she would have to settle for the one her head said would be a good match. But was a mine manager too far out of her reach?

Around noon on Tuesday, Mr Ashworth entered the bakery, and Rose smiled as he approached the counter.

'Good morning, or is it afternoon now?' he asked in a broad Scottish accent. He looked at his silver pocket watch for confirmation and said, 'Good afternoon, miss.'

'Good afternoon, Mr Ashworth,' she replied, 'What can I get you?'

He looked a little taken aback when she called him by name.

'It's a small town, sir,' she explained. 'Everybody knows everybody around here.'

'You're the lady from the kirk, aren't you?' he asked.

'The kirk?' she asked.

'The church,' he clarified.

'Ah! Yes, I am,' she said. 'I saw you on Sunday.'

'Aye, I thought so,' he said. 'May I have a minced beef pie and a fruit cake, please?'

As Rose wrapped the items in paper, William took a leather money bag from his pocket and paid for them. He then tipped his hat and smiled at her before leaving the shop.

Fruit cakes were among the more expensive items in the shop, and Rose thought he must live more extravagantly than most people she knew, who only had fruit cakes at Christmas, weddings and funerals.

Once again, Rose dreamed about a different way of life, where she wouldn't have to work in a bakery or do housework, washing and cooking. She would have servants to do all that for her, and she could afford the red satin dress and wear it whenever she wanted.

Later that night, Daniel was waiting for Rose when she went out into the garden at bedtime.

'Hello, Rose,' he said. 'I've been waiting all day to see your beautiful face.'

He jumped over the wall, stood before her, and looked deeply into her eyes. Her heart beat rapidly. His love for her was apparent in the way he looked at her, in the way he touched her, and in the way he kissed her.

Rose didn't know what to say to him, but the more she saw of him, the more she knew she wanted to be with him, and the harder it would be for them to part when they must.

Could she say I love you, Daniel, but we can't be together because of where you were born and baptised? That was the truth, but it was a hard truth, and there was nothing he could do to change it.

'What is it, Rose?' he asked. 'What's troubling you?'

'I really don't know how to say this, Daniel,' she said, 'but we can't be together. Not ever.'

He looked puzzled for a second, and then the reason dawned on him.

'Ah! I see,' he said. 'Aye, I know things will be difficult with you being a Protestant and me being a Catholic, but that doesn't prevent us from loving each other, or from getting married if we want to. Lots of couples do.'

'But you don't understand. My mother would never speak to me again if I married you, and she'd make sure my father and sisters didn't either. You have no idea what she's like.'

'Oh, I think I do,' said Daniel. 'I heard what she called me the other night. What was it? A dirty Irish bugger?'

'You heard that?' said Rose, her eyes wide. 'I'm so sorry, Daniel.'

'It's alright, Rose. I know that's not what you think of me.' A dreamy look came over his face, and he said, 'I wish I could take you away from here—away from all the prejudice and hatred. We could live on a farm on a hilltop, miles from anywhere, miles from everyone, and we could stay there, just the two of us, happily ever after.'

Rose felt tears pricking the back of her eyes. What a lovely romantic image he'd painted, but how impractical, she thought. He was a dreamer.

'That sounds idyllic,' she said sadly, shaking her head, 'but it can't happen.'

'What are you saying?' asked Daniel, his voice breaking. 'Are you giving up on us?'

Rose nodded. 'I'm so sorry, Daniel. There's no way it can work. We might as well stop seeing each other right now.'

Daniel sniffed loudly and wiped his eyes with his sleeve.

'Is that final?' he asked. 'You won't change your mind?'

'Yes, it's final,' she nodded, knowing that it was not what she wanted, but it was what she must say to him.

'Remember this,' he said, leaning forward and whispering softly in her ear, 'No matter what, Rose, I will always love you.'

Daniel kissed her cheek and climbed over the wall, leaving her alone. She pulled her shawl around her and walked back to the house, determined not to let the tears fall before she reached the privacy of her bedroom.

10

Chapter 10

Tow Law, County Durham
May, 1881

The following day promised to be dry and sunny, but a cool wind blew along the High Street as Rose walked to work. She saw a smart-looking horse in the distance and thought it might be Mr Ashworth's, so she deliberately slowed her step so the horse and rider would pass her before she reached the bakery.

As he approached, Rose saw that it was Mr Ashworth, and presumed he would be on his way to work at this time in the morning. When he saw Rose smiling coyly at him, he slowed his horse from a trot to a walk and raised his hat in greeting.

Rose beamed back at him. She couldn't believe he had slowed to acknowledge her, a mere miner's daughter. Thrilled by his attention, she didn't stop smiling all day.

Just before the bakery closed that afternoon, Mr Ashworth entered the shop.

'Hello again,' he said.

'Good afternoon,' said Rose, 'What would you like today, Mr

Ashworth?'

'I'd like to know your name, young lady,' he said with a lopsided smile, which was quite endearing. 'I didn't think to ask it yesterday.'

'Rose Lawson,' she replied, blushing slightly at his interest in her.

'Rose—that's a good name,' he said. 'It suits you.'

Smiling at her, he winked before turning away and walking out of the shop.

Rose wondered if he had come into the shop to ask her name or had forgotten to buy whatever he intended. If it was only to ask her name, then her plan to be noticed by him must be working, she thought.

Rose was still thinking about the encounter when eating dinner with her parents that evening.

'What do you think of your new boss?' she asked her father.

'I've not seen a lot of him, to be honest,' said Sam. 'He works in the office most of the day, and I'm underground, but from what I've heard, he seems to be a firm but fair sort of man.'

'He's been in the bakery a couple of times,' said Rose. 'He seems nice.'

'Aye, he would buy his food at the bakery. He's not as lucky as me. He hasn't got a wife or daughter to cook for him,' said her father, taking a bite of the jam-filled sponge cake Rose had made and licking the crumbs from his lips. 'This is lovely, Rose. The fella doesn't know what he's missing out on. He should find himself a wife that can cook and bake like you.'

Rose smiled at the compliment. She hoped William Ashworth would find himself a wife and that the wife would be her.

When Rose went to the garden that night, she expected to

see Daniel, but he wasn't there. She was disappointed. Even though she had ended their romance the previous evening, she had still expected him to be there for her.

She waited outside the netty for as long as she dared but gave up after five minutes or so and went back indoors, wondering if perhaps this time Daniel had finally taken notice of what she'd said, even though he'd never stopped pursuing her before.

Lying in bed that night, Rose felt sad and lonely, with thoughts of Daniel foremost in her mind. She remembered that he'd said no matter what she told him, he knew how she felt about him and that he would always love her, or words to that effect. She reasoned that what he'd said was meaningless, or he would have been there for her.

There may be a perfectly rational reason for his absence. It was possible that Daniel hadn't been there because he'd gone out with Jimmy to a fight or for a drink.

Rose hoped she would see him the following night. She was already missing his sparkling blue eyes, soft accent and loving kisses, and it had only been twenty-four hours since she'd last seen him.

Where was he? What was he doing? Was he missing her as much as she missed him?

She desperately hoped he wasn't out searching for another lass; she would hate to see him with another woman on his arm.

The following day, Hannah McKenna, Rose's next-door neighbour, came into the shop and asked for a large meat pie and three fruit scones. Despite her mother's strong feelings for Hannah McKenna, Rose had always found her to be pleasant, and whenever she came into the bakery, Rose spoke to her as she would any other customer. She had no grievance with the woman.

As Rose put together her order, Hannah said, 'I've only got three lodgers staying tonight. It hardly seemed worth baking for just three of them.'

'What happened to the others?' asked Rose, fearing it might be Daniel and Jimmy who had moved out.

'I don't know,' Hannah shrugged. 'They seemed settled here. Then, out of the blue, they announced they'd gone and got jobs over at Evenwood Colliery. The two of them left first thing this morning.'

'Is it Daniel and Jimmy who have gone?' Rose asked. She felt awkward asking the question, but she needed to know.

'Aye, it was them two,' said Hannah. 'It's a shame 'cos they were no bother, unlike some of the boarders I've taken in.' She picked up her baked goods and said, 'Thank you, Rose.'

After Hannah left the shop, Rose sighed. Daniel really had taken notice of her words, hadn't he? Evenwood was near Bishop Auckland, about ten miles away. She was hardly likely to bump into him ever again. She felt desolate, yet shouldn't she have expected him to leave after what she'd said to him? How could they have continued to see each other daily and not be together when they loved each other? It would have been torture for them both.

Rose could not get Daniel out of her mind in bed that night. She never thought he'd leave the town and was annoyed at herself for forcing him to go. She missed him so much.

Eventually, her disappointment at his leaving turned to anger, and she convinced herself that Daniel had deserted her. He was out of the picture for good, so she had to move on.

Rose vowed to concentrate all her efforts on Mr William Ashworth, yet she still cried herself to sleep.

11

Chapter 11

Tow Law, County Durham
May, 1881

As the extended Lawson family had their usual meeting on Sunday morning, Mr Ashworth rode by, inclining his head in Rose's direction. Then he dismounted and tethered his horse before walking towards the church gates, passing close by the family.

'Good morning, Rose. It looks like it's going to be a beautiful day,' said Mr Ashworth, lifting his hat, before continuing up the path to the church.

Rose saw the shocked look on her parents' faces and blushed furiously.

'By heavens!' said her father. 'The boss man speaking to my daughter—and calling her by her Christian name. What's the world coming to? Eh?' He grinned at his daughter.

'Who was that?' asked Daisy, her eyes following the well-dressed man up the path to the church.

'Mr Ashworth,' said her father. 'He's the new boss at our

pit.'

Daisy raised her eyebrows at Rose and smiled.

Her father undoubtedly approved of Mr Ashworth, and her sister seemed to as well.

As he had called her Rose, they must be on first-name terms now. She wondered if thinking of him as William rather than Mr Ashworth was proper. Using his first name sounded much more personal, even in her head.

William caught her eye several times during the service, and Rose smiled radiantly at him each time. When they left the church, he caught up to her and said, 'I don't know many people in Tow Law yet. Perhaps you would be kind enough to introduce me to your family?'

'Yes, of course,' said Rose. 'Mr William Ashworth, this is my father, Mr Samuel Lawson.'

The two men shook hands.

Her mother flushed scarlet when Rose introduced William to her, and he lifted her hand and kissed it as a gentleman would.

Rose then introduced each of her sisters and their husbands, but not their many children, who stared at the stranger.

'Thank you, Rose,' said William. 'Hopefully, I'll see you again soon.'

He walked to his horse, mounted and rode away, watched by every member of the Lawson clan.

'What a peculiar state of affairs,' said her mother. 'Since when did people like him take an interest in people like us?'

'Since our bonny lass caught his eye, I'd say,' said Sam proudly. 'Did you see the way he looked at our Rose?'

'Well, she could do a lot worse than him around here,' said her mother. 'A lot worse, if you ask me.'

Rose wanted to cover her ears and shut out their conversation. How could they talk so openly about William? Their relationship, if she could call it that, was a private matter.

'Daisy,' said Rose. 'Would you like to go for a walk again this afternoon?'

'I'm sorry, I can't today,' said Daisy. 'Me and Bobby are going over to his mother's for tea later.'

Rose nodded as though it didn't matter very much, but she was disappointed. She would have liked to discuss everything that had happened with Daniel and William with her sister as there was nobody else she could speak to about them. She couldn't talk to her mother, especially about Daniel, as her mother was the main reason they couldn't have a future together and why he had moved away. Would she ever see her beloved Daniel again?

She realised she resented her mother for standing in the way of her happiness. She was sure that she would have been happy with Daniel, even if marriage to him meant having lots of children and tiresome chores to do.

Of course, it wasn't just her mother who was prejudiced against the Catholics in Tow Law; many people were, but most were not as vocal about it as Jane Lawson.

Rose's thoughts turned to William Ashworth. What did she think of William? Could they be happy together as man and wife?

From what little she'd seen of him, William appeared to be a pleasant and decent man—a gentleman, even. She admired the care he took over his appearance and the position of authority he held at the mine. People looked up to him. As a husband, he could provide her with a lifestyle she had only dreamed of, and more importantly, nobody could object to their marriage.

It was several days before Rose saw William again. It was a dull, wet day, and the streets were almost empty as she walked home from the bakery. William stepped out of the bank on the High Street and pulled up the collar on his coat. When he spotted her, he ran over the road, took her arm, and led her into a narrow cut between the houses.

'Rose, my darling,' he said, placing his hands on her shoulders and pushing her backwards until her back was pressed against the wall, 'I've been longing to get you alone, you little tease.'

He kissed her passionately, pushing his body up against hers, and then took her hand and held it over the bulge in his trousers, groaning at the contact.

'See what you do to me?' said William. 'I must have you, Rose, right now.'

He began to unbutton his trousers.

'No!' said Rose, shocked by his behaviour. She wanted to move away from him, but there was nowhere to go. William had pinned her against the wall. 'Not here. Not like this.'

'Hmm,' he said thoughtfully, leaning back slightly to look at her face. 'Are you a virgin, my dear Rose?'

Her cheeks flushed, and she nodded.

He looked into her eyes, recognising their truth, and nodded in return. He said, 'Another time then, my dear Rose, but I will make you mine. You can be sure of that.'

Rose was shaking when William left her and wandered over to his horse. She stayed in the cut until she saw him ride away. His words were going around in her head, and she didn't know if they were a threat or a promise. What had he meant by them?

Did William intend to wait for another opportunity to present itself where he could either persuade her to lie with him or force himself on her? Or might it be marriage on his mind?

Walking home, she reflected on his behaviour. Was that how men behaved with women when they were courting? She had imagined that couples spent their time getting to know one another, holding hands when they walked out together and kissing in secret as she and Daniel had done, and that nothing further would happen until after they married. William's behaviour had frightened her a little, as had his words.

'Are you feeling alright?' asked Jane as Rose walked into the house. 'You look a bit peaky.'

'I'm fine, Mother,' she said. 'Just tired, that's all.'

'You sit yourself down, and I'll fetch you a cup of tea,' said Jane. 'It fixes most things does a good cup of tea.'

Rose didn't think that a cup of tea would bring back Daniel or mend her broken heart, or prevent her from being wooed or raped by one of the most influential men in the town. And who would believe her word against his if the latter were to happen?

She silently prayed that William's intentions towards her were honourable.

Chapter 12

Tow Law, County Durham
May, 1881

Rose had just sat down at the dinner table the following evening when there was a knock at the door. Her parents looked at one another in surprise. Nobody knocked at their door. Their family, friends and neighbours walked straight in off the street.

'I'll get it,' said Rose, rising to her feet. She opened the door and gasped. William Ashworth stood on the doorstep in the rain.

'Is your father at home, Rose?' he asked. 'I would like to speak with him.'

She heard her father get up from the table and move towards the door.

'Aye, come on in, Mr Ashworth,' said her father. 'It's good of you to call on us.'

'Good evening, Mr Lawson,' said William, removing his wet hat.

'I'll take that and your coat if you like,' said Jane. 'I'll hang them up for you. They're soaking wet.'

William removed his coat, and Jane hung it on a hook behind the door.

'I'm sorry to interrupt your meal. May I speak with you privately, Mr Lawson?' asked William, looking at Jane and Rose.

'Please, could you give us a few minutes, ladies?' asked Sam. 'Mr Ashworth here wants a word with me in private.'

Jane ushered Rose into the kitchen and closed the door behind them, looking very smug.

'Why do you think he's come to the house?' asked Rose. 'Could it be something to do with the pit, do you think?'

'Your father has worked in that pit for ten years and no manager has called on him at home before,' said her mother. 'I reckon it's you he's come to talk about.'

'Me?' asked Rose, her voice high. 'What have I done?'

Her mother smiled at her knowingly.

'I think you've found yourself a husband,' said Jane, grinning, 'and a fine one at that.'

Rose wondered if her mother was right. The meaning of what William had said to her in the alley was unclear. Had his intentions been honourable after all? Was he asking her father for her hand in marriage?

Sam opened the kitchen door and smiled at Rose.

'He wants a word with you, hinny,' he said, winking at her. 'Me and your mother will stay in here for a few minutes to give you a bit of privacy.'

Apprehensively, she moved to the door, glancing back at her parents, who were grinning at her.

'Go on,' said Jane, shooing her daughter through the door.

'You're keeping the man waiting.'

Rose opened the door slowly and closed it behind her so her parents couldn't hear William and her speaking in the front room.

'My dear Rose,' said William, walking over to her. 'I'm sorry, I think I may have scared you yesterday. That was not my intention. The way you smiled at me made me think you were more experienced, shall I say? Anyway, I have spoken with your father, and he has consented to our marriage.'

William got down on one knee, looked up into Rose's eyes, and said, 'Would you please do me the great honour of being my wife?'

Rose hesitated momentarily as the words sank in, and then she smiled.

'Yes, William,' she said. 'I would love to be your wife.'

William stood up, kissed her lightly on her lips, and said, 'Thank you, my dear Rose. I'll sort out the arrangements. All you need to consider is what you'll wear to be my bride.'

He drew her into his arms, held her until he felt her relax against him and kissed her again gently. Before either of them could say anything else, they heard a knock at the kitchen door. They parted, and Sam and Jane joined them in the front room.

'Mr Lawson,' said William, 'I'm pleased to tell you that your daughter has consented to be my wife. We'll be married as soon as I can get a licence. I've explained to Rose that I'll make the arrangements. All that will be left for you to do is walk her down the aisle and give her away.'

'But what about the costs?' asked Sam. 'The father is supposed to pay for his daughter's wedding.'

'Don't worry about that, Mr Lawson,' said William. 'I will take care of everything.'

'That's very good of you, Mr Ashworth,' said Sam, shaking his hand firmly. 'Thank you very much, sir.'

'As I'll soon be your son-in-law,' said William, 'perhaps you should call me William from now on.'

'Aye, I'll do that. Mebbe not at work though, eh?' said Sam.

'Maybe not at work,' said William. 'Yes, that's good thinking.'

'You can call me Sam, and my wife, here, is Jane.'

William nodded at the couple, put on his coat and picked up his hat to leave.

Rose walked him to the door, and he turned to her.

'Perhaps you would like to come to my house on Sunday after church,' he said. 'You should see your future home before we are married.'

'Thank you, I'd love to,' said Rose enthusiastically.

'Very well,' said William. 'We'll walk there after church, and I'll bring you back later in the day, perhaps after tea. I'll see you then.'

Rose watched him run across the street to where he'd tethered his horse beside a water trough. She felt sorry for the poor animal standing outside in the pouring rain, soaking wet. She watched William ride away at a trot, unable to believe that such a presentable, well-mannered man would soon be her husband.

After William's visit, her parents wanted to know everything about how she and William had met and when they had seen each other. Rose told them everything, apart from the meeting in the alleyway the previous day, which still made her feel a little uncomfortable.

'Congratulations,' said her mother. 'He's a fine man. I'll ask around about a wedding dress. You'll need to wear something special when you're marrying into management.'

'I can't believe my little girl is going to marry the pit manager,' said Sam, shaking his head. 'You're moving up in the world now, hinny. It's very decent of him to foot the bill an' all.'

Rose felt as though she was the luckiest girl alive. Soon, she would be Mrs William Ashworth, the wife of a mine manager, and she could look forward to a more affluent and leisurely married life than her sisters.

13

Chapter 13

Tow Law, County Durham
June, 1881

Rose wore her best dress and asked her mother to help with her hair on Sunday morning. She wanted to look her best for the visit to William's house after church.

When she stepped outside, she shivered, and goosebumps appeared on her arms.

'You need your shawl,' said Jane.

'I can't wear that old thing to go to William's house,' said Rose. 'I'll be fine.'

Rose sat in the church, wishing she had brought her shawl. It was almost as cold inside the building as it had been outside. After the church service, she said farewell to her family and walked over to William, who stood outside the church chatting with the vicar.

She heard Reverend Hardy say, 'I'll see you tomorrow evening,' before William turned to Rose and offered her his arm. They strolled along the lane leading to the town's main road.

'What's on tomorrow evening?' asked Rose, wondering if it might be a social event she might like to attend.

'Football practice,' said William. 'The vicar is the team captain and I've just been recruited to join the club.'

'Have you played football before?' asked Rose.

'A little,' he said. 'But I hope to improve. When I was in Scotland, I used to watch the matches in Glasgow.'

Although his accent indicated that he was Scottish, that was the first reference he had made to his home country. Rose was keen to learn more about the man she would soon marry.

'Where are your family from?' she asked.

'From the west side of Scotland,' said William vaguely as they reached the edge of the town and then stopped.

They stood before a large, detached, double-fronted stone house, surprisingly similar to how she had imagined William's home to be. It had a front garden, with a stone-flagged path leading to the door and a lawn on each side surrounded by borders full of flowers in bloom.

'This is Laburnum House,' said William.

'It's beautiful,' said Rose. 'The garden is very pretty.'

'Wait until you go inside. The interior of the house is even more impressive.'

He opened the garden gate and followed her up the path to the front door, which he opened, and then welcomed her into his home. He removed his coat and hat at the entrance and hung them on a wooden stand.

Rose felt chilled after the walk and was grateful that the house was warm.

William led the way into a room he called the drawing room, which Rose thought sounded rather grand for a front room.

'The house was furnished when I moved in,' he explained. 'The house and everything in it belongs to the company—the Weardale Iron and Coal Company, that is. My family and I will live here for as long as I manage their colliery.'

He looked her directly in the eye when he said the word family, and Rose blushed slightly, knowing he was referring to her and any children they might have together.

Rose looked around the pleasant room. It was as large as the downstairs of their terraced house on Charlton Street. The walls were decorated with dark red wallpaper, contrasting nicely with the white marble fireplace, mantelpiece and painted woodwork. The large bay window had open shutters and lit the room well, and an enormous red and blue mat covered most of the wooden floorboards. It appeared sparsely furnished compared to her parents' home, where everything was crammed into one front room. There was a large potted plant on the table, several paintings hanging on the walls, and a few ornaments on various surfaces.

'It's very nice,' she said.

'The dining room is across the hall. This way,' he said, showing her to another door in the hallway.

She peered past him into a similar-sized room decorated in green. It had a long table at the centre with twelve chairs around it. She was impressed by its sheer scale. She imagined her and William hosting dinner parties there and felt excited at the prospect.

Next to the dining room was the kitchen, where they found a woman taking heated plates from the oven.

'Mr Ashworth!' she said, 'I didn't expect you to come in here.'

'Rose, may I introduce my housekeeper, Mrs Newton. Mrs

Newton, this is Rose Lawson, my fiancée.'

'Very pleased to meet you, Miss Lawson,' said the house-keeper.

Rose smiled at her and said, 'And you too, Mrs Newton.'

She was glad to see William had servants to help in the house.

'We'll be ready for lunch in half an hour, and we'll have tea at four,' said William as he ushered Rose out of the kitchen. Next, he showed her the breakfast room with a door leading into the most beautiful conservatory. Inside, Rose was surprised to see some very exotic-looking plants.

'What's this?' she asked, pointing to a plant in a large pot.

'This is an orange tree,' said William, running a large, waxy leaf between his fingers. 'And on the wall behind you is a grapevine.'

Rose was impressed. She had never known anyone at Tow Law to grow oranges and grapes. The only fruits in her father's garden were blackcurrants, gooseberries and rhubarb—although her father insisted that rhubarb was a vegetable. She loved rhubarb crumble with custard, so it must be a fruit, she reasoned. Who would eat a vegetable with custard?

'It's very warm in here,' she said.

'Yes, it's artificially heated,' said William. 'These plants wouldn't grow at this altitude without a lot of extra heat. The climate here is not conducive to growing very much, really. It's just as well I get free coal as a perk of my job or else I wouldn't be able to afford to indulge in my passion for tropical plants. This place would cost a small fortune to run!'

'It's a beautiful house, William,' said Rose, delighted that she would soon live there.

'Would you like to see the upstairs?' he asked. 'There are

four large bedrooms and a dressing room.'

'Yes, why not!' she replied, knowing they were not alone in the house.

William led the way up the wide staircase to the first floor. Pointing to another stairway that led to the attic, he said, 'There are servants' rooms up there, but they are not used. Mrs Newton has her own accommodation in the town.'

He opened each door on the landing, showing her the spare rooms and the small dressing room. Finally, he opened the door to the master bedroom.

The room had pale wallpaper with a delicate floral pattern. Pale blue curtains hung at the window, and a darker blue mat covered the floor around a double bed. Rose blushed again, thinking that William would bring her to this very bed on their wedding night, and this was where he would make her his, as he had worded it.

'You're very quiet, Rose,' said William. 'This will be our bedroom. What do you think of it?'

'It's the nicest bedroom I've ever seen,' she said, which was the truth.

'I'm glad you like it,' he said, taking her into his arms and gently kissing her lips. She returned his kiss, and after a few moments, he pulled away and sighed.

'What's wrong?' she asked, wondering if she had done something to upset him.

'If we kiss any more,' he said, his eyes dark, 'I will drag you onto that bed, right now.'

Rose's eyes widened at his words. She turned to go back down the stairs, but he grabbed her arm and turned her to face him.

'Don't worry,' said William, his voice low. 'You're safe for now, my dear Rose, but it won't be long until I have a marriage licence and then I can do whatever I want with you. Come on, let's have a look out the back of the house.'

Taking her hand, he walked her down the stairs and to the back door, which he opened and let her pass.

Out the back was a flagstoned yard, a lawned area with a washing line hanging along the far edge of it next to a low wall, a stable for his horse, a lean-to shed for storing gardening equipment, and an outside toilet. Beyond the far wall were fields and an area of woodland in the distance, which provided an excellent view.

Accustomed to the noise in the centre of the crowded town, Rose noticed how quiet it was there. The house and grounds felt very private, not being overlooked by any other properties. She smiled, thinking she would love to live at Laburnum House. There was so much space; it would be perfect to raise a family.

William and Rose went indoors and sat in the dining room at opposite ends of the table. There was a considerable distance between them, and Rose had to raise her voice to make herself heard.

Mrs Newton brought in plates of hot food and placed them in front of Rose and William. The meal smelled delicious—roast beef, roast potatoes and vegetables, with Yorkshire puddings and gravy, all cooked to perfection.

Rose ate heartily and finished the meal before William, who looked astonished at the speed she ate.

'It's not a race to finish first, my dear Rose,' he said. 'You should eat more slowly and savour your food. It's so much better for the digestion.'

She had devoured the meal because she was hungry, and the Sunday dinner was delicious. She felt as though she'd been reprimanded by her future husband for it, but perhaps she was being over-sensitive.

The couple went to the drawing room, where they spent the afternoon chatting amiably in front of a low fire until it was time for tea.

'Will you eat in here, sir?' asked Mrs Newton.

'No, we'll take tea in the breakfast room, thank you,' replied William.

William led the way and waited for Rose to sit before he sat beside her.

Rose was pleased they weren't eating in the dining room again. This room was much more comfortable.

Mrs Newton brought in a tray with a teapot, cups, and saucers and then returned immediately with plates containing fancy sandwiches, scones, and a cake, all of which looked amazing.

Rose delicately ate a sandwich and then had one piece of cake, which she cut into small pieces as William did. She could have eaten more but didn't want William to comment on her eating habits again, and she vowed to be more ladylike in his company from now on.

When they finished eating, William said, 'I'll be playing in a football match on Saturday afternoon. Perhaps you would like to come and watch?'

'Yes, I would like that very much,' said Rose. 'My father goes to the Tow Law matches. I'm sure he wouldn't mind if I went with him.'

William smiled and said, 'I'll look out for you. I should see you home soon. I don't want your parents to worry about you.'

As they left the house, William noticed Rose shiver. 'You should have worn a coat or shawl today. Even though it's June, it's far too cold for a thin dress. Wait here a moment.'

He went back to the house and returned carrying a woollen shawl, which he placed around her shoulders.

'It's Mrs Newton's,' he said. 'She's not going home for a while yet. When I told her your plight, she insisted you wear it to walk back to the town.'

'Thank you,' she said, feeling ridiculous having to borrow a shawl because she had been too proud to wear her own.

William held out his arm, and Rose rested her hand on it as he walked her home.

She felt fortunate to have caught William's eye when he first arrived at Tow Law, and she was excited about her future at Laburnum House as his wife.

14

Chapter 14

Tow Law, County Durham
June, 1881

When Rose got home that evening, she told her parents about William's wonderful house, Mrs Newton's excellent food, and that William had joined the town's football team.

'He asked me if I would go to watch the match on Saturday,' said Rose.

'Tow Law's playing Crook Excelsior,' said her father. 'It's just a friendly game, but Tow Law are the favourites to win.'

'Can I go with you?' she asked.

'Aye, of course, you can,' said her father, pleased that one of his daughters was showing an interest in the sport.

'Are you not supposed to be working at the bakery on Saturday?' asked her mother.

Rose frowned. 'Yes, I am. I'll work the morning and ask Mr Merritt if I can take the afternoon off. It's never busy when there's a football match on.'

Rose was surprised that her mother didn't argue about her

taking time off work. If she went to the match, she'd have a few pennies less in her pay packet. Her weekly earnings went straight to her parents for her bed and board, so they would lose out if she took the afternoon off. No comment or complaint from her mother meant she approved of Rose's forthcoming marriage to William.

On Saturday, Rose left work after the midday rush. She walked home briskly and changed into a violet dress, which she thought was perfect for a sunny afternoon.

Her father was standing by the door looking at his watch when she went downstairs.

'We'd better get a move on,' he said. 'They'll be kicking off soon.'

They marched to the football field together, where quite a large crowd stood around the edges, waiting for the match to start.

The teams stood by the edge of the pitch, one on each side, huddled together.

'They're talking tactics,' said her father knowledgeably.

William waved at Rose as the players moved to their half of the pitch, and a whistle sounded at the start of the game.

Her father gave Rose a running commentary on what was happening throughout the game, and she was grateful that he was there to explain the rules.

She watched her fiancé run around the pitch, tackling other players for the ball and attempting to score a goal. She was amazed at his stamina and skill.

At half-time, the score was nil-nil. William wandered over to Rose and Sam, wiping the sweat from his brow.

Rose noticed he wasn't out of breath, yet he'd been running around the field for ages.

'Thank you for coming,' he said. 'Are you enjoying the game?'

'Yes,' she said. 'It's a lovely day to be outside, and Father's explaining what's going on.'

'That's great!' he said. 'I'd better get back to my team.'

He jogged up the pitch and drank some water before the whistle sounded for the second half.

A Crook Excelsior player scored a goal within the first few minutes of play, and the Tow Law team tried hard to even the score, which they eventually did. Then, they scored another goal in quick succession. Just minutes before the final whistle, a Crook Excelsior player looked like he might score again to make it a draw, but William ran at him and tripped him over. The Tow Law team supporters cheered, and the Crook Excelsior supporters booed.

'He did that on purpose!' said Rose. 'He shouldn't have tripped him over like that, should he?'

'No, he shouldn't have by rights,' said her father. 'It was a foul and he was lucky to get away with it. The referee mustn't have seen what he did. Either that, or he supports Tow Law!' Her father laughed loudly.

'If this is supposed to be a friendly game,' said Rose, 'it doesn't seem very friendly to me.'

'Oh, Rose,' said Sam, still chuckling. 'That's not what a friendly game is about.'

Her father didn't explain what a friendly game was about because the match ended with Tow Law winning two-one.

A win was a win, and the townspeople would celebrate for the rest of the day, but Rose didn't feel comfortable about William's methods. He hadn't played a fair game. The score could have been two-two if he hadn't prevented the Crook player from scoring a goal.

A photographer approached the Crook team to take a team photograph. The men brushed back their hair with their hands and posed in three rows: the taller men standing at the back, the shorter men standing in front of them, and the rest kneeling at the front.

After taking their photograph, he carried his equipment awkwardly across the field to the Tow Law team. As the men prepared for the picture, William made his excuses, bade them farewell and hurriedly left the field, waving at Rose as he went.

She waved back at William, wondering where he was going in such a hurry. She thought it was a shame he'd had to leave before the photographer had taken the team's photograph.

The photographer watched him run away and looked vexed that his photograph for the local newspaper would be missing one of the team members.

Rose and her father walked back together as far as the street corner, where they parted. Sam went into the pub for a celebratory drink, and Rose went home deep in thought about her future husband.

15

Chapter 15

Evenwood, County Durham
June, 1881

Daniel and Jimmy worked together in the pit at Evenwood. One picked at the coalface while the other cleared the hewn coal and loaded it into tubs that conveyed it to the surface.

Working in darkness didn't bother Daniel, nor did knowing there were hundreds of tonnes of rock above his head. He felt safe enough underground. But the cramped conditions in which they worked were torturous for a man of his build.

The seam they worked was only two feet deep. Daniel could hardly move in the shallow workings and struggled to use a pick in the limited space. He was aware that Jimmy was doing more than his fair share of the work.

Jimmy's slight build allowed him to move more freely in the crevice and hold his pick with both hands, and he could remove much more coal than Daniel in the same amount of time.

Daniel wiped the sweat from his brow with his dust-covered shirt. His face was already black with coal dust, so what did it matter?

'Are you alright in there?' Daniel shouted.

'Aye,' came Jimmy's muffled reply. 'I'm coming out for my bait now. I'm starving.'

Jimmy shuffled backwards, and a few seconds later, he climbed out of the seam into a five-foot-high passageway with iron rails on the floor for the tubs that the pit ponies pulled.

Daniel passed him his bait bag, and they sat together on the damp floor of the dimly lit tunnel, leaning against the wall.

'I'll take the next shift,' said Daniel.

'No, you won't,' said Jimmy, taking a bite of his cheese sandwich. 'You can't be expected to work in there. Not a man of your size.'

Daniel didn't disagree.

'I'm surprised they don't have boys working at the coal face down here,' said Jimmy. 'They send them up chimneys, which are about the same size.'

'God forbid!' said Daniel. 'It's bad enough that they have them opening the trap doors. Can you imagine sitting on your own all day in the dark at ten years old?'

Jimmy shook his head sadly. Changing the subject, he said, 'I know you wanted to get away from Tow Law and I understand the reason for it, but I don't know why you agreed to come and work in a seam like this. It was a stupid thing to do.'

'It's the only seam that wasn't being worked by anyone else,' said Daniel.

'That may well be at this mine, but we could have looked elsewhere. There are plenty more mines around here,' said Jimmy, shaking his head. 'I dunno, it feels like you're punishing yourself, cramming yourself into a small space where you can hardly breathe, never mind work.'

Was Daniel punishing himself? He knew he had always been one for hiding his emotions by taking on hard labour. The harder, the better. It was what he did to keep control. Hard work relieved his anger, frustration, sadness and disappointment, which he had suffered from at various times in his life, but this was different.

Rose's absolute refusal to have anything to do with him when he knew that she loved him was the hardest thing he'd had to deal with. And he was in no doubt about what he felt for her.

Jimmy was right. He was punishing himself. He had been trying to control his emotions and survive Rose's brutal rejection.

'I don't know if I should tell you this,' said Jimmy, finishing his sandwich.

Tell me what?' asked Daniel.

'A lad from Tow Law was set on here this week, and I got talking to him. He told me that Rose Lawson is getting married.'

'She's what?' asked Daniel, getting to his feet and banging his head on the low roof of the tunnel. 'Ow!' he said, rubbing his head.

'Sit yourself down, will you?' said Jimmy, taking Daniel's arm and pulling him to the floor. 'I hope that might have knocked some sense into you.'

'Rose is getting married,' said Daniel in a daze.

'Aye, apparently so,' said Jimmy. 'She's the talk of the town. It seems she's done very well for herself. She's marrying the manager of the Black Prince pit.'

Daniel couldn't believe that she was engaged to another man already. He'd only been gone for a month. She hadn't wasted any time looking for somebody to replace him, and she'd bagged herself a manager at that. Although, that didn't surprise him. She was by far the bonniest lass in Tow Law, and she was kind-hearted and fun. Why wouldn't one of the bosses want her for his wife?

'I've had enough of this,' said Daniel. 'We should go back to Tow Law. You'll get taken on at Inkerman again in the blink of an eye, I'm sure of it. You liked it there. And I'll look for something else—maybe on a farm or at the brickworks— something working outside. I've had enough of coal mines.'

'She's engaged to be married, Daniel,' said Jimmy, looking his cousin in the eye. 'Are you sure you want to go back there?'

'Aye, I'm sure,' said Daniel. 'Come on. Let's get out of here.'

The men picked up their bags and walked through the tunnels to the cage that would lift them to the surface.

16

Chapter 16

Tow Law, County Durham
June, 1881

William barged into the bakery, caught Rose's eye, and waved a sheet of paper in his hand. When Rose finished serving a customer, he approached the counter.

'I've got the marriage licence!' he said triumphantly. 'I'm on my way to see Reverend Hardy right now. I hope he has time to marry us this week.'

'This week!' said Rose. 'I haven't got a dress yet.'

'I don't care what you wear, my dear Rose,' said William. 'If you turned up at the church in the clothes you're wearing now, I'd still marry you.' He grinned his lop-sided grin.

Rose laughed. Her work clothes were old and plain and sprinkled with flour.

'I'm sure I can do better than this,' she said.

'Where's your boss?' William asked, looking into the bakery at the back of the shop. 'I'd like to speak with him if he's around.'

Rose found Mr Merritt taking a tray of pies from the oven and asked him to come into the shop.

'Hello,' said William, offering his hand to the baker, who shook it. 'I'm William Ashworth, Rose's fiancé. We will be married very soon, hopefully this week, so I'm afraid she won't be able to work here any more. Today will be her last day.'

The baker looked devastated to lose her and stumbled over his words.

'William!' said Rose, annoyed that he had done this without speaking to her first. 'There's no reason I can't work here for a while longer.' Lowering her voice so only William could hear, she said, 'Perhaps until I'm with child.'

'My dear Rose,' said William. 'I know you are only trying to help this man, but it's not befitting for the wife of a colliery manager to work, and we can certainly manage without the extra wage. You'll finish your shift today, he'll pay you what you are owed, and then the next time you set foot in here will be as a paying customer. Now, I really have to go to the vicarage,' he said, waving the marriage licence again.

'I'm sorry, Mr Merritt,' said Rose when William left the shop. 'I didn't think we'd be getting married so soon.'

'It's alright, lass, I'll find someone else. There's always someone needing a job.' He shook his head. 'I don't know what's wrong with getting married the traditional way with banns. It gives the couple time to think about what they're doing and it gives other people a bit of notice about what's going on.'

Rose pondered over his words as she cleaned the shop at closing time. Were she and William rushing into marriage? How long had she known him? Thinking back, it was early in May that she had first seen William at the church, and it was now almost the end of June. That was less than two months. Was it long enough to get to know somebody?

When she arrived home after work, her mother greeted her enthusiastically.

'I'm pleased you're back,' said Jane. 'Mrs Smith from the High Street sent a lovely dress round for you this morning. She was from a well-to-do family and married beneath her, the poor woman, but her wedding dress is beautiful. Wait 'til you see it. It's perfect.'

'Where is it?' asked Rose.

'I laid it out on your bed,' said Jane. 'Come on up and have a look.'

Her mother led the way upstairs, and when they entered Rose's bedroom, Rose stared open-mouthed at the cream-coloured satin dress with a lace overlay.

'It's gorgeous!' she said, running her fingers over the delicate material.

'When Mrs Smith heard who you were marrying, she insisted you wear it,' said her mother. 'It's just on loan though, so be very careful with it. Her daughter wore it and she hopes her granddaughter will wear it one day an' all.'

Rose tried on the dress, and it fit her very well. She felt fabulous in it as she twirled in front of the mirror. She had never worn anything so beautiful.

The red satin dress in the shop window came to mind. Now that she would be Mrs William Ashworth, the dream of wearing it no longer seemed as fanciful as it had once done.

Jane smiled at the vision of her daughter in the wedding dress, and then she cocked her head. 'I think there's someone at the door. Make sure you change out of that before you come down.'

Her mother was talking with William in the front room when Rose went downstairs.

'There you are,' he said, stepping forward to meet Rose and taking her hands in his. 'I've got some great news. We can be married tomorrow.'

'Tomorrow is Friday,' said Rose, rapidly considering the implications of marrying on a weekday. 'My father will be at work.'

'Luckily, I know your father's boss and can put in a word,' he said, winking at her.

Rose laughed and said, 'Thank you, William. I'd like him to be there.'

'Come to the church at ten o'clock in the morning,' said William. 'After the ceremony, we'll go to Laburnum House. Mrs Newton will prepare a luncheon for around noon. Your family would be most welcome to join us.'

'Thank you, William. I'm sure my sisters will come but their husbands will be at work,' said Rose. 'Oh! I have a dress now.'

'I can't wait to see you in it,' he said. 'Anyway, I should probably leave you to it. I'm sure you have a lot to do. I'll see you at ten in the morning. Please don't keep me waiting.' He laughed nervously.

'I'll be there,' said Rose, with a reassuring smile.

As soon as William left the house, Jane hugged her daughter.

'I can't believe my youngest little girl is getting married and will be leaving us tomorrow,' she said tearfully.

'I'm not moving far away,' said Rose. 'I'll still see you often enough.'

The following morning, Rose woke with butterflies in her stomach. Thankfully, her mother was calm and organised, and Rose was pleased to have her there to help her bathe and wash her hair before styling it and getting dressed.

Jane handed her a bunch of pink roses, their stems de-thorned and wrapped in a white ribbon, for a bridal bouquet.

'Bonny roses for our bonny Rose,' said her father proudly, with a tear in his eye.

Rose walked to the church with her parents and stood outside with her father while her mother went inside to check what was happening. A few minutes later, she returned.

'William is here,' she said. 'The vicar is ready, and our Lily, Violet and Daisy have all come. The older bairns are at school and they've left the little ones with friends. Now, I'd better get back inside, because they want to get started. I'll be in the front pew on the left, Sam. Once you've given her away, you come and sit next to me. Are you both alright?'

Rose and her father nodded and smiled at each other.

Jane rushed back into the building, and when Rose and Sam heard the wedding march playing on the church organ, Sam held out his right arm. Rose took a deep breath to steady her nerves before taking it, and then Sam walked his daughter up the aisle to meet her future husband.

She noticed her sisters smiling at her from a pew near the front of the church. Then she saw William standing at the front, staring at her as she walked towards him.

With her father standing by her side, Reverend Hardy began to speak, and then, before long, her father moved away and sat beside her mother. Just she and William stood in front of the vicar.

Rose didn't hear much of what the vicar said, but she repeated the words she needed to repeat. When he asked if she would take William Ashworth to be her husband, she said

83

loudly and clearly, 'I do.'

William slipped a gold ring onto her finger before kissing his bride.

'Who will be your witnesses to the marriage?' asked the vicar.

'It doesn't matter,' said William. 'Choose whoever you think best?'

Reverend Hardy asked Sam and Jane Lawson to join the newly married couple, and he led them all into the vestry to sign the marriage register. He said as he opened a large book on the table. 'William, if you could sign here, please.'

William signed where the man indicated and handed the pen to Rose.

'You need to sign here, Rose,' said the vicar, pointing to the following line.

Rose hesitated. The pen felt foreign in her hand as she held it above the page.

'If you can't sign your name, you can leave your mark,' said the vicar kindly. He pointed at an earlier entry in the register and added, 'Most people draw a cross like this.'

Rose looked up at William, who appeared horrified that she couldn't sign her name. She felt so embarrassed. She wished her parents had sent her to school, but they hadn't seen the need for a girl to learn to read or write and hadn't wanted to waste money on an education she wouldn't use.

She placed the pen tip on the paper and awkwardly drew an X beside her name.

'Thank you,' said the Reverend. 'Mr Lawson, if you could sign right here.'

Sam picked up the pen and wrote his name slowly, carefully forming the letters.

'And last but not least, Mrs Lawson, your signature goes below that of your husband.'

Jane drew a cross, as Rose had done, and finally, the vicar signed his name.

'That's everything done,' said Reverend Hardy, smiling at the newlyweds. 'I hope the two of you will be very happy together.'

William handed the vicar some money, thanked him, and shook his hand. The couple returned to the church, walking up the aisle together as husband and wife, and Rose saw tears of joy in her family's eyes. They were all so happy for her, and she was delighted, too.

Outside, a small crowd had gathered to see the newly married couple emerge from the church. William held Rose's hand as they walked through the door.

Standing at a distance, Rose saw Daniel Kelly watching them. He didn't look at all happy. He glared at her and then, almost imperceptibly, shook his head.

Well-wishers surrounded the couple. The Lawson's friends and neighbours came forward to meet Rose's new husband and congratulate them. A voice in Rose's ear, one that she had missed so much, said, 'You didn't waste any time, did you? I've only been gone a month. But believe me, Rose—I meant every word I said.'

She turned around, but Daniel had disappeared into the crowd.

Rose was annoyed that he had come to her wedding after he had abandoned her, running away without saying goodbye. She had been distraught when he left, but since then, she had proven that she didn't need Daniel Kelly in her life. She was now Mrs William Ashworth.

Then, she chided herself for even thinking about Daniel on her wedding day. Today was about her and William, not Daniel Kelly.

The wedding party followed the couple to the large house at the edge of the town. The housekeeper prepared an extravagant meal in the dining room. Rose's family sat around the table, chatting merrily and enjoying the fancy food.

'This dinner is nice,' her father whispered to Rose. 'I'm glad your new husband is paying for it. It must have cost a pretty penny.'

When the plates were empty, William invited everyone into the drawing room for drinks. Rose's sisters made their excuses to leave, as they had husbands and children of their own to feed, and her parents followed William and her into the drawing room.

As it was a special occasion, Jane accepted a glass of sherry, and Rose followed her lead. Her father chose malt whisky, and William had brandy.

Sam raised his glass to the happy couple and wished them all the best for their future together.

It wasn't until his toast that Rose realised William had not invited any family or friends to the wedding, which she thought was rather strange. Surely, someone from Scotland would have wanted to attend his marriage. Maybe he didn't have any family, and that was why he never talked about them.

They heard a knock at the door. Moments later, Mrs Newton introduced the photographer Rose had seen at the football match.

'He's come to take a picture of you and your husband on your wedding day, Rose,' said Sam. 'It's a little gift from me and your mother.'

Rose was excited to have her photograph taken for the first time. The photographer placed a chair in front of the fireplace and asked Rose to sit on it. William stood by her side with his arm on the back of the chair. He was looking at his bride rather than the camera, and she smiled sweetly up at him.

'That's it,' said the photographer. 'Hold still, please.'

Rose found it difficult to sit still for so long and retain her smile, but the photographer said they had both done very well. She looked forward to seeing the image, which he promised to bring the following week.

By mid-afternoon, everyone had left Laburnum House, including the housekeeper, and Rose and William were finally alone.

William approached her slowly, his eyes darkening as he took her hand and led her upstairs to the master bedroom. He drew the curtains and then pushed her down onto the bed.

'Now, Mrs Ashworth,' he said. 'I will have what's rightfully mine.'

Without another word, he pulled up her dress sharply. Rose heard the fabric tear and cringed, remembering the dress was on loan. He quickly removed her underwear, undid his trouser buttons and climbed on top of her.

Afterwards, he pulled up his trousers, smiled briefly at her, and left the room.

Rose was dazed and sore. Was that what the marriage bed was all about? It wasn't how she had imagined it. She thought the act would be more loving, fun and pleasurable and that it would last longer.

Her mind returned to Daniel, and she was sure he would not have just done the deed and left her lying alone like this. She closed her eyes and imagined Daniel kissing and caressing her beforehand and folding her in his arms afterwards, making her feel wanted, his eyes shining with love for her.

She realised William had not once said he loved her.

Feeling very disillusioned, Rose slid off the bed and removed the wedding dress, which was terribly crumpled. She was relieved to see that it was a seam that had torn with William's rough handling, not the fabric, so the repair should be straightforward. Silently, she cursed her husband for not taking more care of the wedding dress—and of her.

William spent the rest of the day reading in the drawing room while Rose explored the house and gardens more thoroughly.

Mrs Newton had left some food for them in the kitchen. They ate their evening meal in the dining room with a glass of wine. Rose had never had wine before and felt a little tipsy after drinking two glasses.

That evening, when the couple retired to bed, William wanted her again, and Rose lay back, hoping it would be over quickly, which it was. Then William rolled over and soon fell asleep, snoring lightly.

Chapter 17

Tow Law, County Durham
June, 1881

The following morning, Rose washed, dressed in her green Sunday dress—even though it was Saturday, and pinned up her hair before she went downstairs. William was waiting for her in the breakfast room, reading a newspaper.

'Mrs Newton,' he called, 'We're ready for breakfast.'

Rose sat beside him at the table, and Mrs Newton carried in a tray containing a pot of tea, two plates of poached eggs and a toast rack.'

'Will that be all, sir?' asked the housekeeper.

'There is one more thing,' said William, folding the paper and placing it on the table. 'Now, that I have taken a wife, your services will no longer be required.'

Rose guessed the look of surprise on her face must have reflected that on Mrs Newton's.

'I'll sort out your wages and a reference after breakfast,' he said, taking a piece of toast and buttering it.

'Thank you, sir,' said Mrs Newton.

Rose noticed the tears in Mrs Newton's eyes as she turned to leave the room. She couldn't believe how heartless William's dismissal of his servant had been. The woman looked upset by the news, and he hadn't shown any compassion. Rose didn't know Mrs Newton's circumstances but women didn't work unless they needed the money. Perhaps she was a widow and had a family to support, or maybe she had been abandoned by her husband and left to fend for herself. Whatever the reason for her needing to earn money, losing her job would certainly bring hardship her way.

'My dear Rose, you look miles away,' said William.

Rose looked at her husband and smiled. She couldn't cross William about a matter like this, not while she was still getting to know him. What did she know about managing servants anyway?

'As the lady of the house,' he said, 'you will be in charge of the housekeeping from now on. You will have a generous allowance. I'm sure you're more than capable of caring for a place of this size—shopping, cooking, cleaning, et cetera. Oh! And laundry. Mrs Newton always did that on Mondays. I have a man who tends the garden twice a week, but perhaps you may like to take that on once you've settled in. You'll need something to fill your days until we have a child for you to care for. Everything you'll need for the garden is in the shed out the back.

Rose nodded at William, showing that she understood him, but she felt so stupid believing she would have servants taking care of her, her husband and the house. She never considered that William would dismiss his servants and expect her to do the work of two.

After breakfast, William left on his horse to go to the mine office. Rose wandered around the house feeling disheartened. Everything was clean and tidy as Mrs Newton had only just left her position, so there was little for Rose to do.

In the bedroom, she held the crumpled and torn wedding dress in her hands and shook her head sadly. She carried it downstairs, laid it over the back of a chair and set the iron to warm by the fire. She placed a blanket over the kitchen table, laid the dress out flat, and ironed it carefully as the antique lace was very delicate. Once she had removed the creases, Rose looked at the damaged seam. She wasn't convinced her sewing skills were good enough to repair such a fine dress, so she decided to ask the dressmaker for assistance.

She placed the dress in a basket, wrapped a shawl around her shoulders as the wind was chilly, and set off for the High Street.

When the dressmaker examined the torn seam on the wedding dress, she gave Rose a questioning look but didn't comment, for which Rose was grateful. She couldn't tell anyone how the damage occurred, and she didn't want to lie.

The dressmaker worked quickly and efficiently, and when she had finished, the dress looked as good as new. Rose paid her for the work and thanked her very much.

Then, she walked further up the High Street and knocked on a house door.

'Good morning, Mrs Smith,' said Rose brightly.

'Well, if it isn't Rose Lawson,' said the old woman. 'What is it that they call you now?'

'Ashworth. Mrs Rose Ashworth.' The name felt strange on her lips.

'I wish I could have come to the church to see the wedding,

but my legs have been bothering me lately.'

The woman was standing barefoot on the doormat, her feet and ankles so swollen that she could never have squeezed them into shoes or boots.

'I'm sorry,' said Rose. 'Is there anything I can do to help?'

'No, love,' said Mrs Smith. 'Don't you worry yourself. I have plenty of people around me to take care of me, but thank you very much for offering.'

Rose handed her the wedding dress.

'It was very kind of you to lend me your dress for my wedding,' she said. 'Thank you!'

'You're welcome, lass,' said Mrs Smith. 'I hope it brings you luck.'

Rose smiled wistfully and nodded as she turned away. She hoped she would be happy with William, but the events of the previous day and that morning had put doubts in her mind.

On her way home, she made a detour to her sister's house. When Daisy opened the door, she said, 'Rose! I didn't expect to see you so soon after the wedding. Is everything alright?'

Rose fell into her sister's arms and began to cry.

'What has he done to you?' Daisy asked, leading her sister into the front room and setting her on a chair.

Rose sniffed loudly, and Daisy handed her a handkerchief.

'Come on, Rose,' said Daisy. 'It's me, your favourite sister. You can tell me anything—you know that.'

The reference to her favourite sister made Rose smile. It was true. Daisy was her favourite sister and always had been. She wiped her eyes and her nose.

'William finished his housekeeper this morning,' she said. 'He expects me to do all of the housework and all of the gardening from now on.'

Daisy stepped back, her eyes wide open, her hand covering her mouth, and then she laughed.

'What did you expect?' she asked when her laughter subsided. 'It's your house now. Of course, he'd expect you to look after it. We all have to roll up our sleeves and get on with it, Rose. It's easy when it's just the two of you. Our Lily says it's ten times harder when you've got bairns to look after an' all.'

Daisy smiled reassuringly at her younger sister. 'Is there something else bothering you?' she asked, still concerned about her sister. 'To come knocking on my door the morning after your wedding night, I have to ask—did he treat you alright? Has he done anything to you that you didn't think he should?'

'No, it's nothing like that,' said Rose, shaking her head. Although her wedding night hadn't gone as expected, she didn't want to tell Daisy that William didn't love her and that his lovemaking left much to be desired. 'It was just a shock when he asked Mrs Newton to leave when we were having breakfast, that's all.'

Rose knew that she had entered into the marriage because of William's job and status, which she assumed would lead to an easier life and a more privileged lifestyle, as well as to please her parents. Now, she suspected he had married her so he would have an unpaid housekeeper, gardener and a woman in his bed.

'It's strange at first—being married,' said Daisy, 'moving away from home and living with a man you hardly know. You only really get to know your husband after you've moved in with him, but I'm sure you'll be fine. You'll soon get used to each other's ways, and when you have your first child, it will cement you together as a family and you'll forget what life was like before.'

Rose hugged her sister, thanking her for her advice, and then went home to an empty house.

When William came home later that afternoon, he greeted Rose and looked her up and down. 'I should buy you some new clothes,' he said decisively. 'Something befitting a lady who lives at Laburnum House.'

Rose looked down at her Sunday dress, the best dress she owned, and wondered what was wrong with it. She had always liked it, but she would never turn down the offer of new clothes. She loved to wear new clothes.

'There's a dressmaker's shop on the High Street,' she said, remembering the lovely red dress she had seen in the window.

'Very good. We should go there and order some clothes to be made up for you. I'll take a break from work on Monday and meet you there at one o'clock.'

Rose's smile was genuine. She couldn't wait to get some new clothes and hoped to persuade her husband to buy her the red dress while they were there.

18

Chapter 18

Tow Law, County Durham
June, 1881

On Sunday morning, Rose looked around the kitchen to see what she could make for breakfast. She didn't know what William liked to eat except for eggs, which they'd had the day before, so she decided to make soft-boiled eggs and toast.

Before she started, she laid the table as it had been the previous morning, with cutlery, a butter dish, and salt and pepper pots.

Rose boiled the water in a pan, ready for when she heard William walking down the stairs. When she did, she dropped three eggs into the water.

'Good morning,' he said, popping his head around the kitchen door. 'My newspaper is usually on the table. Do you know where it is?'

'I don't know,' said Rose, shrugging. 'Did Mrs Newton buy it for you?'

'If I knew that, I wouldn't have asked,' he said curtly.

Rose gasped. She realised that, with William interrupting her, she had forgotten to time the eggs. Guessing how long they had been boiling in the pan, she lifted them out and placed them in china egg cups, then carried the eggs, the toast, and a pot of tea on a tray to the table in the breakfast room.

William cut the top off one of his eggs with a knife, and the liquid egg white flowed over the shell and down the sides of the egg cup.

'These eggs are not cooked!' said William. 'No newspaper. Raw eggs. You're useless. I could have done a better job myself!'

Rose was livid. Nobody had ever spoken to her like that in her life. Her family had laughed if she'd ever made a mistake when cooking at home. They would never have made her feel like an absolute failure.

'If you can do better, be my guest!' she said, standing up and flouncing from the room.

'Rose, don't you dare leave the table before I'm finished.'

She turned around in the hall and said, 'Too late! I already did.'

William leapt up from his chair, bounded across to her and grabbed her arm.

'I will not be disobeyed by my wife in my own home,' said William through gritted teeth. He looked directly into her eyes, making her feel very uncomfortable. His grip on her arm was hurting, and she thought it might leave a bruise.

'I'm waiting for an apology,' he said.

'I'm sorry,' she said.

He released his hold and said, 'Don't let it happen again. Remember, on Friday, you promised before God that you would obey me.'

William returned to the table, buttered a piece of toast, and ate it sullenly while Rose sat beside him, unsure what to think, but she was too upset to eat.

Later that morning, Rose and William walked to the church, and she stopped outside to chat with her family, as was the family tradition.

Even though she had left home only two days earlier, Rose had never been more pleased to see her parents and sisters. She felt like she had aged two years or perhaps more in those two days. She had certainly grown up.

Her sisters fussed over her and asked if she was enjoying married life. She smiled sweetly and told them what they wanted to hear. Rose noticed Daisy studying her and her new husband and wondered what was going through her sister's mind.

Whenever Rose moved away to speak to someone else, William followed her and joined in the conversation. She found it frustrating that she couldn't say anything privately to anyone in her family. William was always there.

As usual, most of the gossip was about what was going on in their lives and those of their friends and neighbours.

Sam said, to nobody in particular, 'I see Mrs McKenna has a full house again. The boxer and his mate have moved back in.'

This statement set his wife off on a rant about there being too many Irish ruffians in the town.

Rose hoped her surprise at hearing the news of Daniel and Jimmy moving back to Tow Law was not evident on her face. She had been shocked to see Daniel on her wedding day but hadn't considered that he might have moved back to the town.

She hoped their paths wouldn't cross too often because seeing him and hearing his words at her wedding had been painful. She couldn't deny that she still had feelings for the man, and now, after spending just two days as William's wife, she regretted more than ever that family and religion had stood in the way of her and Daniel's courtship.

William took Rose's arm and led her into the church.

The following day, Rose spent the morning washing clothes and pegging them out on the washing line to dry. At midday, she couldn't eat. She was too excited about going to the dressmakers with William to order new clothes.

Rose arrived at the dressmaker's shop early. After about ten minutes, William's horse came into view, and Rose waited until he dismounted outside the shop before going inside.

'Good afternoon, Mr Ashworth, Mrs Ashworth,' said Mrs Collins, the dressmaker.

'Good afternoon,' said William, showing no surprise that the woman had addressed them by name. 'I would like to order a couple of day dresses for my wife. They must be made from good quality material—something hard-wearing so they won't need to be replaced too often. The style should be simple. Nothing too elaborate or fancy.'

'Yes, sir,' said the dressmaker. 'And what about colours?'

'I love lilac and pale green,' said Rose, knowing those colours suited her.

'My dear Rose,' said William. 'You need something more serviceable than lilac and green. Navy, brown, or perhaps black. Yes, it would make sense if one were to be black. It could double as a mourning dress.'

'But I'm not in mourning,' said Rose.

'That might well be the case now, but no doubt you will be at some point in the future. Black would be a practical choice

98

and I prefer navy to brown.'

Rose was disappointed that William had ordered plain dresses in dark colours. She would never have chosen those for herself because they made her complexion look pale and pasty.

He then ordered two silk corsets in pastel colours, four pairs of silk drawers, four pairs of silk stockings with lace trimmings, and fancy garters to match.

Rose was surprised by his extravagant spending on under-garments and wondered if it might be a good time to mention the red dress that was still in the shop window.

'I love this dress, William. Don't you?' Rose asked, pointing to the window display. 'I believe the colour would suit me very well.'

'Yes, it certainly would, ma'am,' said Mrs Collins. 'Would you like to try it on? I can alter it if it doesn't fit.'

'I will not buy that dress for you,' said William. 'It's far too frivolous for a respectable woman and I believe the colour would make you look like a whore.'

The stony-faced dressmaker wrote an order for the two dresses in a ledger and quoted William a price for his purchases. William paid a deposit before he left the shop and returned to work.

Rose stayed longer for the dressmaker to take her measure-ments for the dresses. Then she went home to take in the dry washing from the line, do the ironing, and prepare their evening meal, feeling even more dissatisfied with her new husband and her new life.

19

Chapter 19

Rose tried her hardest to please her husband during the next few weeks. Since he had grabbed her that morning when the eggs were undercooked and demanded her obedience, she had been afraid of upsetting him.

She kept her husband well-fed, the house clean and tidy, and the garden tended. Rose had worked out a weekly routine: laundry on Mondays, cleaning on Tuesdays and Thursdays, gardening on Wednesdays and Saturdays, and baking on Fridays. Sunday was reserved for church and relaxing. It was a manageable schedule but exhausting.

Rose also baked fresh bread, shopped for supplies in town, and prepared their breakfast and evening meals daily. She bought the best meat from the butcher's shop, which her brother-in-law owned. Sometimes, she saw Lily there and chatted for a while, but she rarely saw the rest of her family, except for Sunday mornings at the church, where her father had been advising her about gardening.

Sadly, Rose hadn't set foot in the bakery where she worked before her marriage. As William preferred home-cooked bread, pies, scones, cakes, and biscuits, she never bought baked goods, which was a shame as she would have liked to chat with Mr Merritt and some of the regular customers whom she missed.

With so many responsibilities, Rose had little time for anything else. She was more tired at the end of the day than when she'd worked at the bakery and helped her mother. Whenever there were a few moments to spare, Rose spent it sewing her quilt. She was disappointed it hadn't been completed in time for her wedding night, but it would soon be finished.

Every night since their marriage, William has demanded her attention in bed. Even though she was desperate for sleep, Rose complied with his wishes but never enjoyed their lovemaking and desperately hoped that she wouldn't fall pregnant. She didn't know how she would cope with caring for a child as well as everything else.

One fine Sunday afternoon, William sat on a chair in the back garden, reading a heavy tome on mine engineering. Rose took out a cup of tea, smiling as she admired the neatly trimmed lawn and the new flower bed she had created along one edge. She was proud of her work and silently thanked her father for his advice because she would not have known where to start without him.

A man walked along the path by the garden wall and con-tinued towards the woods. Rose was sure it was Daniel Kelly. The man was the right height, build and colouring. Did he know where she lived, or was it just a coincidence that he was walking past her house?

'Is that for me?' asked William, holding out his hand to take the cup and saucer. 'Thank you, that's very kind of you.'

'You're welcome,' she said. 'I wondered about visiting our Daisy or my parents later this afternoon. Would you mind if I did?'

'Why would you want to visit them this afternoon when you saw them this morning at church?' asked William. 'Are you finding it difficult to settle into the role of my wife, Rose? Or don't know how a wife should behave?'

Rose didn't know what to say to him.

'In that case, I'd better explain,' said William, taking her silence as affirmation. 'A married woman should not go out walking or visiting without her husband or a companion. It's not the done thing. And I'm afraid I don't have the time to go anywhere with you today as I must get through this book. I'm sure you can find something to occupy yourself while I read.'

'I miss talking to people,' blurted out Rose. 'We have a lovely dining room. Perhaps we could invite someone over for dinner one evening. It would be fun to entertain, don't you think?'

'There is nobody I would like to invite into our home,' he said, 'now if you don't mind...'

William returned to reading his book.

Rose went to the drawing room and admired the rows of leather-bound books in the oak bookcase. She wished she could read; it would help to fill the time on Sunday afternoons when she wasn't supposed to work. Why had she thought she'd like having servants and more leisure time? She only had one afternoon a week that she didn't work and was already bored. She would have dearly loved to have some company and friendly chatter; William hardly talked to her apart from at mealtimes.

Rose turned to look at the mantelpiece where the framed wedding photograph took pride of place. When the picture was taken, she was sitting on a chair with William standing by her side, and they were looking at each other and smiling. Nobody seeing it would ever guess that the couple in the photograph were not in love.

Feeling lonely, Rose went into the kitchen to prepare their evening meal, even though they would not be eating for several hours yet.

The following day was laundry day. Rose washed the clothes and hung them out around mid-morning. She checked several times during the afternoon if the washing was dry, but it wasn't. Dampness was hanging in the air, and Rose feared they might not dry outside. As it was getting late, she would have to prepare their evening meal soon, so she went to bring in the clothes.

She unpegged each item, placed the pegs in a cotton bag slung over her arm, roughly folded the clothes and put them in a large wicker basket.

'Hello, Rose,' said a voice she hadn't heard since her wedding day, Daniel's soft Irish lilt, and she spun around to face the path.

'Daniel!' she said. 'What are you doing here?'

'I came to ask you if you're happy with him,' he said, looking directly into her eyes.

She looked down when she answered quietly, 'Of course I am.'

When she returned her gaze to meet his, she could tell he

didn't believe her.

'Is he good to you, at least?' he asked, with a pained expression.

'Aye,' she said and didn't elaborate.

Once again, she could see the doubt in Daniel's eyes.

'I hear you've moved back to Tow Law,' she said, steering the conversation away from herself.

'Aye,' said Daniel. 'Our Jimmy's back at Inkerman. He's well suited to coal mining. I didn't care for it, so I'm working on a farm just outside the town. I'll be walking past here on my way home every day but Sunday. I found this path at the weekend, and I like it. It's nice and quiet, and if I'm lucky, I might get to see you.'

Rose smiled wistfully.

'If you're ever in trouble, Rose,' said Daniel, 'or if you need to talk to somebody, look out for me, won't you? You know I'd do anything for you.'

'Thank you, Daniel, but I'm fine, really,' she said. 'It is good to see you though.'

Those were the first truthful words she had spoken to him, and his smile showed he appreciated her saying them.

He tipped his cap at her and continued to his lodgings.

Chapter 20

Tow Law, County Durham
August, 1881

Rose found her new life hard and lonely. Apart from William, who she discovered was a man of few words and a couple of shopkeepers in the town, she saw hardly anyone throughout the week and her family only on Sundays. William wouldn't allow her to visit them alone, and he never had the time to accompany her.

She missed the banter in the bakery where she had worked and chatting with her parents—even her mother.

Rose settled into her routine, which soon included seeing Daniel.

On Mondays, she washed, dried, and ironed the laundry. Desperate for companionship, she began taking in the washing when she knew Daniel would be walking home from work. She longed to chat with someone, and she enjoyed his company more than most.

Then, on her gardening days, Wednesdays and Saturdays,

she ensured she was in the back garden to see him when he passed.

Fridays were baking days. She baked cakes, pies, scones and biscuits, and soon, she made a few extra and took them out for Daniel. He loved her food, especially the meat pies.

On Tuesdays and Thursdays, Rose cleaned and tidied the house. In the late afternoon, she stood by a window overlooking the garden and waved to him as he walked along the path at the back of the house.

Daniel always stopped to spend a little time with her when she was outside, and Rose looked forward to seeing his friendly face and hearing his gentle voice. Whenever she saw him, she remembered the nights they spent together in the back gardens of Charlton Street and the few loving kisses they had shared.

Rose and Daniel became closer as the weeks passed, sharing their secrets and dreams. Their intense attraction remained, and they found it increasingly difficult not to act on it.

William was just as demanding in bed as when they were first married. When he touched her, Rose closed her eyes and began to imagine that it was Daniel's hands on her body, and she found herself responding to her husband's touch, much to his surprise and delight.

One wet Tuesday afternoon, Rose was cleaning the master bedroom when she heard a knock at the front door. She put down her duster, ran downstairs, took off her apron before she reached the door, and opened it.

'Hello, Rose!' said Daisy, 'I thought I'd come over to see you. I hope that's alright.'

'Of course, it's alright,' said Rose, opening the door wider to allow her heavily pregnant sister to enter. 'It's so good to see you.'

'We haven't had a good chat for ages,' said Daisy. 'William sticks to you like a shadow when we see you at the church. How are you? Are you settling in alright?'

'Come into the kitchen,' said Rose. 'I'll make us a pot of tea.'

'No, thank you. I can't stomach tea,' said Daisy. 'Just a glass of water will do me. It's strange how your tastes change when you're expecting.'

Daisy followed Rose into the kitchen, where Rose poured two glasses of water, placed a few ginger biscuits on a plate, and then took them on a tray into the drawing room. Sitting on armchairs facing each other, the tray on a small table between them, the sisters chatted, and once they got talking, they didn't want to stop. Time passed by so quickly.

William returned home from work and hearing women's voices in the drawing room, he stepped into the room.

'Daisy,' said William. 'What a surprise. Rose didn't say you'd be calling today.'

'She didn't know,' said Daisy. 'I was a bit restless this afternoon so I thought I'd have a walk over to see her.'

'Hmm,' said William. Looking at Rose, he said, 'I can't smell any dinner cooking. Are we having salad tonight?'

'Oh!' said Rose, looking at the mantel clock. 'I didn't realise the time. I bought some lamb chops for dinner. They won't take long to cook.'

'You know I like dinner to be ready when I come home,' said William. 'It's not a lot to ask since you're twiddling your thumbs at home all day.'

'I'd better be going,' said Daisy, lifting her heavy body from the chair and squeezing past William on her way to the front door.

Rose showed her sister out, and after Daisy stepped outside, she turned and whispered, 'Are you sure everything's alright between the two of you?'

Rose nodded, and Daisy went home, taking her word for it.

William walked downstairs carrying a feather duster and a cleaning cloth.

'I found these in our bedroom,' he said. 'They don't belong up there. The window is smeared and the furniture is thick with dust.'

'It's not that bad,' said Rose. 'I just dusted up there last week.'

He picked up her discarded apron from the side table in the hall and shook his head.

'This is not good enough, and I don't expect you to answer me back, as you well know,' said William slowly and deliberately, in a tone of voice that made Rose's flesh crawl. He raised his hand, struck her hard across the cheek, and she fell back against the wall, hitting her head and sliding to the floor.

William pulled her to her feet, pushed her into the kitchen, and said, 'Now, make my dinner like a good wife.'

Still a little dizzy, Rose prepared the vegetables, brought them to a boil, placed the lamb chops into a skillet to fry and made a thick gravy with some left-over stock. She didn't have time to think about what William had done or how she felt about it. She wanted the dinner to be perfect for him so that he would be happy and wouldn't hit her again.

The following morning, Rose had a mark on her face. The skin had not torn, but an angry bruise covered her cheekbone, and she suspected she might soon have a black eye. She bathed it with cold water, knowing it was probably too late to help reduce the bruising, but she had to try.

It was Wednesday. She had missed waving at Daniel the day before because of Daisy's unexpected visit and she knew he would be worried if he didn't see her in the garden that afternoon, but she couldn't let him see her bruised face.

After doing her morning chores, she went into the garden, wearing a bonnet with a wide brim to shield her face. It was a bright, sunny day, so the bonnet didn't look out of place.

To avoid seeing Daniel that day, she worked in the front garden at the time he was due to finish work. It upset her to do that because she loved to see him, but avoiding him was better than letting him find out that her husband hit her. There was no telling how Daniel would react.

Rose cut the grass and was about to push the mower back to the shed when she heard Daniel's voice behind her. Although her instinct was to turn to him, she didn't. She pretended that she hadn't heard him and went around the side of the house and to the shed.

Daniel leapt over the front wall and followed her. He reached for her arm, and she noticeably flinched at his touch.

'Rose, what's wrong?' he asked. 'Have I done something to upset you?'

Had he done something to upset her? How could he think that? Daniel would never do anything to upset her. He was nothing like William.

'Leave me alone,' she said, fumbling to open the shed door.

He gently took her arms and turned her to face him, gasping when he saw her face.

'Oh, my God!' he said, running his finger slowly down her face and cupping her chin. He gently kissed her bruised cheek.

'Did he do this to you?'

She nodded.

'It was my fault though,' she said. 'He was upset because our Daisy came round and I hadn't finished cleaning or made his dinner when he got home from work.'

'Rose, look at me,' said Daniel, lifting her chin. 'There is no excuse for a man to hit a woman. He did this. That makes it his fault, not yours.'

Rose's face crumpled, and she fell into Daniel's arms, crying softly at his kind words and tender touch. He held her close, whispering comforting words in her ear.

'He doesn't deserve you, Rose,' said Daniel. 'Do you remember when I said I'd like to take you away, somewhere a long way from everyone else? I wish to God I had, and then I would never have lost you.'

Rose lifted her face to look at him, and he wiped away her tears. She wondered if that was still possible. Could she and Daniel disappear from Tow Law and live together away from everyone else, somewhere nobody cared what religion they were, somewhere she could feel happy and safe?

Unable to resist the temptation any longer, she reached up and kissed his lips, and after only a slight hesitation, he responded. They kissed passionately for the first time and then withdrew from each other's arms, breathing heavily, slowly stepping backwards, aware that they had crossed a line.

Rose was a married woman. She should not have kissed a man who wasn't her husband, and she should not have enjoyed it so much.

'I'd better go,' said Daniel. He crossed the back lawn, jumped over the low wall onto the path, and looked back at Rose before he walked away.

Rose returned to the house, her heart beating rapidly after Daniel's kiss. She sat on a chair in the kitchen until it calmed, but her mind was far from settled. Glancing at the wall clock, she saw there was an hour before she had to start making dinner for William, so she took out her quilt. It would take her mind off what had just happened, and she may have time to finish it. It had taken her two years, but it was almost complete.

Half an hour later, she spread the finished item over the dining room table to admire her handiwork. The stitches were so tiny that they were hardly visible, and the patchwork colours were perfect for their bedroom. The quilt would look lovely on their bed.

21

Chapter 21

Tow Law, County Durham
August, 1881

After her encounter with Daniel and finally finishing her quilt, Rose was happy. She sang to herself as she cooked dinner that evening. William was already seated in the dining room when she carried the plates to the table, and she sat next to him to eat their meal.

'How was your day?' asked Rose as she picked up her cutlery.

William raised his eyebrows at her interest and said, 'Very good, as it happens. We set on some more men this morning.'

'That's good. The pit must be doing well,' said Rose.

'I'm sure you're aware that Black Prince is the largest colliery for miles around,' he said proudly. 'And it's doing very well indeed under my management.'

William continued to talk about the mine and didn't ask Rose about her day, for which she was grateful. Daniel was her secret, and he must stay that way. His kiss had made this day the best she'd had in months.

Rose didn't notice William eyeing her suspiciously as she cleared the dishes.

That evening, when they went to bed, William saw the homemade quilt on the bed and pulled a face.

'Wherever did this come from?' he asked, lifting a corner and feeling the material. 'It feels cheap.'

'I've spent the last two years making this quilt,' said Rose, 'and I would like it on our bed.'

'No, I'm sorry. You've wasted your time,' said William. 'I much prefer the one that was on the bed before. Put it back on while I undress for bed.'

With tears in her eyes, Rose removed her precious quilt, folded it, placed it in the cupboard, and put the old one back on the bed. She loved her quilt and was angry at William for not liking it and making her take it off the bed, but she didn't dare say anything to him.

Rose and Daniel continued to meet regularly for the next week or so, but instead of chatting over the garden wall as they had done, Daniel came into the back garden. There were several secluded places where they couldn't be seen from the little-used path, and there was nobody in the house to see them either.

They talked at length, held each other close and kissed over and over again, but neither of them was willing to take their romance any further and do what they both longed to do. They never discussed it, but Rose knew it would never happen.

She was a married woman, and she could do nothing to change that. The only way her marriage would end was if her husband were to die, and as far as she could tell, William was an extremely fit and healthy twenty-eight-year-old man, so that was unlikely to happen any time soon. She was stuck with him.

One fine afternoon, when Daniel was about to leave the garden, the couple hugged each other.

'What the hell is going on here?' yelled William as he flew through the back door. 'Get your hands off my wife!'

William launched himself at Daniel, who moved to one side, but William caught him and the contact unbalanced him. William took advantage of this, turned around, and punched Daniel hard in the stomach, winding him. Daniel grunted and doubled over in pain.

Seeing a garden spade by the side of the shed, William grabbed it, lifted it into the air and swung it at Daniel's head. Daniel's hand reached for it, but it was too late to soften the blow by much. He clutched his head, blood flowed down his face and neck, and then he fell silently to the ground.

'No!' shouted Rose, trying to reach Daniel.

William grabbed his wife by her hair and dragged her back into the house, kicking and screaming.

Once they were inside, William turned on Rose. She hardly recognised her husband. His bulging eyes, flared nostrils, and bared teeth made him look insane. She cowered before him and flinched when he slowly lifted his fist to show her what was coming. He punched her first in the face and then in the stomach. Rose screamed and shouted Daniel's name, enraging her husband even more. She screamed again as he hit her repeatedly until she fell to the floor. Rose tried to crawl away from him to protect herself, but the blows kept coming.

22

Chapter 22

Tow Law, County Durham
August, 1881

Daniel crawled to the outside tap on the back wall of the house and turned it on. He put his head under the cold water, which washed away the blood from his head, face and neck, stemmed the flow of blood from the wound, and cleared the haze in his brain.

He heard Rose's cries coming from the house, so he got to his feet, stumbled to the open door and went inside.

Rose was lying on the floor in the hallway, not moving, with blood around her nose and mouth. He feared she might be dead. At seeing Daniel, William backed up against the wall and slid down until he sat with his back against it.

Daniel grabbed William's shirt with his left hand and pulled him up to his full height. With his boxing training, he instinctively drew back his right arm and punched William's face as hard as he could, feeling some of his teeth dislodge with the contact.

'That's for what you've done to her!' said Daniel through gritted teeth.

William's hand went to his bloody mouth, and he spat out a tooth.

Daniel went over to Rose, who lay on the floor, pale and still. He could see her chest gently rising and falling, and he let out the breath he was holding.

He picked her up and carried her out of the back door without knowing where to go. He couldn't take her to her parents because they wouldn't allow him to see her, and he suspected it would be the same with her sisters. He'd have to carry her through the town to get back to his lodgings, and everyone would want to know what had happened.

He lifted her over the stone wall and carried her towards the farm where he worked. There was a small barn set away from the main farm buildings where they would be safe for a while.

Rose started to regain consciousness as he carried her through the open fields, and by the time he laid her down on the fresh hay, her eyes were open.

'What happened?' she asked. 'Where are we?'

'Do you remember that William hit me?' asked Daniel.

'Yes,' she said, her eyes going to his head. 'Are you alright?'

'I'll be fine.'

'Do you remember what happened after that?' asked Daniel.

'He stopped me from going to you. He took me inside and... and he hit me.'

'He hit you and kicked you until you passed out,' said Daniel bitterly. 'But he'll not touch you again if he wants to keep the teeth he has left.'

Rose drew her eyebrows together and asked, 'You knocked his teeth out?'

'Just a few of them.'

'I wish you'd killed him,' she whispered under her breath.

'If I had killed him,' said Daniel, holding her hand tightly, 'I'd hang for his murder and then we'd never be together. I know what you English people think about us Irish but I'm not that daft.'

Rose sat up, groaning with the effort. She placed her hands on either side of Daniel's face. 'I don't care that you're Irish, Daniel Kelly. I love you, and I think I always have. I should never have married William. My heart was already yours. I should have run away with you when I had the chance.'

'Oh! Rose,' said Daniel. 'I love you so much. Months ago, I told you that I loved you and I always will, and that's the truth. We could still run away together. We could pretend to be man and wife. Who would know any different?'

'Could we?' Rose asked, with so much hope in her voice that Daniel wanted to believe they could.

'You need to recover first,' he said. 'You're badly hurt. Do you want me to go for Doctor Fawcett, or should I fetch our Jimmy over?'

'Why Jimmy?' asked Rose.

'With him being a boxer, he's had plenty of practice healing cuts and bruises. He's as good as any doctor with fight wounds—and I trust our Jimmy to keep his mouth shut.'

Rose wondered if she and Daniel could hide from William for as long as it would take them to get well enough to travel. It wasn't just her that needed to recover. Daniel had a nasty cut and swelling on his head from where William had hit him with the spade.

'Go and fetch Jimmy,' she said.

23

Chapter 23

Tow Law, County Durham
August, 1881

Rose must have fallen asleep. She woke to a crack of thunder, and her heart began to pound in her chest. She was alone. She tried to sit up but couldn't. There wasn't anywhere on her body that didn't hurt. To take her mind off her injuries, she watched the flashes of lightning through the barn door and listened to the rumbles of thunder, counting the seconds between the two. The storm was almost directly overhead. The heavens opened, and the sound of the downpour hitting the tin roof was deafening.

Daniel and Jimmy ran into the barn, soaking wet. They removed their jackets, and then Jimmy approached her. His face told her all she needed to know about how she looked. He stood with his hands on his hips and slowly shook his head.

'Hello, Rose,' he said, kneeling beside her. 'I'm going to take a look at your head and your face first. Is that alright?'

'Aye,' she said.

Jimmy expertly felt her skull to feel for fractures and then her cheekbones and jaw.

'Can you open your mouth for me?' he asked.

He pressed on her teeth to see if any of them were loose.

'So far so good,' he said. 'I'm afraid you'll need to remove your clothing so I can check the rest of your body for injuries.'

'Can't you do it through her dress, Jimmy?' asked Daniel, trying to save Rose from the embarrassment of undressing in front of two men.

'I suppose I could,' said his cousin, 'but I might miss something.'

'If that's what needs to be done,' said Rose. 'I'll do it.'

She was in so much pain that she no longer cared about etiquette or even common decency. She just wanted someone to make her feel better.

Daniel helped her to her feet, and Rose groaned loudly. She was unsteady, so he reached out to support her.

'You'll have to help me,' she said. 'I don't think I can lift my arms. I feel sore all over.'

Daniel unbuttoned the back of her navy dress, something he had longed to do, but not in these circumstances. He pulled it up and slipped it over her head, revealing a beautiful, dusky pink silk corset.

'The underskirt as well?' asked Daniel, trying not to look at Rose's cleavage, which was inches from his face.

Seeing Rose blush, Jimmy said, 'That can stay on.'

Jimmy ran his hands over her shoulders, feeling her collarbones, and then down both arms to her fingers and thumbs. He stood behind her, and she could feel his firm hands moving down her spine to her hips and then along each rib, and Rose cried out with the sudden pain.

'If you take off your shoes and pull up your underskirt,' said Jimmy, 'I'll check your legs and feet.'

Daniel helped her to pull up the cotton undergarment, revealing pale stockings with lacy tops and garters, as well as massive red bruises on her thighs and shins.

Daniel closed his eyes briefly and took a deep breath, wishing he had done more damage to William for his mistreatment of Rose. He reached for her hand and held it firmly, wondering if her body hidden beneath her corset was bruised too.

When Jimmy finished his examination, he said, 'We're done now. You can sit down if you like.'

Daniel helped Rose lower herself onto the hay and then sat beside her. Taking her hand in his again, he asked Jimmy, 'What's the verdict?'

'He's made a right mess of you, Rose,' said Jimmy. 'You must be in a hell of a lot of pain right now and I can tell you from experience that it'll get worse before it gets better. Well, first off, you have a broken nose.'

Seeing Rose's look of horror, he quickly added, 'Don't worry about that, I'll soon have it looking as good as new. Mine's been broken three times and you'd never know!'

'That's right,' said Daniel. 'He's not just saying that to make you feel better.'

'It's a hazard of the job for me,' said Jimmy, clenching his teeth. 'But it should never happen to a woman—especially at the hands of her husband.'

He cleaned the blood from around Rose's nose and mouth, fiddled with the area around the bridge of her nose and then stuck adhesive tape on either side.

'See! That's all there is to it,' said Jimmy, looking proudly at his handiwork. 'Now, you have a broken rib on your right side, maybe two. After that, it's just a few small cuts and a hell of a lot of bruises.'

'How long will it take for her ribs to heal?' asked Daniel, knowing that was the worst injury. He was concerned that it might prevent them from escaping.

'About a month. As long as she keeps that corset on, the ribs will be protected and shouldn't be too painful,' said Jimmy. 'The doctor would give her laudanum for that, but the best I can do is a bottle of good old Irish whiskey. It works in pretty much the same way.'

He took a bottle from his jacket pocket and handed it to Daniel, saying, 'Take good care of her.'

'I intend to,' said Daniel.

'Thank you, Jimmy,' said Rose. 'Would you have a look at Daniel's head before you go?'

'There's no need to fuss about me,' said Daniel.

'Are you hurt?' asked Jimmy, going to his cousin and parting his hair to search for an injury and finding it. 'Bloody hell! This wasn't done with a fist.'

'William hit him with a spade,' said Rose.

'The cut is between three and four inches long,' said Jimmy. 'You're going to need some stitches in here.'

'Can you do that?' asked Rose.

'Aye. Me and Daniel have stitched each other up several times,' said Jimmy, taking a needle and bobbin of black thread from his coat pocket. 'Isn't that right, Daniel?'

'Aye, he's right,' said Daniel, chuckling. 'We're better with a needle than a lot of women.'

Daniel picked up the whiskey bottle, moved to where a streak of moonlight shone through the door and sat on the floor. Rose tried to go to him, and Jimmy helped her to sit by Daniel's side.

Daniel took a swig of whiskey and held the bottle out to Jimmy.

Rose hoped Jimmy wasn't going to drink before stitching Daniel's wound, but instead, he dipped the needle and a length of thread in the alcohol before turning his attention to Daniel's scalp.

Rose took Daniel's hand and looked into his eyes as Jimmy carefully stitched the wound. When he had finished, twelve stitches later, Rose kissed Daniel's brow.

'Thanks, Jimmy,' said Daniel, getting to his feet and patting his cousin's shoulder.

'Any time,' said Jimmy. 'But don't go making a habit of it, will you?'

Daniel laughed loudly.

'Shush,' said Rose. 'Someone might hear you.'

Jimmy put on his jacket and left the barn, glad the rain had stopped, and the sky had cleared somewhat.

'I can't believe that we're finally going to spend the night together,' said Daniel, taking Rose's hand to help her up, 'and that I'm going to put that dress back on you and keep my hands to myself.'

Rose's eyes were wide, and her heart beat loudly. How could she feel desire for Daniel when her body was so broken? She was finally going to spend the night with the man she loved, and she wished the circumstances were different. She didn't doubt that they would have spent the whole night making love if they were.

Daniel dressed her carefully, and afterwards, they sat together and shared the whiskey, taking turns drinking from the bottle. He talked to her constantly in an attempt to take her mind off the pain, telling her about his experiences of growing up in Ireland and his reason for coming to England.

As night fell, Rose lay back on the hay with Daniel by her side. She moaned as she turned towards him, rested her head on his shoulder and wrapped her arm around his body. This man had rescued her from her husband. Feeling safe and protected, she soon fell asleep.

24

Chapter 24

Tow Law, County Durham
August, 1881

William was furious that the Irishman had had the gall to hit a man of his standing and even more so because he'd knocked out two of his bottom teeth. He had to admit that he was annoyed with himself, too, for he'd not had the courage to stand up to the man and fight back. He'd just sat there like a miserable coward and allowed the Irishman to carry his wife out of the house and take her away. The bloody nerve of the fellow.

He knew he shouldn't have beaten Rose as severely as he did. It had shocked him when he'd realised she was unconscious. But he'd been so angry when he'd seen her in the arms of the Irishman, looking at him with love in her eyes. He'd wanted to teach her that it wasn't acceptable to consort with other men now she was married. She was his wife, for God's sake. What had she been thinking?

But he had not intended to go so far as he had. If the Irishman hadn't come in when he did, William wondered if he might have killed her. Then, he really would have been in trouble.

As things stood, if the Irishman took Rose to the doctor's house, the doctor wouldn't say a word because, in the eyes of the law, there was nothing wrong with a husband beating his wife; it happened all the time. The police never got involved in domestic disputes.

It was so embarrassing for him that Rose had turned to another man within months of their marriage, suggesting she found him lacking in some way, and doubly so when she'd married him, a middle-class gentleman, yet he'd found her in the arms of a working-class man.

Perhaps that was his mistake, he thought wistfully. He'd chosen a wife from a poor background, but from the moment he'd first set eyes on Rose, he had been unable to resist her. Initially, he had intended to take her as a lover, but when he learned she was a virgin, he wasn't entirely comfortable deflowering her and then leaving her. Marrying her had seemed to be the best option at the time; that way, he could have her to himself, or so he'd thought.

William wondered if Rose was just infatuated with the Irishman's dark good looks and Irish charm or if he had discovered their secret liaison too late. Had she given herself to the Irishman already? He hoped he'd caught them together before they had gotten too close, but even if Rose had lain with another man, he wanted her back. She was his wife and his property, and she would return to Laburnum House where she belonged.

He picked himself up off the floor and washed the blood from his face, turning the water in the bowl red. He looked in the mirror. Already, a fist-shaped bruise was starting to form on his jaw.

Wondering where the Irishman had taken Rose, William saddled his horse and set out to look for her.

His first stop was at Doctor Fawcett's house, where he dismounted and tethered his horse. He took a deep breath to calm himself before knocking at the door, which the doctor's wife opened.

'Good evening, Mr Ashworth. It looks like you've run into a spot of bother,' she said, looking at his face. 'Come in, and my husband will take a look at you.'

'It's not for myself that I've come,' said William. 'I wondered if your husband might have seen my wife today. Mrs Rose Ashworth.'

'No, it's been a quiet day. Nobody's been here and he's not been called out anywhere. He's been tending his garden most of the day.'

'Thank you for your help, Mrs Fawcett,' said William. 'I'm sorry to have disturbed you.'

'That's quite alright,' she said. 'I hope you find your wife.'

Next, William rode to Charlton Street, where Sam and Jane stood outside their house chatting with another couple he didn't recognise.

'Oh! It looks like you've been in the wars, William,' said Jane. 'Do you want me to have a look at that?'

'No, thank you, Jane,' said William. 'I'll be fine. It's your daughter I'm looking for. I wondered if she might be here.'

'Why would you think she's here?' asked Sam. 'She hasn't set foot in this house since the day you married her'.

Although a little riled by Sam's comment, William ignored it and said, 'It's just that she's not at home. I wondered if she might be visiting family. I'm sorry to have bothered you.'

William turned the horse around and noticed a suspicious look pass between his in-laws. He realised it must seem strange for a wounded man to be searching for his missing wife. But what else could he do? He had to find her.

He knew Rose was on good terms with her sister, Daisy, so he went to her house, dismounted and knocked at the door.

'Hello, William,' said Daisy. 'Is there something wrong?'

'No, of course not. I'm sure it's nothing to worry about,' rambled William, flustered by her direct question. 'I wondered if you've seen Rose this afternoon?'

'I've not seen her since that day I called round to your place,' said Daisy. 'Isn't she at home?'

'No, and I don't know where she's gone,' said William. 'I've already been to your parents' house and she's not there. If you see her, please will you let her know I'm looking for her?'

'Aye, of course, I will,' said Daisy, obviously concerned for her sister's well-being. She watched him mount his horse and ride away.

As William rode up the High Street, forked lightning lit up the sky. A loud thunderclap spooked his horse; the animal reared, and William struggled to keep his seat. He urged the horse forward and regained control.

A little further up the road, William stopped outside O'Riley's public house, thinking the Irishman might be there or one of the customers might know who he was and where he could be found. He tied his horse outside and entered the low, dark building. It was still early in the evening, but the room was full of men drinking beer or whiskey, and their chatter stopped when they became aware of his presence. They all turned to look at him.

'What are you doing in here, Mr Ashworth?' said a short

man, walking over to him. 'This is an Irish bar. You'll not get a good reception in here.'

William recognised the man as a hewer from his colliery.

'Do any of you know a young Irishman,' said William, raising his voice so everyone could hear him. 'He's a little taller than myself, with dark brown hair and blue eyes?'

The men continued to stare as though they had not understood the question.

'They'll not tell you anything about any Irishman, Mr Ashworth,' said the miner. 'Whether they know who you're asking about or not, they'll not let on either way.'

'I appreciate your help,' said William, and promptly left the bar, thinking he would have got more information if he'd asked a brick wall. Clearly, the Irish were loyal to each other and wouldn't give up one of their own.

William rode around the town indiscriminately after that, drenched by the torrential rain that stotted off the house roofs and the road beneath him. He didn't know where else to look. He didn't know where the Irishman lived or where he worked. The Irishman wasn't a pitman at his mine; William was sure of that. His skin didn't look stained with coal dust, so perhaps he wasn't a miner. There was another ironworks in the town. Maybe he worked there?

He hastened to Bond's Foundry and rode up and down the surrounding streets, looking through windows into front rooms not concealed by curtains.

If the Irishman were lodging in the town, he would be unlikely to take an unconscious woman back to a lodging house, but if he had his own home, he could have taken her there. His dear Rose could be spending the night with the Irish rogue who had stolen her away from him.

He was becoming frantic in his search and desperately wanted to scream, but recalling the look that passed between Sam and Jane, he stopped himself. He thought he must look mad enough without making even more of a spectacle of himself.

Eventually, he gave up for the night and returned home alone, frozen to the bone. After stabling his horse, he entered the house, dried himself with a towel and poured a large glass of brandy to warm him.

25

Chapter 25

Tow Law, County Durham
August, 1881

When the dawn broke, Rose opened her eyes and wondered where she was. She tried to move, but a sharp pain shot through her ribs, and she screamed.

'Rose,' said Daniel, his worried face appearing above her, 'What's wrong?'

'I tried to get up,' she said wearily.

'I'll help you,' said Daniel, standing up and pulling Rose to her feet.

'Daniel,' she said, cupping his face with her hands and looking into his lovely blue eyes. 'Thank you for what you did yesterday.'

Daniel's anger rose at the memory of what William had done to Rose the day before, and his fists clenched involuntarily.

'As much as I wish we could, we can't stay in this barn forever,' said Rose. 'Somebody will find us. What are we going to do?'

Gently wrapping his arms around Rose's body, he said, 'Don't you worry about that. I have a plan.'

'You won't take me back to him, will you?' asked Rose, her eyes full of fear.

'No!' said Daniel firmly, 'Don't worry about him, Rose. You'll never have to see him again.'

Rose sighed and leaned heavily against Daniel, grateful for his support.

A knock on the barn door startled the couple, and they parted quickly, eliciting a moan from Rose.

'It's only me,' said Jimmy. 'I've been to the bakery this morning, and I've brought you a bag of food. There's bread and cake in here. I hope that's alright. It's all Mr Merritt had ready this early in the day. The cake is probably from yesterday, but I didn't think you'd mind if you're hungry.'

'Thank you,' said Daniel. 'How much do I owe you?'

'Nothing,' said Jimmy, shaking his head. 'I spent the night thinking things through. You know you have to get away from here, don't you? This barn is less than a mile from the town. There's a good chance you'll be found if you stay here much longer.'

'Aye, we've worked that out as well,' said Daniel.

'Rose's husband was out looking for her last night,' said Jimmy. 'He even went into O'Riley's and asked about you. Rest assured, nobody said a word. Anyway, I've brought your things from Mrs McKenna's. I didn't think you'd want to risk going back to get them.'

'Thanks, Jimmy,' said Daniel, taking the small bag from his cousin. 'Will you stay here at Tow Law?'

'Aye,' said Jimmy. 'I've got a decent job that pays well—and there's a lass I've got my eye on.'

The cousins hugged.

'Good luck to you both!' said Jimmy as he left the barn.

Daniel wondered if he and Rose should leave right away. He was concerned that someone might have seen Jimmy coming to and going from the barn or might stumble across them accidentally. It was possible that William might have raised a search party to find his wife, and if he enlisted the help of his entire workforce, there would be nowhere safe for them to hide in and around the town.

The bruising on Rose's face had darkened overnight. If anyone saw it, they might ask questions. She was in a lot of pain and couldn't get to her feet without his help. Was she strong enough to travel? Considering the enormous risk they would take by staying in the barn another night, he realised Rose would have to manage whether she was ready or not.

Daniel helped Rose to sit on the hay and sat by her side.

'Listen carefully, Rose,' he said. 'Jimmy's right. We need to get out of here before somebody finds us. We should go to your house first to get you some clean clothes and pick up anything else you might need.'

Rose started to shake, and Daniel put his arm around her shoulders. She leaned into him for comfort.

'It's alright,' he said. 'I'll come with you.'

'But what if he's there? What if William is at home?' asked Rose, her face losing its colour.

'He should be at work today,' said Daniel, 'but as I said, I'll be standing right next to you. If he's there, just remember, I'm bigger and stronger than he is.'

'But William doesn't fight fair,' said Rose, remembering the football match where he tripped a player who had been about to score a goal and the spade he'd picked up to hit Daniel with.

132

If William had been stronger, that blow to Daniel's head could have been fatal.

'Don't worry about me, I can look after myself—and you!' said Daniel, stroking her hair away from her face. 'There's nothing we can do to hide the tape on your nose because we want it to heal properly, but there must be something we can do to cover these bruises.'

'Face powder might help,' said Rose, 'and I have that hat with a wide brim that hides the sides of my face. You know, the one I wore when he hit me before.'

Daniel remembered that day well and the hat she'd worn to hide her face from him. He wished so much that he'd taken Rose away at that first sign of trouble, and then William wouldn't have had the opportunity to beat her again—to beat her until she lay unconscious at his feet. Dear God, why hadn't he suggested going away to her then?

He persuaded Rose to drink the rest of the whiskey to relieve her pain and then filled the empty bottle with water from a nearby spring. After eating some of Jimmy's food, Rose and Daniel set off for Laburnum House.

Rose put her hand on the back door handle, turned it, pushed the door inwards, and was surprised when it opened. She wondered if William hadn't locked the door when he went to work that morning or if he might still be in the house.

She removed her muddy boots in the hallway, and Daniel did the same. She didn't want to leave dirty footprints on the floor, and she would make less noise walking through the house with stocking feet.

Rose crept through the hallway and slowly climbed the staircase, with Daniel following close behind her. She froze on the landing when she heard a noise in the master bedroom.

Her eyes widened when she turned to Daniel, silently asking him what they should do. Before they could decide, a figure stepped out of the room and faced them.

'Mrs Ashworth!' said Mrs Newton, struggling to see over the dirty bed linen she carried in her arms. 'I didn't expect to see you today. Mr Ashworth said you'd gone away for a few days. He asked me to come in and see to things until you got back.' Lowering the laundry, she said, 'Whatever has happened to your face, ma'am? And who is this fella that's with you?'

Rose swallowed loudly, unsure of what to say.

'Mr Ashworth attacked Rose yesterday afternoon,' said Daniel. 'He beat her until she passed out on the floor. Luckily, I heard her shouting for help. I came into the house, found her like this, and took her somewhere she would be safe overnight.'

'If Daniel hadn't taken me away from here,' said Rose. 'I might not have survived the attack, Mrs Newton. I'm covered in bruises from head to toe. I was too frightened to come home by myself, so I asked Daniel to come with me in case William was here.'

'Oh, my good Lord,' said Mrs Newton, stepping back. 'I spent most of my life looking just like you do when my Frank was alive. I know I shouldn't speak ill of the dead, but I was glad when my Frank passed away. He was a violent man when he'd been drinking, and he drank most of the time. If you can get away from your husband, you do it, ma'am. I would never have thought the master would do something like this; he doesn't seem the type, and unfortunately, everyone will think the same as me. I hope the day never comes when it's your word against his, but if you need a witness to say what he's done to you, I'd be happy to oblige.'

'Thank you, Mrs Newton,' said Rose sincerely. 'I've just

come back for some clean clothes and something to hide the bruising on my face and then we're leaving.'

'I'll help you change into some clean clothes and I'll pack a bag for you, ma'am,' said Mrs Newton. 'Then I'll see to your face. I'm an expert at hiding bruises. I had years of practice. Now, why don't you go downstairs, young man, and make us all a pot of tea? We'll be down shortly.'

Mrs Newton put the washing she held on the floor and returned to the bedroom.

'She seems like a good woman,' said Daniel. 'She understands what you're going through. I think we can trust her.'

'Yes, I'm sure we can,' said Rose, and followed the house-keeper into the bedroom.

Daniel went downstairs, filled the kettle, put it on the stove, and then went back upstairs and waited on the landing. When Rose came out of the bedroom wearing a clean outfit, he helped her down the stairs.

While he made a pot of tea, he watched her go to the dresser in the kitchen and take some money from a drawer. He wondered at how small and fragile she looked against the massive piece of furniture. How could anyone want to hurt her?

They sat at the kitchen table to drink the tea, and before long, Mrs Newton came into the room carrying a travel bag in one hand and some small pots in the other.

She placed the bag by the door and said to Rose, 'Please turn to face the light, ma'am.'

Rose groaned in pain as she turned on the chair to face the window.

Mrs Newton gently smoothed some lotion onto Rose's skin and dabbed face powder over it with a brush. 'The lotion will help the powder to stay in place,' she explained, placing the two pots and the brush in the travel bag.

'Do you know where Rose's wide-brimmed hat is?' asked Daniel.

'Yes. I'll go and fetch it,' said Mrs Newton.

When Mrs Newton left the room, Daniel looked closely at Rose's face. The marks were still there, but from a distance, they were not at all obvious, and he thought their chances of getting away had just improved. It was a shame about the tape, but he didn't dare remove that yet.

Mrs Newton returned with the hat and put it on Rose like she was a child, fastening it securely under her chin. 'There, you go,' she said with a smile. 'You look so much better than you did when you came in, you poor thing. Take good care of her, lad. I wish you both the best of luck.'

Daniel disappeared into the drawing room and returned with a small, leather-bound book.

'Take this with you,' he said.

'Why?' asked Rose. 'I can't read.'

'Pretend you're reading whenever you're sitting down,' said Daniel. 'People will be less likely to strike up a conversation with you if you look like you're engrossed in a book, and you can keep your head lowered to hide the tape on your nose.'

Rose smiled. She would never have thought of that.

The next part of Daniel's escape plan would be the most challenging to execute successfully.

Rose left by the front door and walked into town. She went to the railway station and bought a ticket to Bishop Auckland, then sat on an iron bench with a wooden seat on the platform and pretended to read the book, glancing up occasionally.

She noticed Daniel walking to the ticket office, carrying her travel bag. He, too, bought a ticket to Bishop Auckland. They avoided eye contact while they waited for the train to arrive, and when it pulled into the station, they climbed into separate carriages for the first leg of their journey.

Nobody who had seen them at Tow Law station that morning would have guessed they were travelling away to start a new life together.

26

Chapter 26

Tow Law, County Durham
August, 1881

When William returned home from work that afternoon, Mrs Newton had his dinner ready for him as he liked. He glanced around the house and noticed that the blood splatters in the hall had gone, and he was pleased to see that everything was clean and tidy. He went to the dining room, sat at the head of the table, and Mrs Newton served his meal.

'Thank you, you may go now,' he said.

'Thank you, sir,' she replied.

William heard the housekeeper put on her coat and close the front door as she left the house.

After he had eaten, he went to the bedroom to change his clothes. While there, he looked in Rose's drawers and wardrobe, searching for any clue as to where she might have gone.

The new navy and black dresses he had bought for her were hanging in the wardrobe, and the old clothes she'd brought with her when she moved in had disappeared.

He pursed his lips, knowing she had been wearing the navy dress when the Irishman carried her out of the house. That image was burned into his mind. He deduced that Rose must have returned to the house to change her clothes and collect her old dresses.

The housekeeper had been in the house for most of the day. She must know something. William ran down the stairs, out of the house and sprinted to Mrs Newton's cottage. He knocked loudly at her door, which she opened within seconds.

'Mrs Newton, I'm sorry to bother you,' he asked, his eyes narrowing slightly. 'Have you seen my wife today?'

'No, sir,' said Mrs Newton, who had been expecting his visit. 'You said she'd gone away for a few days.'

'She must have come back to the house at some point today and taken her clothes. Some of her dresses are missing.'

'Maybe she took them with her?' suggested Mrs Newton. 'Are you alright, sir? You seem a little confused this evening.'

'I'm perfectly alright,' said William sharply.

Realising that he wouldn't glean any information from Mrs Newton, he said, 'I'm sorry to have bothered you. I must be mistaken.'

As he walked home, he wondered what it was about the people in this small town that made them so protective of each other. Last night, the Irishmen in the bar wouldn't give him any information about the man his wife had been seeing, and now his house servant wouldn't reveal anything about his wife's visit to the house.

Where he'd come from in Scotland, he'd never witnessed loyalty like he'd seen at Tow Law. Up there, he would likely have found someone with a grudge who would have gladly told him what he wanted to know. It may have cost him the price of a drink or a few shillings, but he would have gotten the information out of them somehow.

When he returned home, William poured himself a glass of brandy and went into the drawing room, trying to work out what to do next.

Spotting the wedding photograph on the mantelpiece, he picked it up and examined it. His dear Rose was beautiful, smiling at him like she cared for him. He threw the photograph down onto the hearth in disgust, smashing the wooden frame and the glass.

He had to get Rose back. Telling people she had gone away for a few days might work for a while, but in time, they would ask questions and demand to know more. He had no idea where she had gone. He didn't know if she was with the Irishman or not. Where was she?

William came to the conclusion that he wouldn't find her without help. He finished his drink and bent to pick up the slightly damaged photograph. Smiling to himself, he decided to visit the office of the *Durham Advertiser* the following day. He folded the picture in half so only Rose faced him. William didn't want his picture to appear in the newspaper, just hers. He was fortunate to be able to offer a reward for information about her whereabouts, and he didn't doubt that somebody would come forward for the money.

People in the town would find out that Rose had left him one way or another. At least this way, he could control the story and hopefully reduce the gossip.

Chapter 27

Bishop Auckland, County Durham
August, 1881

Rose and Daniel disembarked from the train at Bishop Auckland. Separately, they went to the ticket office and bought tickets for the next train to Darlington. Then, they waited at opposite ends of the platform for the train to arrive, not paying attention to each other or the other passengers.

While looking at the words on the page in front of her, Rose heard a man shout, 'Daniel! Daniel Kelly! It's me, Davy Morrison!' Looking across the platform to where Daniel stood, she saw a man about the same age as Daniel approach him with his arms wide open. The men hugged, a massive grin on Davy's face.

She recalled that, as they'd set out on this journey, they had both dreaded meeting people they knew—people who might ask questions. On the train to Bishop Auckland, she recognised several of her fellow travellers, but as it was market day in the town, nobody would consider it odd to see her there.

But this man was completely different, and Rose was concerned about him. He clearly knew Daniel well, for they talked and laughed like old friends. She wished she could hear what they were saying, but she was too far away from them.

When the Darlington train arrived at the platform, Rose gingerly climbed up the steps and entered a carriage. She chose a window seat from where she could watch Daniel and the man. She saw Daniel pat the man on his back and shake his hand before running to catch the train just seconds before it pulled out of the station. He entered the carriage where Rose sat and took the seat behind her without saying a word or showing any signs of recognition.

Rose longed to ask him about the man he'd been talking to, but that would have to wait until it was safe for them to speak. Even so, she felt more relaxed simply knowing Daniel was nearby, so she put the book down and sat back to enjoy the scenery on the ride to Darlington. It seemed the further away she travelled from William, the safer she felt.

She and Daniel had agreed that when they reached Darlington, they should buy their tickets for the next leg of the journey separately and not sit together on the train to York. Even though Darlington was over twenty miles from Tow Law, many people visited the large market town.

The train pulled into York station in the middle of the afternoon. Rose and Daniel met at the ticket office, bought tickets for the last part of their trip together, and sat side by side on a bench on the platform to await the train.

'Who was that man you were talking to at Bishop Auckland?' asked Rose, anxious to know if he was a risk to them.

'That was Davy Morrison—a fella from our village back home in Ireland,' said Daniel. 'He's come here looking for work. I told him he'd find our Jimmy at Tow Law.'

'Did he ask where you were going?' asked Rose.

'I told him I hadn't settled in the coal mines and that I didn't get on with the farmer I worked for so I was heading to Hartlepool to try my hand on the fishing boats. If anyone wheedles that bit of information out of him, it'll send them on a wild goose chase.'

'That was very clever of you,' said Rose.

She wished Davy hadn't seen Daniel at the station, especially when he was heading to Tow Law and could potentially end up working at William's mine.

Rose and Daniel sat together on the train to Doncaster and ate some of the food Jimmy had given them that morning, and when the train reached its destination, Daniel held Rose's hand to help her down from the train.

Rose couldn't help looking over her shoulder to see if they were being followed. Could it really have been that easy to get away from her husband?

'Welcome to Doncaster, Mrs Kelly,' said Daniel, winking at her.

She grinned at him.

How she wished she was Mrs Kelly and not Mrs Ashworth! Why had she allowed silly prejudices and her own stupidity and selfishness to get in the way of marrying this wonderful man?

They walked out of the station together and into the town, where Daniel approached a road sweeper.

'I'm looking for work,' he said. 'I've heard there are coal pits around here. Can you point me in the right direction, please?'

'My son works at Denaby Main,' said the man, leaning on his broom. 'He said they're taking men on. It's about six miles from here, but you can get a train there.'

Daniel and Rose returned to the station and bought tickets to Denaby Main Colliery Village at the ticket office.

'Are you alright, Rose?' he asked, looking at her pallid face.

'I'm just weary with all this travelling,' she replied, although she was suffering dreadfully with pain. Each time she took a breath, her ribs hurt. 'This will be the fifth train we've been on today.'

'And it will be the last, I promise,' he said, taking her hand and squeezing it gently.

When they arrived at Denaby Main, they discovered it was a small village. At first glance, it looked to be little more than a coal pit surrounded by workers' houses, but on their way to the mine gates, they spotted a school, a church, a chapel, a few shops, and several public houses. All the buildings looked fairly new.

'Wait here for me,' said Daniel. 'I'll go in and see about getting a job.'

'Are you sure you want to work in a coal mine?' asked Rose. 'I know you didn't like it before, and William might have contacts at some of them.'

'There's always work available in the coal mines and married men can usually get a company house for their family for free,' said Daniel. 'It'll be alright, you'll see.'

Daniel's optimism didn't rub off on Rose. She stood fidgeting by the gate, trying to recall if William had told her where he'd worked before moving to Tow Law. He had worked at a mine somewhere in Scotland, but that was all she remembered. She didn't think he'd mentioned Denaby Main or Yorkshire, but then again, how much did she know about his past?

Daniel came through the gates grinning, holding a house

key in front of him, and Rose returned his smile. She was glad he'd secured a job and somewhere for them to stay so quickly.

They walked along streets of terraced houses until they found the one they were looking for—Clifton Street.

He unlocked the door, and they stepped into their new home. He closed the door behind them, turning the key in the lock, and then he took Rose into his arms and held her close, careful not to hold her too tightly.

'We're here, Rose,' he said with wonder. 'You're safe now.'

Rose's eyes filled with tears of joy as he kissed the top of her head. They had done it. She had escaped from her violent husband. She was safe in Daniel's arms, and despite her pain, she had never felt happier.

They explored the tiny house together. The downstairs room was partially furnished with a table and two chairs, and there was a cast iron range similar to that in her parents' home. The upstairs room had a double bed and a mattress but no curtains or bedding.

Rose opened her travel bag and hung her dresses on the curtain rail. They blocked out the moonlight and would stop anyone from seeing into the room. At the bottom of her bag was the quilt she had made. She lifted it out and spread it over the mattress.

'That's lovely,' said Daniel. 'Where did you get it?'

'Thank you,' said Rose, pleased that he liked it. 'I made it myself.'

'You're beautiful and talented,' said Daniel, and then yawned.

'We should get some sleep,' she said. 'It's been an exhausting day.'

Daniel helped Rose remove her dress, and he took off his

waistcoat, shirt and trousers. In just their underwear, they climbed into bed, pulling the quilt over them. Rose slept peacefully that night, wrapped in Daniel's arms.

Daniel lay on the bed holding Rose, and he couldn't believe his luck. He had loved Rose from the very moment they had met, and now she loved him, too. She loved him enough to leave her husband and run away with him and pretend to be his wife.

He was aware, despite trying her best to hide it, that Rose's injuries were causing her a great deal of pain, and as much as he longed to make love with her, he would be patient. Jimmy said it would be about a month before her ribs healed. Daniel would wait as long as it took. Now that they were together, miles away from Tow Law, there was no hurry.

He kissed Rose lightly on her brow, snuggled into her and fell into a deep sleep.

28

Chapter 28

Denaby Main Village, Yorkshire
August, 1881

The following morning, Rose woke early. Daniel helped her out of bed and to dress. He hurriedly put on his clothes. Downstairs, they ate the remains of the food Jimmy had given them and drank water straight from the tap at the end of the street.

Rose wished Daniel luck as he left for work and kissed him. She stood in the doorway and watched him walk to the end of the street in the morning sun. The sky was clear and blue, promising a warm and dry day ahead.

Then, she looked around her new home. It wasn't a quarter of the size of Laburnum House. The windows were small and grimy, and the rooms dark and dusty, but she felt happier there than she had ever felt in William's grand house.

She powdered her face as Mrs Newton had shown her, put on the wide-brimmed hat and went to the village shop to buy food and everything she would need to clean the house. As little as she enjoyed housework, Rose was surprised to find she was actually excited to clean and furnish the house for Daniel and herself.

A man stood behind the counter and greeted her as she entered the shop. Rose told him what she wanted, and he picked the items off the shelves and placed them in a large paper bag.

After she paid for the goods, Rose said, 'We've just moved here. There isn't much in the house. Do you know where I can buy curtains, bedding, pots and pans, and things like that?'

'You don't sound like you're from around here,' he said, studying her face. 'You sound like you're from up Newcastle way.'

Rose was reluctant to reveal any information about where she had come from, so she nodded in agreement.

'Aye, I thought so,' he said. 'We've had a few miners here from up your way.'

Rose hoped that nobody from Tow Law worked at the pit.

'To answer your question, there's a shop at t'other end of the village that deals in furniture and that kind of thing, Mrs...'

'Mrs...Kelly.' Rose stumbled over the name and blushed at her near mistake. Touching her shiny gold wedding ring, she said, 'We just got married.'

'Congratulations,' he said sceptically, looking at the tape on the bridge of her nose. 'I hope you'll be happy here at Denaby Main.'

'Thank you, and you are?' asked Rose.

'Mr Crowther,' said the shopkeeper. 'Pleased to meet you.'

They shook hands, and Rose gathered her shopping bag in her arms, wincing as she lifted it and held it against her chest to carry it back to the house.

She opened the windows and spent the rest of the morning cleaning downstairs. When she finished, it looked much better and felt fresher, too.

After a lunch of bread and butter with a thin spread of strawberry jam, Rose went to find the other shop in the village that Mr Crowther had mentioned. She stood outside and looked in the shop window. There was a vast array of household items on display, and she quickly went inside to look at everything they had to offer.

She bought far more than she intended, in fact, everything that they would need for the house: two pairs of curtains, two sheets and a blanket, an oil lamp, a small chest of drawers, a kettle, a pan, a teapot, a set of crockery—with several missing pieces, and some cutlery. With everything being second-hand, she thought the total price was very reasonable.

When she handed the money to the shop owner, he said, 'Thank you. We'll drop everything off at your place this afternoon.'

She gave him her name and address, remembering to use the name Kelly rather than Ashworth or Lawson, and left the shop smiling.

When she returned home, she began to clean the bedroom, and it wasn't long before she heard a horse and cart pull up outside the house and voices by her door. She went downstairs to open it, and the man and his son carried in the small items first and put them on the table; then, they took the chest of drawers upstairs and placed it against the wall in the bedroom.

'You'll soon have this place ship-shape again,' said the shop owner, looking around the room and smiling reassuringly at her. 'If there's anything else you need, you know where to find us.'

'Thank you,' said Rose, 'I'm sure I'll be back.'

When Daniel came home from work, Rose had finished cleaning the bedroom, made up the bed, lit the range with some coal she'd found in the coal house in the backyard, and had a cold meal of ham, cheese and fresh bread ready for him. The kettle was on the stove, and the tea leaves were in the pot.

When he walked through the door, he stepped back, his mouth open and eyes wide.

'I thought I'd stepped into the wrong house for a minute there!' said Daniel in amazement. 'It looks so much better than it did this morning. What have you done?'

'Cleaning, mainly,' she said, smiling at his reaction. 'The curtains are still to hang. I couldn't reach to do that—my ribs hurt when I tried.'

'I'll put them up for you after I've had a wash,' said Daniel. 'The house looks wonderful, but really, you should be resting until you're feeling better.'

Rose pouted. She couldn't have sat in a dirty house, staring at dust and cobwebs until her injuries healed, and anyway, she had wanted to make the house nice for Daniel.

'I think the table would be better by the window,' she said. 'Could you...'

Daniel strode over to the table, lifted it effortlessly, and placed it in front of the window. Then, he carried the two chairs over and put them by the table.

'Thank you,' said Rose, smiling.

Daniel washed his hands, arms and face while Rose laid out the food and made the tea. They sat down to eat their first proper meal together. After Rose cleared up and washed the dishes, she directed Daniel as he hung the curtains in both rooms.

Then, they decided to walk out and explore the village. They strolled around the lanes holding hands, looking every bit like a newlywed couple to the villagers they passed on their way. The powder and a wide-brimmed hat concealed her bruises well.

Rose found it easier to maintain the pretence of being Daniel's wife than expected. Because she wore a gold ring on her wedding finger and she and Daniel were clearly in love, nobody questioned that they were married to each other.

A few nights later, when they went to bed, Rose undressed in front of Daniel, purposely showing off her body.

Daniel knew he should avert his eyes, but he was fascinated by the sight of her and took pleasure in watching her undress. The bruises on her skin were beginning to fade. If her ribs weren't broken, he would have swept her off her feet and kissed every inch of her body, letting her know how much he loved her and driving her crazy with desire. He fought strongly to control his urge to take her there and then. He worshipped Rose and wouldn't do anything to hurt her.

Rose hoped that her display would spur Daniel into action. She didn't care that her ribs still hurt; the need she had for him was painful, too. For months, she'd imagined what it would be like to make love with Daniel, and she craved his touch. Now that they were together, as far as she was concerned, there was nothing to stop them.

Naked, she slipped between the sheets and looked up at him through her lashes.

Daniel removed his clothes, leaving his underwear on, and climbed into bed beside her. Rose turned towards him and stroked his chest with her hand. Daniel raised her hand to his mouth, kissing it to soften his refusal.

She placed her leg over his, moving her foot up and down his calf, and kissed her way up his arm to his shoulder.

'I know what you're doing, Rose,' said Daniel. 'And I'm very sorry, but I can't. Not until your ribs have healed.'

'That could take weeks,' moaned Rose.

'I don't care how long it takes,' he said. 'I'll wait. I don't want to hurt you.'

'I care how long it takes,' she said huffily.

Daniel smiled, pleased to know that Rose wanted him as much as he wanted her. He drew her close and kissed her brow.

'Go to sleep, Rose,' he whispered. 'You've had a hard time lately and you need to rest.'

Rose snuggled into Daniel's side. She couldn't wait to find out what it would be like to make love with Daniel and silently prayed for her ribs to heal quickly so she wouldn't have to wait too long to find out.

29

Chapter 29

Tow Law, County Durham
August, 1881

First thing in the morning, William went to the newsagent's shop to buy a paper. He folded it neatly, tucked it under his arm and strode home, eager to read it. He sat in the breakfast room, spread the paper out on the table, turned the pages until he found what he was looking for, and read it attentively.

Tow Law Woman Missing: Mrs Rose Ashworth of Laburnum House, Tow Law, disappeared from her home on the fourteenth day of August. Twenty-year-old Rose is described as five foot four inches tall, with straight, fair hair and no distinguishing marks of note. She was reported missing by her husband, Mr William Ashworth, manager at Black Prince Colliery in the town. Understandably, her husband is keen to find her. A generous reward will be given for any information regarding Mrs Ashworth's whereabouts that leads to her discovery. A photograph of Mrs Rose Ashworth and her husband taken on their wedding day earlier this year is shown for identification purposes. If you have seen this woman or know where she is currently residing, please forward any information, along with your details, to the office of the Durham Advertiser.

Underneath the text was the wedding photograph showing both Rose and himself.

William shook the paper angrily, threw it down on the floor in disgust and paced the room. He was livid. He'd explicitly told the editor not to print his photograph in the newspaper, and he'd handed the man the folded photo showing only Rose. He wished he'd torn it in half, and then there could have been no mistake.

Glancing at the newspaper image staring up at him from the floor, William noticed that where he had folded the photograph, a sinister-looking jagged line ran down the picture between Rose and himself, appearing to divide the couple. Not wanting to see the image again, he picked up the paper, folded it, and placed it on the sideboard.

Then, he grabbed a bottle of brandy, poured himself a large glass, spilling a little on the table, and drank it in one go. He knew he should be at work already, but how could he concentrate on his job when Rose was missing, and probably giving herself willingly to an Irish labourer?

By now, everyone in the town would know Rose had left him. Questions would be asked. And to top it all, the newspaper had printed his photograph against his wishes. He felt as though the walls were closing in on him.

What would he say to Rose's family? He couldn't tell them the truth. If he said she'd run away with an Irishman, the news could kill Jane, and if he said he'd beaten their daughter until she was unconscious, Sam would kill him.

He poured another glass of brandy, his hand still shaking, and gulped it down. He had to get his story straight. He paced the room, pondering what that should be.

Eventually, he decided to keep it simple. If anyone asked about Rose, he would tell them that the house was empty when he returned from work that day. Rose was not there, and some of her clothes and the housekeeping money were missing.

That would imply Rose had planned to leave him. He would be viewed as the victim in the matter and would hopefully garner the locals' sympathy. After all, who would dispute the word of a mine manager?

30

Chapter 30

Denaby Main Village, Yorkshire
August, 1881

Rose loved the little house she shared with Daniel. She loved shopping for them, making their food and caring for him. If she had any doubts whatsoever that she loved him, there were none now. Her heart was his and would be forever.

As annoyed as she had been at Daniel's refusal to lie with her, she knew he had done it for the right reasons. She could see in his eyes that he was just as frustrated as she was, and she couldn't wait for her injuries to heal so they could finally consummate their love.

Rose cleaned the glass panes in the front room window and saw an elderly man step out from a house on the opposite side of the street. His hair was long and white, his back stooped, and he walked with a stick. The man struggled to carry a dining chair and his stick simultaneously and paused several times before placing the chair in front of his window and sitting down on it. After a few minutes, she noticed he took a pipe from his jacket pocket, lit the tobacco in the bowl and held the stem to his mouth. Puffs of smoke rose into the air around him, and a smile crossed his face. Rose wondered what the man was thinking about to make him smile that way.

When he stood up and tried to lift the heavy chair, she ran outside to help.

'Good morning!' she said. 'Can I carry that inside for you?'

'Thank you, that's very kind of you,' he said, looking up into her face. 'You must be our new neighbour.'

'Yes, I live across the street. I'm Rose and my husband is Daniel.' The lie came easily to her lips as she carried the chair into the man's front room.

'Arthur Robinson,' he said, sitting on the chair heavily when Rose placed it by the window. 'I've seen you both through the window. You make a nice couple. You know, you remind me of my wife. Bess had lovely hair like yours.'

His eyes misted over, and that smile she'd seen outside when he'd been smoking his pipe returned to his face. Rose wondered if he'd been thinking about his wife then.

'She passed five years ago,' said Arthur sadly. 'The flesh fell off her and she faded away to nothing. The doctor could do nowt for her.'

'I'm sorry, Mr Robinson,' said Rose.

'Please, call me Arthur.'

'It was nice to meet you, Arthur,' said Rose, stepping towards the open door.

'Thank you for coming to see me,' he said. 'I don't see many people now that I don't get out much, and it's not often the weather's nice enough to sit outside, especially this summer. It's been a cold one, hasn't it?'

'It has,' said Rose. 'I'll call again soon, if that's alright with you?'

The old man's smile told her he would be glad to see her again. She closed the door behind her and ran home.

The following day was cold and gusty, and Rose knew Arthur would stay indoors. As she prepared the meat and vegetables to make a pan of beef stew, she wondered what Arthur ate when he was alone and couldn't walk to the shop. She made a little extra to take him a portion.

When the food was ready, Rose filled a bowl and took it over the road. She knocked at the door and heard Arthur shout for her to come in.

'I've brought you a bowl of stew,' she said, placing the bowl on the table. 'Be careful, it's very hot.'

'You didn't have to go to any trouble,' he said. 'But thank you. It smells lovely.'

'It wasn't any trouble and you're very welcome,' said Rose, who turned to leave.

'I hope it wasn't your young man that broke your nose,' said Arthur, watching her face for a reaction.

'No!' she said, turning to him and shaking her head. 'Daniel wouldn't hurt a hair on my head.'

'Who was it, then?' asked Arthur directly, as she noticed elderly people tended to do.

'I was attacked by another man before we moved here,' said Rose, not able to keep the hatred and fear she held for William from her voice.

'I'm sorry to hear that, Rose. I hope your young man will keep you safe,' said Arthur. 'If you were my wife, I wouldn't let you out of my sight.'

Rose smiled wistfully and left the house, thinking his old rheumy eyes saw much more than most.

She continued to take warm meals and baked food over to Arthur's house, and one day, she took a pair of scissors and cut his hair, for which he was grateful. They were good company for each other while Daniel was out at work and often shared a pot of tea. Arthur loved to reminisce and share his memories, and Rose enjoyed hearing tales from his younger days.

She had never known either of her grandfathers, as they had died before she was born, but she began to think of Arthur as a kindly old grandfather figure who watched over her.

31

Chapter 31

Tow Law, County Durham
September, 1881

William returned from work tired and weary. He removed his jacket and hat and sat at the dining table to wait for his dinner.

Mrs Newton put a large plate containing minced beef, suet dumplings, mashed potatoes and carrots on the table.

'Thank you, Mrs Newton,' he said. 'This smells delicious.'

'You're welcome, sir,' she said as she poured red wine into his glass.

William's mouth watered at the prospect of the hot, tasty meal after a hard day's work, but before he had time to pick up his cutlery, the housekeeper said, 'A letter came for you this morning, sir.'

He had been anxiously waiting for news from the newspaper office day after day since the article had appeared in the paper, but no news about Rose's whereabouts had been forthcoming as yet. He had been beginning to lose hope of finding her.

'Fetch it to me!' said William.

Mrs Newton went into the hall and brought the sealed envelope to him.

'Thank you, Mrs Newton. You may go now.'

When he heard the door close behind her, he ripped open the letter, read the contents and grinned broadly. It was what he had been waiting for. An informant named Mr Crowther had given the newspaper the address of a house where a woman fitting Rose's description was living with a young dark-haired man.

Tomorrow, he would travel to Yorkshire to see if Rose was living there, and if she were, he would bring her home. He had missed his dear Rose.

32

Chapter 32

Denaby Main Village, Yorkshire
September, 1881

Lying on his belly in the mine, Daniel picked at the coalface in the dim light, reflecting on the month he'd spent with Rose at Denaby Main—a month that had been almost perfect, in his opinion. He and Rose got on so well together that if ever there was a couple that was meant to be, he thought it was them.

He already considered Rose to be his wife, even though he had not made love with her yet. But now that Rose's injuries had healed, he knew that would happen very soon. They longed to come together, and it had been so difficult waiting all this time when they shared the same bed.

Saturday night would be the night, he decided. He ran through the evening in his mind. He would finish work, and they'd eat together as usual. Then he'd have a bath in front of the range to wash the coal dust from his skin and hair, and rather than get dressed again, he would dry himself off and take Rose upstairs for an early night, and he would open her eyes to how much pleasure a man and a woman could share.

And after that landmark occasion, he would be her husband, to all intents and purposes, he told himself.

Today was Friday. Tomorrow was Saturday. Just one more day, and he couldn't wait for it to arrive.

Rose no longer had certain days on which she did specific chores as she had at Laburnum House. The tiny house on Clifton Street hardly took any time at all to look after, and Daniel was not as demanding as William about cleanliness, mealtimes and food preferences.

Daniel was much more relaxed about everything, and Rose enjoyed the freedom to do what she wanted when she wanted. Without a garden and lots of rooms that were rarely used to clean, she found she had much more free time. She thought it was strange that she'd married William because she imagined he would be the means to a more leisurely life when, in fact, it was much easier and enjoyable being the wife of a coal miner.

Rose was incredibly happy with Daniel at Denaby Main. Her only fear was that William might be searching for her and that one day, he would discover where she was living. She looked over her shoulder every time she left the house, something her neighbour, Arthur, had not missed.

Around noon, Rose glanced out the window and saw Arthur had taken his chair outside and was sitting by his window. It was a bright but cool day. She carried a plate of sausage and mashed potatoes across the street for him, and they chatted for a few minutes before Rose took the meal inside and returned to her house.

She had just sat at the table to eat her meal when she heard a loud knock at the door. Startled, she looked around wildly, wondering who it could be. Nobody had been to the door since the furniture delivery men when she'd first arrived in the village. Worried it might be William, she fled up the stairs and hid behind the bedroom door.

Rose was shaking, and her breathing was rapid and shallow. The tiny hairs on the back of her neck and her arms stood on end.

She heard the door handle turn and the door open on its squeaky hinge. Muffled footsteps came from the room below, and then they were on the bottom step of the wooden staircase, climbing slowly up the stairs one step at a time, halfway up, almost to the top.

Rose jumped when she heard a man curse loudly, and then tumble down the stairs, followed by a thud as he landed on the floor at the bottom of the stairs.

She was frozen to the spot, cold sweat trickling down her spine, trembling with fear. She didn't know how much time had passed since the man had fallen down the stairs, but there had been no more sounds since. Had he left the house, or was he still there, lying at the bottom of the stairs?

Eventually, Rose moved from her hiding place, crept to the open doorway and peered around the door frame.

At the bottom of the stairs lay William Ashworth, her husband, the man she had been so frightened to see again. He had tracked her down. Looking at him lying there, she felt numb. She couldn't tell if he was unconscious or dead—and she didn't think she cared one way or the other.

As she stood there, she realised that if William were dead, she would be free to marry Daniel. She didn't care what her parents or anyone else said anymore. She would convert to Catholicism to be his wife or even live with him in sin. Nothing mattered except being with Daniel.

But if William was unconscious, he could come round at any moment, capture her and take her back to Tow Law, and he had every right to do so because she was his wife.

She walked cautiously down the stairs, stepped over William's legs, and went out onto the street.

Arthur lifted his walking stick high into the air, grinned and winked at her. She waved at him in thanks, realising Arthur must have tripped William on the stairs with his stick. Her new friend had saved her from her husband.

Rose sprinted to the pit and barged into the office, breathing heavily from the exertion.

'My God, woman! What's got into you?' asked the manager.

'I need to see Daniel Kelly, right away!' she said.

'Mr Kelly's shift doesn't finish until six o'clock,' said the manager with an air of authority. 'You can see him when he comes back up to the surface.'

Rose's face was pale, her body was shaking, and she flinched at every sound.

'Can I go down to see him?' she asked. 'I have something very important to tell him.'

The manager laughed, as did several other men in the office.

'We can't let women go down the mine,' he said. 'Goodness knows what would happen.'

Rose crumpled into a heap on the floor and started to sob uncontrollably.

'Clayton,' she heard the manager say, 'Fetch your wife over to see to Mrs Kelly, would you?'

Rose heard the footsteps of a man she presumed to be Clayton leaving the building. She wondered if she'd be safe staying with Mrs Clayton, a woman she had never met before

165

until Daniel finished his shift at six o'clock. What time was it now? She looked at the office clock—it was only half past one. Heaven help her!

Her head spun, and her heart thumped loudly in her chest.

She wished she knew if William was dead and no longer a threat to her or if he was still alive and very much a threat. If he were alive, he would never give up his search for her; she knew that much about her husband.

33

Chapter 33

Denaby Main Village, Yorkshire
September, 1881

William opened his eyes, raised his hand to his throbbing head and realised he was lying in a twisted position at the bottom of a staircase. He remembered that he'd been searching for Rose; an informant had given the newspaper office this address as the house where he thought Rose was staying.

He had married Rose, taken her out of poverty and given her an elevated position in society, and in return, she had run away with an Irish thug, the lowest of the low, and was living with him in sin. Anger raged through his veins when he thought of his wife giving herself to the Irishman.

That's the thanks he got for trying to do the right thing by her. He should have taken her in the alleyway when he'd had the chance that day and cast her aside as he had initially intended. He could easily have taken her there and then. Nobody had been around. Nobody would have known. If she had accused him of rape after the event, he was confident that his word would be believed over hers, and if she had a child as a result, he would have denied it was his and blackened her name.

William wished he had just used Rose to satisfy his crush on her rather than marry the damned girl. What had he been thinking? Life would be a lot less complicated if he had. But now that she was his wife, and she had shown him up by running away with another man, he had to get her back and ensure she could never leave him again.

He was as sure-footed as a cat. How on earth had he fallen down the stairs? He shook his head and immediately regretted it as a shot of pain went through it, and he screwed up his eyes. After a few moments, he stood up gingerly, checking himself for injuries. He felt alright, apart from a sore head and a few bruises.

William searched the house again, but it was empty. Rose's dresses were hanging in the bedroom, and that dreadful quilt that reminded him of his humble upbringing in a hovel in Glasgow was on the bed, which meant Rose had been staying in that house, and the warm meal on the table meant she was probably there when he arrived.

Had Rose pushed him down the stairs?

William didn't think so. He was sure he would have remembered if she'd been there when he fell. So what had happened?

Standing by the front door, William wondered what he should do. He had learned the name of the Irishman who left Tow Law when Rose disappeared. Daniel Kelly. As Denaby Main was a pit village, the major source of employment would be the coal mine, so William decided to see if Kelly worked there. If he did, Rose wouldn't be far away, and if he was in luck, Kelly might lead him straight to her.

William walked to the mine, went through the large iron gates and headed to a building that looked like it should be the mine office. It was similar to his own. As he approached, a man left the building in quite a hurry.

The door was closed when he reached it, so he knocked and went inside, where he saw Rose sitting on the floor, her red eyes wide open, staring at him. Then, she opened her mouth and screamed.

The manager stood up, faced William, and said, 'I'm Mr Holdsworth, the manager at this colliery. Can I take your name, sir?'

'I'm William Ashworth and this lady is my wife,' said William, holding his hand out to Rose. 'Come on Rose, you're coming home with me.'

'No!' she shouted, scrambling along the floor to get further away from him.

'Is this man your husband?' the mine manager asked.

She stared at him and didn't speak.

'I have our marriage certificate here to prove it,' said William, handing the document to the man.

'So, you're a mine manager too, Mr Ashworth,' said the man, reading the document and seemingly impressed with what he saw.

'Yes,' said William. 'I manage Black Prince Colliery at Tow Law in County Durham.'

'I've heard good things about Black Prince,' he said. 'I considered applying for the job there myself.'

'It's a very profitable pit and it comes with a lovely house,' said William. 'Unfortunately, my wife didn't appreciate it and ran off with an Irishman by the name of Kelly.'

'I see,' said the manager, turning his head towards Rose and looking disgusted by what he'd heard.

'I ran away from home because you beat me black and blue!' shouted Rose.

Seeing her distress, a mining engineer asked, 'Should we get the policeman over here to sort this out, sir?'

'The constable won't get involved in a dispute between a man and his wife,' said the manager. 'If she is his wife like he says, and she hasn't disputed, we have no choice but to let him take her.'

Rose put her hand over her mouth and wailed inconsolably. If William took her home, he would never allow her to see Daniel again. All her hopes and dreams of a future with the man she loved had been crushed. She might as well be dead.

William took her arm, pulled her to her feet, and said, 'Come on, Rose, we have a long journey ahead of us.'

He helped her out of the office and held her arm firmly as they walked to the railway station.

Rose felt nothing at all. It was as if her body was a shell, and everything inside it had shrivelled and died. There was nothing left for her to feel.

William and Rose took a train to Doncaster and another to York, and in all that time, William never released his hold on her arm. He booked a hotel room in York for the night, and they climbed the stairs to their bedroom.

The large room was light and nicely decorated. A double bed covered with a yellow quilt was in the centre of the room. Rose realised that she would be sharing the bed with William that night, and she accepted her fate because there was nothing she could do to prevent it.

William removed his jacket and hat, placed them tidily on a chair, and then looked at Rose. For the first time since Daniel had taken her away from Laburnum House, they were alone.

He walked around the bed, stood in front of her and slapped her hard across her cheek. Rose didn't make a sound.

'You are my wife,' said William through clenched teeth. 'When you became my wife, you promised before God to obey me and to be faithful to me. You have broken both of those promises. Let God have mercy on you because I sure as hell won't! I have never been so humiliated in all my life. Things are going to change from now on, my dear Rose, and not for the better. You will no longer have the freedoms that I once afforded you and you will never have the opportunity to stray again. Do you understand?'

Rose nodded compliantly.

'Now get undressed, clean yourself and get into that bed. Be ready for me in ten minutes. And I expect you to behave like the whore that you are, not the timid virgin I married.'

William left the room, locking the door behind him, and Rose assumed he'd gone downstairs to have a drink in the hotel bar.

There was no point telling William that she had not lain with Daniel because he wouldn't believe her, and anyway, if she'd had her way, she would have done so.

She quickly undressed and climbed into bed, dreading the moment that William would return and join her. As she lay there waiting, she thought that no matter what William did to her body, her heart would always belong to Daniel.

34

Chapter 34

Denaby Main Village, Yorkshire
September, 1881

When Daniel stepped out of the cage at the end of his shift, Mr Holdsworth was at the shaft top to meet him.

'Daniel Kelly?' asked the mine manager.

'Aye, that's me,' replied Daniel.

'There's something I need to discuss with you. Come with me to the office.'

Daniel followed the man to the office building, and they went inside.

'Take a seat,' said Mr Holdsworth.

Daniel sat on a chair and looked up at his boss's solemn face, wondering why he'd been singled out by the manager.

'What is it?' asked Daniel. 'Have I done something wrong?'

'This afternoon, your *wife* came here looking for you,' said the manager. 'She was in quite a state.'

'Where is she?' asked Daniel. 'Is she alright?'

'Shortly afterwards, she was followed by her *husband*!' said

Mr Holdsworth. 'I must inform you that Mr Ashworth has taken Mrs Ashworth home.'

'No!' said Daniel, leaping up from the chair. 'Why didn't you stop him? He beat her to within an inch of her life. That's why she left him. God only knows what he'll do to her now—'

'That man is her husband,' said the mine manager, 'and nobody has the right to come between them—not you, not me, not even the law.'

The man who had suggested involving the policeman earlier gave Daniel a sympathetic look.

Daniel frantically ran his hands through his hair. He had never felt such despair in his life. William had come for Rose as she feared, and he hadn't been there to protect her. He had failed her. But what, if anything, could he do now?

Mr Holdsworth's voice cut into his thoughts.

'It appears you lied to me when you came here looking for work and that you got your house by deception. You are not a married man with a wife, and as you well know, you should not have been provided with company accommodation. Single men are expected to stay in lodgings.'

'I'll move out of the house,' said Daniel despondently. He didn't want to stay there if Rose wasn't with him.

'You'll do more than that,' said the manager sternly. 'You'll be paid for your work up until today and then you'll leave this village and you will not return. Do you hear me?'

Daniel nodded.

'We don't like liars in our midst, nor men that steal another man's wife!' said Mr Holdsworth. 'Go on, get out. Wait outside.'

Daniel stood outside the office door with his shoulders stooped, waiting for his wages. His perfect life had just been shattered. He had lost Rose, their home and his job. He desperately tried to think what he should do.

The office clerk brought out Daniel's pay and went back into the office without saying a word. Daniel didn't care. Nothing at Denaby Main mattered any more. The only thing that mattered to him was Rose.

There was only one thing he could do, he decided. He had to return to Tow Law, see Rose and reclaim her if that's what she wanted. He didn't know if Rose had returned with William of her own free will or if she had been forced, but he guessed by Mr Holdsworth's words that it had been the latter.

Daniel recalled what the manager had said about nobody coming between a man and his wife. That was wrong. The way some men treated their women, they deserved to have them taken away from them. Even so, Mr Holdsworth had sown a tiny seed of guilt in Daniel's mind for what he'd done—but, if given half a chance, he would do the same again. He would take Rose away to somewhere more secluded, with fewer people, and he would never leave her side.

On his way past the second-hand goods shop, Daniel asked the shopkeeper if he could take everything back from the house on Clifton Street and handed the man the house key. In return, the shopkeeper gave him back half of the money Rose had spent on household goods. It was more than enough to cover the cost of his rail fare back to Tow Law.

When he returned to the house on Clifton Street, the door was ajar. His heartbeat quickened. Might Rose still be inside?

He opened the door slowly. There were blood splatters on the door jamb. He prayed it wasn't Rose's blood. He looked in both rooms. Nobody was in the house, but Rose's clothes were still there. He filled her travel bag with their clothes, her quilt and food, and left the little house that was full of sweet memories and where he'd hoped they would make many more.

Across the road, an old man was peering out of the window at him and nodded in his direction. Daniel nodded, thinking the fellow Rose had befriended would probably have seen what happened that afternoon. Had he witnessed William going to the house? Or Rose fleeing to the mine?

Daniel didn't stop to ask. He knew enough about what had happened. William had taken Rose away, back to Tow Law, and he had to follow them. He walked briskly to the railway station to begin the journey back to County Durham.

35

Chapter 35

Tow Law, County Durham
September, 1881

The following day, William and Rose disembarked from the
train at Tow Law. He held her arm possessively as they walked
through the town to Laburnum House, ignoring the stares and
fingers pointed at them.

As they passed the dressmaker's shop, Rose glanced at the
window display and saw that the beautiful red dress had gone.
The dressmaker had replaced it with a plain blue dress without
any lace; in her opinion, it was nowhere near as lovely as the
red one. She was disappointed it had been sold and wondered
who might have bought it, thinking perhaps one of the mine
managers, mine engineers, or the owner of the ironworks had
bought it for his wife or daughter. The dress was ideal for an
evening of entertainment in a grand house. It would have been
perfect for a lady living at Laburnum House, too, she thought
sadly.

William opened the front door and allowed Rose to enter

before him.

Mrs Newton came from the kitchen to meet them in the hallway, her hands covered in flour. She welcomed the couple home and offered to make a pot of tea. Rose remembered how kind the housekeeper had been after William had beaten her and smiled wistfully in her direction. Mrs Newton's face remained impassive.

William and Rose waited silently in the drawing room for the tea, and after it had been served, William closed the door so Mrs Newton could not overhear what he was about to say.

'As I mentioned last night, my dear Rose,' he said, 'your recent behaviour has been far removed from what I expect from a wife. However, on this occasion, I am willing to forgive your misdemeanours and take you back, but there are certain conditions that must be met. As I am now aware you can't be trusted, I have arranged for you to have a chaperone whenever I am away from home. I have spoken to Mrs Newton and she has agreed to return to work here in that capacity. She will accompany you every single time you leave the house, for whatever reason, whether it's to shop, visit friends and family, work in the garden or use the lavatory. Understand this—you will never be alone again and you will never have the opportunity to leave me again.'

Rose wanted to protest against his harsh treatment but thought it better to remain quiet. After all, she had broken his trust by running away with Daniel, but he had behaved badly, too. If he hadn't beaten her in the first place, she wouldn't have left. He'd broken her trust that day. She had always believed a husband should be his wife's protector and the one person she could trust and always be safe with.

'You will have no money of your own or access to any money

177

for housekeeping,' said William. 'You will order goods from the shops on account and I will settle the bills directly with the shopkeepers at the end of the month.'

Rose realised William had put a lot of thought into this plan, and she knew he was right in what he said—she would never have the opportunity to run away again.

With that knowledge, her heart sank even further. She would never see Daniel Kelly again, hear his soft Irish voice or feel loved and safe in his arms. She had enjoyed every moment she shared with him at Denaby Main and had hoped they would share a wonderful future together there. But William had found her, and now she must face the consequences of her actions.

'You will continue to do the housework and gardening as you did before,' said William. 'After today, Mrs Newton will merely be your chaperone and she will report directly to me. She is no longer a housekeeper or servant in this house. You cannot ask her to do your chores because she has been forbidden to do so. And you will continue to sleep in my bed at night and do your duty as my wife.'

As William listed his commands, Rose became increasingly annoyed with him. What he was demanding was unfair.

William stopped momentarily to take a sip of tea. When he replaced the cup in its saucer, he said, 'Those are my conditions. What do you have to say?'

'I hate them,' said Rose, unable to hide her feelings any longer. 'I hate every single one. Your conditions are mean and cruel—like you!'

She saw a flash of anger in his eyes a split second before he lashed out and punched her hard in the chest.

Even though she had expected William to react, Rose was

shocked by the force of the blow with which he had hit her. The chair she was sitting on fell backwards, and she screamed when her head hit the wooden floor.

'Do you agree to them?' asked William, standing over her.

'Yes,' she said through gritted teeth, moving her hand to her head, which was wet with blood.

'Thank you,' said William. 'Get up off the floor and drink your tea. Then you can go and change into one of your new dresses. That old thing you're wearing should be disposed of. It looks like something you've bought off a rag and bone man.'

There was a knock at the drawing-room door.

'Is everything alright in there?' asked Mrs Newton. 'I thought I heard something.'

'Yes,' said William as the housekeeper opened the door to check. 'As you can see, everything is perfectly fine.'

Rose stood by her husband's side. His hand twisted her arm painfully behind her back, warning her to keep quiet.

Mrs Newton nodded and left the room, but the show did not convince her. She knew what she had heard, and she noticed the congealed blood in Rose's hair and the strained look on the girl's face. She had hoped the master would never find the mistress and her young man, but he had and he'd brought her home.

What kind of life would the lass have to endure now? She vowed to do what she could to help her. That's why she'd accepted the job as chaperone, as unjust and twisted as it was. She could protect Rose to some extent while she was in the house, but unfortunately, she wouldn't always be there.

The following morning, there was a large bruise between Rose's breasts, and it hurt to fasten her corset. As she dressed, her hands shook. The thought of facing her family for the first time after what she'd done filled her with dread. She felt a mixture of shame and guilt for abandoning her husband, even though it had been his fault, and for leaving town without saying a word to her parents. They must have been terribly worried about her.

'I think you should wear the black dress for church,' said William from the bedroom door.

Rose didn't question him. She put on the black dress as he suggested.

William held Rose's arm securely as they walked through the town, declaring that he and his wife were together again and that everything between them was fine.

Outside the church gates stood her parents. Although she had only been away for a month, she thought they looked older than she remembered. Their faces had become more wrinkled, her mother's hair had more grey in it, and her father's bald patch appeared larger. Her mother had large grey bags under her eyes and looked like she hadn't slept in a month. Had her leaving town with Daniel upset them that much?

William marched Rose up to meet them and stood before them.

'Sam, Jane,' he said, 'you'll be pleased to see that I have found your wayward daughter and brought her home—and that I have forgiven her for what she's done.'

'That's very gracious of you, William, I must say, all things considered,' said Sam, and then turning to Rose, he said, 'Where the hell do you think you've been, young lady? You've disgraced your family good and proper, running off and leaving William like that. He's been very worried about you. You're lucky he's taken you back. He's a good man is William.

Most fellas would have thrown you out on your ear after what you did, and that's no more than you deserve.'

Her father's harsh words brought tears to her eyes. He had never spoken to her like that before.

She hadn't once thought about how her leaving would affect her parents or family. Her father wasn't aware of what William had done to her. He might have killed her that day if Daniel hadn't come to her rescue. Even now, William had bruised her body, but nobody would ever know because her dress hid the marks.

'You're a selfish little so-and-so, that's what you are. While you've been off gallivanting with that fella,' her mother almost spat out the last word, 'our Daisy...our Daisy had a little boy.' Her mother choked up and cleared her throat before saying, 'You should have been here with your sister in her time of need.'

Rose had not given her sister a thought since she left Tow Law. How could she have forgotten about Daisy and her baby so easily? When she left Tow Law, the only thoughts on her mind had been escaping from William and being with Daniel. Her mother was right; she was selfish.

'How are they?' asked Rose.

Jane shook her head and walked away.

'Daisy had a rough time of it,' said her father, looking down at his feet. 'She died when the bairn was born.'

Rose looked from her father to her mother, who was standing by the church gates. They were both wearing black clothes, as was she.

'Did you know about this?' Rose turned to William, her eyes filling with tears.

He nodded.

'And you didn't think to tell me?' she asked.

'You weren't here,' he said. 'If you had been, then I would have broken the news to you respectfully at home.'

Rose turned away and wiped her eyes with a handkerchief, thinking William was an evil man for withholding that information, knowing that she and Daisy had been close. He knew she would find out about Daisy's death from her family in a public place and that she was unlikely to be able to control her grief.

She wondered if he had done it on purpose. If everybody saw her in tears at the church, she would look remorseful and repentant for what she'd done. Was her husband that calculating?

Rose had never loved William but now she hated him. What he'd just done was crueller than the beatings and the strict rules he had imposed on her, and she would never forgive him for it.

When Lily and Violet appeared with their families, and Bobby arrived carrying his motherless infant, they completely ignored Rose, wandering into the church and sitting in a pew together.

Rose sat beside William throughout the church service with a stony face, determined not to show any emotion. She would not give him the satisfaction of seeing her break down in public. She could shed tears for Daisy another time when she was alone.

36

Chapter 36

Tow Law, County Durham
September, 1881

When they left the church, Rose's family turned their backs on her and walked away without speaking. Mr Merritt glared at her as he passed, shaking his head and tutting.

Is this what life would be like now in Tow Law—everyone letting her know how disappointed and disgusted they were at what she'd done? But what had she expected when she returned, that they'd welcome her back with open arms?

William held her arm firmly as they walked along the narrow lane to the High Street. Rose thought she spotted Daniel standing at the edge of the main road, staring down the lane towards the church, but when she looked again, he had gone. She dismissed the sighting as her mind playing tricks on her because she knew how much she longed to see him again.

When the couple returned to Laburnum House, Rose went into the kitchen to prepare a dinner of roast beef, roast potatoes and boiled vegetables, while William read a book in the drawing room.

While she peeled and chopped the vegetables, Rose's mind was on her husband's behaviour. He treated her courteously enough in company, and anyone who saw them together would think he had forgiven her for leaving and generously taken her back. However, in private, his behaviour was much more volatile. He usually behaved like the gentleman she had presumed him to be when they first met. Still, occasionally, especially when he was angry, he became unpredictable and violent, and from previous experience, she knew she must be careful not to rile him.

When she challenged him about his new rules the previous day, he responded by hitting her and knocking her to the floor. There had been no room for discussion or negotiation; he had to be obeyed.

She shook her head. She couldn't understand why he thought he was the one who had been slighted by her disappearance when he had been the cause of it.

Of one thing, she was sure. Somehow, she had to get away from William and Laburnum House. She couldn't spend the rest of her days with him, living in his house, being paraded in public as his wife, but being treated no better than a slave and a whore in private.

If she had gone to her parents when William had first hit her, she wondered if they would have helped her. She doubted it. They would probably have agreed with the mine manager at Denaby Main that nobody should come between a man and his wife.

Rose was William's property to treat as he wished, and neither she nor anybody else could do anything about it.

She had heard of married couples getting divorced, and although it was becoming more common, only the very wealthy could afford to divorce their spouse. She had no money. Divorcing William was not an option for her.

She would be William's wife until either she died or he did, and that thought filled her with despair as they were both young and healthy. She wished he'd never come to Tow Law and that she'd never met him.

Rose hoped that one day, Daniel might return and whisk her away again. She had never been as happy as in the weeks she spent with him in Yorkshire. For the brief time she had been in the presence of her family at church that morning, she had been ashamed of what she'd done, but thinking back to those wonderful weeks, she knew she would do anything to spend just one more night in Daniel's arms, no matter the consequences.

'Get upstairs! Quick!' said William, barging into the kitchen looking flustered. 'And don't come down until I tell you to. Do you understand?'

Rose drew her eyebrows together, puzzled by his request, but nodded, put down the knife, and did what he said, leaving the joint of beef roasting in the oven.

From her bedroom, she heard voices coming from the front of the house, and she peered around the curtains to see what was happening outside.

She gasped.

Daniel was there.

He was standing by the garden gate, pleading with William to allow him to see her.

Rose's hand went to her chest, where her heart was beating rapidly. Daniel had come for her as she hoped he would.

She was surprised by William's arrogant stance in the front

garden. He didn't appear to be afraid of Daniel in the slightest, even though Daniel was larger and stronger than him, and a trained boxer. She wondered what trick William had up his sleeve.

Rose watched in horror as four stockily built men appeared from the back of the house, carrying shovels—miners whom William must have paid to guard the house in case Daniel should come for her. She recognised the tallest of the men to be Bill Wheatley, who had tormented Jimmy McNally and made the mistake of challenging the young boxer to a fight.

She stood there, helpless, with her hands clutched to her chest, wishing Jimmy was standing by Daniel's side right now; he had never needed his cousin more.

Daniel looked from William to the four men surrounding him. He stood his ground, his face impassive. Rose knew he was weighing up his odds against the five men and didn't fancy his chances. She could scarcely breathe.

The miners closed in on Daniel menacingly, and Daniel bolted onto the road and ran towards the town.

One of the men pitched his shovel at Daniel, and the metal blade hit Daniel's lower back, bringing him to an abrupt stop, and he fell to the ground. The men rushed over to where he lay on the road and punched and kicked him until, eventually, he stopped moving. The men stepped away from him, and William stood over Daniel's lifeless form.

Through her tears, Rose saw Jimmy McNally and Davy Morrison sprinting down the road towards Daniel.

At the sight of them, William ran back into the house, and Rose heard the door slam shut and the key turn in the lock.

When the two Irishmen reached William's miners, they punched them repeatedly, each taking on two at a time, until the miners fled from the scene, knowing that they couldn't beat Jimmy and Davy in a fight, even with tools as weapons.

Numbed by what she had seen, Rose watched from the bedroom window. Jimmy and Davy lifted Daniel by his arms and dragged him away up the road. His head and face were covered in blood, and his eyes were closed. She feared he might be dead.

'Please, God,' she said to herself. 'If there is any justice in this world that you created, let Daniel Kelly survive this day.'

Rose held back her tears for both Daisy and Daniel until William fell asleep that night. Her silent tears flowed freely in the quiet of the night as she remembered the good times that she had shared with each of them. They didn't stop until sunrise the following morning when Rose climbed out of bed, hurriedly dressed, pinned up her hair and went downstairs to make breakfast, desperately hoping that Daniel was still alive. She would not be able to settle or sleep until she knew one way or the other.

Chapter 37

Tow Law, County Durham
September, 1881

Rose filled Daniel's dreams. She was there with him, and they were smiling and laughing together. Suddenly, they were torn apart by forces over which he had no control, making him feel helpless and powerless and plunging him into the deepest despair.

When Daniel woke and opened his eyes, Jimmy was sitting by his side.

'It's good to have you back with us,' said Jimmy, smiling down at him. He raised his cousin's head and held a cup of water to his lips.

Daniel took a long drink of the cool liquid, which soothed his dry mouth and throat.

'How long have I been here?' asked Daniel, recognising the room he had lodged in at Mrs McKenna's house.

'You've been unconscious on and off for five days,' said Jimmy.

'Five days!' said Daniel. 'Where's Rose? Does she know what happened?'

'Aye, she does,' said Jimmy. 'I went to see her a couple of days ago when her husband was at work. He has a woman guarding her, did you know that? The old biddy was a soft-touch though, and she let me have a few minutes with Rose. I told her that you were alive but still unconscious. She's been frantic with worry about you, I can tell you that. She saw what happened and she thought you were dead.'

'Poor Rose,' whispered Daniel. He remembered what happened and how brutal William's men had been and wondered if they'd been hired to teach him a lesson or to kill him.

Daniel couldn't blame William for wanting him dead because when William had stolen Rose away from Denaby Main, he had wanted to kill William. On the journey back to Tow Law, Daniel had seriously thought about murdering him. That way, he could get Rose back and keep her forever, but killing was not in his nature. He had never shied away from a fight in his life, but killing somebody in cold blood, no, that was not something he could do. And if he were caught for the crime and hanged for it, Rose would be left all alone.

Daniel tried to lift himself off the bed, but pain filled his upper body, and he fell back onto the mattress.

'No!' said Jimmy. 'Don't move. Lie still. It's not just your head that was hurt, Daniel.'

'What's wrong with me?' he asked.

'Where do I start?' Jimmy looked at Daniel and said, 'They beat you so badly that I brought Doctor Fawcett over to have a look at you.'

'Did you tell him what happened?' asked Daniel.

'Aye, I did, and he didn't have any sympathy for you. He said you deserved what you got for stealing a man's wife and that William's men should have finished you off.'

Daniel tried to lift his hand to his head, but it wouldn't move. Panicking, he said, 'Tell me, Jimmy. What have they done to me?'

'Well, that arm is broken,' said Jimmy. 'It's splinted so you can't move it. It will heal in time though.'

'And what else?' asked Daniel, knowing that Jimmy was leaving the worst news until last.

'I've had to stitch cuts all over your body,' said Jimmy. 'The stitches can come out in a few days. Your back bore the brunt of it.'

'And?'

'Your ribs are broken.'

'How many?' asked Daniel.

'Most of them, I think.'

'Is that everything?'

'No,' said Jimmy, tugging nervously at his shirt cuffs and moving to the bottom of the bed. 'Your legs aren't broken— well, only one bone near your ankle is—but neither of them moves, and you can't feel anything when I touch your feet.'

Daniel lifted his head from the pillow and saw that Jimmy was squeezing his toes, yet he couldn't feel any pressure.

'You had an awful bruise on your lower back,' said Jimmy. 'The doctor thought it was caused by something sharp. Maybe the blade of a shovel or a spade. He thinks the paralysis might just be temporary until the swelling on your spine goes down. Time will tell.'

'I'm paralysed!' said Daniel. 'God, no!'

A tear ran down his cheek. He remembered his dream before waking, in which he felt helpless and powerless. Well, now he really was helpless and powerless. As Jimmy said, most of his wounds would heal in time, but if the lower half of his body didn't work, what use would he be to anyone? What use would he be to Rose if he couldn't walk or work or make love to her and give her children?

'You're young and strong, Daniel,' said Jimmy. 'If anyone can get over something like this, it's you!'

Mrs McKenna opened the bedroom door, approached his bedside, and placed her hand on his shoulder.

'I thought I heard voices up here,' she said. 'Thank God you've come round at last, Daniel. We've been worried sick about you. Jimmy here has hardly left the room since he and Davy brought you back. You must be thirsty and hungry. Can I get you something? A cup of tea or a bowl of soup?'

Daniel shook his head.

'He'll have some soup please, Mrs McKenna,' said Jimmy. 'He needs feeding up.'

'Right, you are! I've got some beef broth ready downstairs. I'll bring some up.' She left the room and descended the stairs.

'I don't want any,' said Daniel despondently. 'I don't want anything. I'd rather be dead than a cripple and a burden to anybody.'

'Don't give up on us now,' said Jimmy, taking Daniel by the shoulders. 'I've sat by your bedside since this happened, and I'll stay here as long as it takes to get you back on your feet. You will get over this, Daniel Kelly, so get that into that thick skull of yours.'

Daniel smiled, grateful that he had a cousin like Jimmy. He thought he must have a thick skull, too, because that was about the only part of him that the miners hadn't managed to break.

'Let's get you propped up so you can eat,' said Jimmy, piling

191

pillows behind Daniel's back and head to sit him up. 'Mrs McKenna will be back soon.'

Daniel's recovery was painful, slow and tedious, and he was grateful for Jimmy and Mrs McKenna's continued support as the weeks passed.

After a month, the bruising had gone, his cuts had faded to pink scars, and the broken bones were almost healed, but he still couldn't move his legs.

Every day, Daniel lay in bed and thought of Rose. He wished she was there with him to lift his spirits, help the time to pass more quickly and give him a reason to live. In his mind, he ignored the fact she was William Ashworth's wife because right now he needed to believe there was a future for them. What other reason did he have to get better?

Jimmy lifted Daniel's legs several times a day, bending and stretching them to prevent the muscles from wasting away and the joints from seizing up. He regularly checked whether or not any feeling had returned, but two more weeks passed without any change.

Then, when Daniel woke one morning and stretched, his left foot felt itchy, and he scratched it with his right foot.

When he realised what he'd done, he shouted, 'Jimmy! I can move my feet!'

Jimmy leapt off his bed, grinning at Daniel, and just to be sure, he grabbed Daniel's big toe.

'Get off!' said Daniel, pulling his foot away.

Jimmy hugged Daniel, and they cried tears of joy.

38

Chapter 38

Tow Law, County Durham
November, 1881

Daniel couldn't believe how weak he felt as he tried to stand for the first time. His legs buckled beneath him, and he fell back onto the bed. Even though Jimmy had been moving his legs regularly to prevent the muscles and joints from seizing up, the muscles had wasted away through lack of use.

'Take it slowly,' said Jimmy. 'Come on, let's try again. Put your hands on my shoulders and I'll take your weight.'

Daniel laughed.

'I'm stronger than I look,' said Jimmy.

'Aye, I know that,' said Daniel. 'I just don't think I can do it.'

'Yes, you can,' said his cousin. 'Don't think I'm going to allow you to be a cripple for the rest of your days, Daniel Kelly, and have anyone waiting on you hand and foot. I'm going to be a tougher trainer than Mr O'Dowd was back in Galway.'

Daniel leaned forward, placed his hands on Jimmy's shoulders and then lifted himself, using his arms rather than his legs until he was standing on his feet.

'There you go,' said Jimmy. 'I knew you could do it. Now, I'll walk backwards and you step forwards.'

Daniel wobbled as he moved his right foot forward and then his left. He walked four faltering steps before Jimmy bumped into the wall. Jimmy turned around, and they walked slowly back to the bed.

'Aye, you'll be running around in no time, chasing them girls again,' said Jimmy and flinched. 'I'm sorry, Daniel. I meant nothing by it.'

Daniel shook his head sadly and sat on the edge of the bed. 'It's alright, Jimmy, and thank you for your help. I want to get back on my feet, but not to chase Rose or any other girls. I'm learning how to walk again so I can get as far away from here and from her as possible.'

'Well, I can see why you'd want to do that,' said Jimmy, putting his hand on his cousin's shoulder, 'and I don't blame you. Now, lie on the bed, put your feet against the wall and push.'

After completing several exercises, Daniel was exhausted and covered in sweat. He removed his shirt and washed himself with a cloth and cool water from a jug by his bed.

Later that day, Mrs McKenna came to Daniel's room and cut his hair, which had grown considerably in the time he'd been there. Then, she brought him a mirror, a razor, some soap and a bowl of hot water and placed them on the small table by his bed.

'I thought you might like to tidy yourself up, now that you're back on your feet,' she said, smiling kindly at him. When she left, he looked into the mirror. He'd changed since the attack; his face was thinner, paler and bearded, and a scar ran down his left cheek, about an inch and a half long. He had seen the scars on his chest and right thigh, and he was grateful that he couldn't see how bad his back was for it had taken the worst of the beating. He'd counted fifty-six stitches when Jimmy removed them. After a haircut and a shave, he felt much better.

As promised, Jimmy was a tough trainer, and Daniel followed his instructions and more. He wanted to get well so he could leave the town. There was nothing for him at Tow Law any more.

In four more weeks, Daniel could walk several miles with the aid of a walking stick. He still felt a bit unsteady at times, but he was improving rapidly.

It was time.

Chapter 39

Tow Law, County Durham
December, 1881

Rose stood by her sister's grave. A light dusting of snow coated the ground. She'd visited the churchyard regularly since she learned of Daisy's death but hadn't known which of the newly dug graves was hers. She couldn't ask anyone; she should have been there for the funeral.

But now, she knew.

A wooden cross stood at the head of one grave, crudely carved with the name Daisy, and Rose guessed Bobby had made it himself to commemorate his late wife.

Rose stood at the foot of the grave and said the words she had waited so long to say.

'My dearest Daisy, I'm so sorry I wasn't there for you and your baby when your time came. It's hard for me to explain why I left so suddenly without telling anyone. I needed to escape from Tow Law and didn't have time to tell you or anybody else the reason for it. I think you suspected something was wrong between William and me from the start. Well, you were right, as usual. You always were a good judge of character. I hate to admit it, even now, but my husband is a violent man. If you had seen the state I was in when I left—what William had done to me—I'm sure you would have understood. He almost killed me, Daisy.

'Now, everybody around here thinks the worst of me for running away with Daniel Kelly. None of them know what really happened. They don't know I left William because he beat me. They don't know that Daniel saved my life and protected me. The gossip in the town is wrong. In the four weeks I spent with Daniel, we didn't have a sordid affair like everyone's saying. Nothing improper happened between us.

'My life is such a mess, Daisy. I'm stuck with a cruel husband. I hate him so much for what he's done. And I love Daniel with all my heart, but it's unlikely I'll ever see him again. I do wonder, in my darkest moments, if I would be better off in that grave instead of you. If I could change places with you and give your baby back his mother, I would.

'I can't believe you're no longer here. I see Bobby with your baby at the church every Sunday and my heart goes out to them. They are both well, but I can see Bobby misses you dreadfully. Rest in peace, my favourite sister.'

By the end of her speech, tears flowed down Rose's cheeks. She took a handkerchief from her pocket and dried her face.

Mrs Newton stood by the churchyard gates, giving Rose some privacy to grieve for her sister. Eventually, Rose walked back to her, and they continued to the house in silence.

After a cup of tea, the ladies sat by the fire in the drawing room, discussing plans for Christmas.

'William wants a tree in this room,' said Rose, 'and he's

asked me to dress it. Would you help me with the decorations?'

'Of course I will, dear,' said Mrs Newton. 'It would be my pleasure.'

Although William's rules were that Rose should do all the work while her companion supervised her, Mrs Newton often helped Rose with the chores without being asked. She wasn't the sort of woman to sit around idly when there was work to be done.

Initially, Rose resented the woman's constant presence because she had been forced upon her by William. Over the last few months though, they'd spent so much time together that Rose realised, begrudgingly at first, that she enjoyed the older woman's company. It was nice to have somebody to talk to.

Rose rarely spoke with anyone except for William and Mrs Newton. She saw her family briefly before church on Sunday mornings, but they hardly had a word to say to her any more. Mrs Newton had become more of a companion to her than a chaperone.

The ladies were writing a list of the items they would need to make the Christmas decorations when they heard a knock at the door.

'I'll get it,' said Mrs Newton, remembering her role as Rose's protector.

Rose heard the unmistakable voice, jumped up, and rushed to the door. Daniel was standing on the doorstep, asking Mrs Newton if he could speak with her.

Rose was overjoyed to see that he had walked to the house, although he was leaning heavily on a walking stick, and she grinned at him.

His eyes looked over Mrs Newton's shoulder, and his face

softened at the sight of Rose in the hallway.

Mrs Newton relented when she saw the love they shared for each other and stepped aside.

'Five minutes,' said Mrs Newton, 'that's your lot. I'll be back in five minutes.'

She went out the back door, leaving Daniel and Rose looking at each other in the hallway.

'You can walk again,' she said with wonder in her voice.

'Aye, I can,' he said. 'It's nigh on a miracle after—'

'I'm so sorry for what William's men did to you,' said Rose. She stepped forward, raised her hand to the new scar on Daniel's cheek, and ran her finger along it.

He grabbed her hand and pressed it to his lips, then lowered his head and kissed her, holding her firmly in his arms.

'I've dreamed about doing that for so long,' he whispered.

'Me too,' she said. 'What are we going to do now, Daniel? Will you take me away from here? Please.'

Daniel looked down at the ground.

'You're not leaving me here with him, are you?' she asked, her voice breaking.

'I'm so sorry, Rose, but I don't have a choice,' he said sadly. 'If we run away together, William will find us again like he did before. You are his wife. That's just the way it is.'

'So, why did you come to see me?' she asked, her eyes glassy with unshed tears. 'Raising my hopes and then stamping them into the ground.'

'I came to say goodbye, Rose,' he said. 'I'm leaving Tow Law soon. I can't stay here and see you with him. It...it would hurt too much.'

'Where are you going?' she asked, her voice sounding high to her ears.

'I don't know yet,' he said. 'I'll travel around for a while and stop when I find work. That's what we Irish do, you know.'

'Kiss me again before you go,' Rose begged.

Daniel kissed her passionately until they were breathless.

'I'll always love you, Rose,' he said. 'Don't you ever forget that.'

Mrs Newton opened the back door and coughed loudly, warning the young couple that she was coming back.

'I'm going now,' shouted Daniel to let her know that it was safe for her to return, and he walked out of the front door without looking back.

Rose ran up the stairs and sobbed uncontrollably on her bed for hours, her heart breaking at the thought that she would never see her beloved Daniel again.

When her thoughts became more lucid, she remembered the dreadful injuries that Daniel had sustained at William's instruction, and she was just glad that he was alive; for as long as Daniel was alive, there was always hope.

After breakfast on Christmas morning, Rose gave William a gift. He smiled as he took it and quickly unwrapped it.

'Handkerchiefs,' he said, unfolding the white squares.

'They are made from the best cotton, and I embroidered your initials on the corner of each one,' said Rose, pleased with her handiwork.

'So you did,' said William. 'Thank you, my dear Rose.'

He placed the handkerchiefs on the table, stood up and walked into the drawing room leaving them behind.

Rose was disappointed by his reaction to her gift. She had spent hours sewing the fine, delicate stitches on each one to perfect the letters W A for William Ashworth.

William returned carrying a gift in brown paper, with a red ribbon tied in a bow at the top.

'For you,' he said. 'Merry Christmas.'

Rose untied the bow and removed the paper to uncover a box.

'Open it!' he urged.

She opened the lid slowly, unsure what to expect from her husband. He had never bought her a gift before. Inside, she saw a business card for the dressmaker's shop on the High Street. Under it was something wrapped in white paper. Her heart skipped a beat. Was it the red satin dress that she had longed for?

Excitedly, she peeled back the white paper and revealed a fancy corset in pale blue silk, a matching pair of garters and a pair of silk stockings.

She tried to hide her disappointment. She smiled and said, 'Thank you, William.'

'I want you to go upstairs and put these on and I will look forward to unwrapping my Christmas gift tonight,' he said with a wicked grin.

Rose went upstairs to change into her new underwear, knowing that for the rest of the day, she would dread the coming evening as much as William would await it with pleasure.

She spent the morning preparing their Christmas dinner, which comprised leek soup, roast goose with roast potatoes and vegetables, and plum pudding with brandy sauce. Mrs Newton had made the pudding five weeks earlier so it was just to warm up. The couple ate the delicious three-course meal in the dining room almost in silence. Now and again, William looked at her and smiled lewdly or winked at her, which Rose found very unnerving.

She raised her eyes to William's face and wondered if, after everything that had happened, she would ever come to love her husband, but when he returned her look with one of pure lust, she felt repulsed by him. It wasn't likely that she could ever love a man she didn't desire.

Rose fondly remembered previous Christmases at her family home. They had always been joyful and lively affairs. Family members had crowded around the table for their Christmas dinner, which had never been as extravagant as the one she ate today, but she had enjoyed it so much more because she had been in the company of people she loved. After their meal, they would tell stories, play games and laugh. They laughed a lot.

Had she ever heard William laugh?

'Perhaps we could visit my parents this afternoon,' Rose suggested. 'Lily and Violet will be there with their families.'

'No,' said William dismissively. 'I don't intend to waste a day associating with drunken men, listening to women's nonsense and avoiding snotty children when I could spend it peacefully here at home. I'll be in the conservatory tending my plants if you need me.'

Rose cleared the table and washed the dishes. This Christmas was her first as a married woman, and she felt utterly miserable. Her thoughts turned to Daniel, as they often did, and she wondered where he had gone and how he was spending Christmas.

40

Chapter 40

Tow Law, County Durham
February, 1882

William whistled to himself as he walked across the yard to the pit to conduct the regular safety inspection. Around six hundred men and boys worked at Black Prince Colliery, and he was responsible for their safety. Today, though, his mind was on Rose as he descended to the coal seams where the miners worked.

After Rose's escapades, she had settled back into Laburnum House as if nothing had happened, and she was more affable and less argumentative than before. She had been more attentive to his needs lately, for which he was grateful. He would never have needed to discipline her if she had behaved in this way when they were first married.

He'd heard that Daniel Kelly had left the town, and good riddance to him. William doubted the Irishman would ever return, not after the beating his men had given him. He would have been happier if they had finished him off, and then he would be out of their lives forever, but they'd failed because that meddlesome boxer and a fellow countryman had come on the scene and saved him. At least his men had scared Kelly enough to make him leave town. That was a decent result.

William smiled mischievously. Rose was his now, his alone, and she always would be.

The coal seams in the area of the mine William inspected were shallow, and he didn't like to venture too far into them. He examined the miners' working conditions as well as he could from a place where he could stand, albeit bending over, and without touching the dirty walls to avoid caking his clothes in wet coal dust—it was horrible, mucky stuff.

The heat was almost unbearable at this depth underground. William didn't remove his jacket because he deemed it inappropriate for a manager to do so, but he understood why many of the miners worked bare-chested and sometimes even bare-legged in the mine.

He asked the men if their canaries were healthy, and they all answered in the affirmative. He then visually checked the air for coal dust. One area had an exceptionally high rate of fine dust particles, and he ordered it to be watered down to reduce the risk of an explosion.

When he finished, William returned to the surface as quickly as possible. He had always been interested in the geology of the coalfields and the methods of working in the mines, but he didn't like spending time underground.

He couldn't work in the cramped conditions that the coal hewers endured day in and day out. Some seams were less than two feet deep, and the miners lay on their bellies for up to twelve hours a day, picking at the coal and moving it out to the waiting trucks, pulled by pit ponies that lived in the bowels of the earth.

The darkness, heat, dust, threat of toxic gases, confined spaces, and the fear of rock falls combined to make the coal mine William's idea of hell.

It surprised him how many men came knocking at the office door asking to work there. He knew it was the wages that drew them to the pits. Coal miners were paid more than most labourers, but they needed to be to work in those dreadful conditions. It was a dangerous job, too. Not all of them would survive it. Luckily, there had been no fatalities at the mine since he took over as manager.

When William reached the mine office, he warmed his hands by the fire, asked his clerk for a cup of tea, sat at his desk and picked up a newspaper. The headline on the front page immediately grabbed his attention. He read the report of a terrible explosion at Trimdon Grange Colliery that had occurred on the sixteenth day of that month. He learned that dozens of men and boys had been killed by a massive explosion and the subsequent fire and that many more had been suffocated by the afterdamp that followed. In total, seventy-four souls had lost their lives.

William's hands were shaking as he folded the newspaper and laid it on the desk, and he wondered if he had carried out his inspection as carefully as he should have done. He had been distracted by thoughts of Rose—she was very distracting—but he shouldn't let his love life interfere with his work. He was the manager at Black Prince Colliery, and he was responsible for the men and boys working at his mine. If a disaster like the one at Trimdon Grange were to happen there, he would never forgive himself.

He got to his feet without drinking his tea and returned to

the pit to carry out another inspection. This time, William was focused entirely on his job. He ordered all areas of the mine to be watered down, not just the dustiest part, reprimanded a miner for riding on a truck in a low tunnel, and told the miners who used midgie lamps for light to use Davy lamps in the future because the naked flames from the candles were a potential fire hazard. As tedious as it was, he checked all the roofs above the workings to ensure they were not at risk of falling and ordered men to add more props in sections of the mine where there was any doubt.

Eventually, he returned to his office, thinking about the accident at Trimdon Grange. The cause would not be known until the coroner investigated further. Still, William was confident that he had done everything possible to prevent a similar accident from occurring in his mine. That was all he could do.

Chapter 41

Tow Law, County Durham
March, 1882

Time passed slowly for Rose after Daniel left town. It had been a long, cold winter. Snow fell heavily in January and February, making the roads impassable for much of that time, but March had been mild, and there were signs of spring all around.

During this time, Rose continued to do everything William expected of her, and life settled back into its routine of house-work during the day and taking care of his needs at night. She was pleased that the snow had stopped her gardening activities for a while, making life a little easier for a few months.

Rose had come to accept that she was William's wife and that this was what her life would entail from now on. She found it difficult not to answer him back, especially when she disagreed with him or disapproved of what he said, but she'd learned the hard way that it was better to keep her mouth shut than to oppose him in any way. She continued to bite her lip, and he had not hit her for quite some time. It seemed they had come to a truce of sorts.

She still missed Daniel terribly but acknowledged they had no future together. Not while William was alive, anyway. She regretted that dreadfully, but it was the truth, and she had to accept that, too.

Rose wrapped herself up and walked to the butcher's shop to buy a duck for their evening meal. Since her return to the town, few people bothered to pass the time of day with her, silently claiming moral superiority. If only they knew the truth, she thought.

When she entered the shop, Lily was standing behind the counter serving a gentleman, and John was making pork sausages in the room at the back of the shop. The customer was talking heatedly to Lily and then turned to leave. When he saw Rose, he tutted, turned up his nose, and walked out without saying a word to her.

Lily greeted Rose and said, 'Take no notice of him.'

The slight had upset Rose, even though the man was a stranger to her.

'I know you always got on better with our Daisy than me with you being nearer in age,' said Lily, 'but no matter what's happened, you're still family. If you need anything, I'm always here.'

'Thank you,' said Rose, swallowing loudly, surprised at her sister's words. She had been coming into the shop regularly since her return, and neither Lily nor John had treated her very kindly.

'I heard you've been visiting Daisy's grave every week,' said Lily. 'I hope you're not feeling guilty for what happened to her. I know Mother blames you for going away, but she shouldn't. If you'd been here, there would have been nothing that you could have done for her, just like there was nothing the rest of us could do.'

'Thank you,' repeated Rose, her eyes glassy. She didn't feel responsible for Daisy's death, but she felt terrible for not being with her sister in her final days and for missing the chance to say goodbye.

Being close to tears, Rose changed the topic of conservation away from Daisy.

'What was that fella in front of me all het up about?' she asked.

'The ironworks,' said Lily.

'What about it?' asked Rose.

'Haven't you heard?' asked Lily incredulously. 'Everybody's talking about it. It's closing down. It's just rumours at the minute, but where there's smoke there's fire, I always think.'

'But why?' asked Rose. 'There must be a thousand men working there. What will they do if it closes?'

'Rumour has it that they'll be offered jobs at the company's other site at Tudhoe,' said Lily. 'It'll be bad for business if that many families move away from here. They're all customers, even if they don't shop here as often as you do.'

So, that was why Lily's attitude had changed towards her. Her sister was concerned about the future of her business. Rose probably spent more money in their shop than anyone else because William demanded expensive cuts of red meat or a whole chicken, duck or game bird at every evening meal.

Rose was grateful that nobody else in her family would be affected by the ironwork's closure; none of them worked there.

At dinner that evening, Rose questioned William about what she'd heard, and he had quite a lot to say on the matter, some of which Rose didn't understand. Still, it seemed the Weardale

Iron and Coal Company thought it better to manufacture their products at one site, and it had chosen the Tudhoe site over Tow Law. He didn't appear concerned about the effect the decision might have on his mine, even though the same company owned it, and most of the coal from it was used at the ironworks that was under threat of closure. William thought the coal he produced might be sent to the ironworks at Tudhoe instead, but if not, there were plenty of other markets for it.

He was particularly cheerful that evening, and even the forthcoming closure of the ironworks and the uncertainly about the future of his colliery didn't dampen his mood.

'Why are you so happy tonight?' she asked, unable to resist asking the question any longer.

'Ah! Is it that obvious?' he chuckled. 'After dinner, I will be packing my travel bag. The company has agreed to give me leave to go to London.'

'You're going to London?' she asked incredulously.

'Yes, indeed,' he said. 'I'm going there to watch the FA Cup Final. I can't wait to see The Old Etonians play against Blackburn Rovers. To reach the final is no mean feat. To get that far, they've already proven that they are the best two teams in the country.'

'That's wonderful,' said Rose.

'Yes, it is,' he replied. 'I might even learn a trick or two from them to improve my game.'

Getting up from the table, he kissed her cheek, and as he rushed upstairs to pack his bag, he shouted, 'I leave first thing in the morning. You can expect me home on Monday afternoon!'

42

Chapter 42

Tow Law, County Durham
March, 1882

On Monday afternoon, Rose and Mrs Newton were baking in the kitchen when they heard a knock at the front door. Rose's heart skipped a beat. Her first thought was that Daniel had returned for her while William was away, and the second was that William had returned early—which was silly because William wouldn't knock at his own front door.

Mrs Newton wiped her hands on her apron and went to answer it.

'Good afternoon,' said Mrs Newton.

Rose didn't hear the reply, but Mrs Newton invited the visitors into the drawing room. Rose hastily washed her hands, removed her apron, and went to see who was calling at the house unannounced. In the drawing room stood a well-dressed gentleman who looked to be in his fifties and a woman just a few years older than herself.

'Please, sit down,' said Rose.

'We'd rather stand if you don't mind,' said the man in a strong Scottish accent. 'My name is Henry Campbell, and this is my daughter, Mrs Adeline Mitchell. We have travelled from Ayrshire in Scotland to come here today.'

'I expect you're looking for Mr Ashworth,' said Rose, remembering that her husband's family hailed from that part of Scotland.

'If that's what he's calling himself these days,' said Mr Campbell.

'I'm sorry, I don't know what you mean,' said Rose, puzzled by his comment.

Taking a newspaper cutting from his jacket pocket, Mr Campbell unfolded it and said, 'I can see that you are the young lady in this photograph.'

He showed Rose a copy of the wedding photograph that had appeared in the newspaper while William was searching for her.

'Who is this man standing next to you?' he asked.

'That's my husband,' said Rose. 'Mr William Ashworth.'

The young woman laughed bitterly.

'This is no laughing matter, Adeline,' said her father sternly. 'Now that we have found the man we sought, Mrs Ashworth, it seems we have a great deal to discuss. Perhaps a cup of tea might be in order.'

'I'll make it,' said Mrs Newton, sensing trouble. 'Perhaps you'd like to sit in the breakfast room.'

The guests followed Rose to the breakfast room and sat around the table. Shortly afterwards, Mrs Newton brought in a tray and poured the tea.

'Please stay, Mrs Newton,' said Rose, as the housekeeper turned to leave. These people were making her nervous. She didn't know them or the purpose of their visit, but it seemed to be of a serious nature.

Mrs Newton poured a cup of tea for herself and joined Rose and the guests. She squeezed Rose's arm reassuringly under the table.

'Where shall I start?' Mr Campbell asked himself. 'I own a couple of coal mines up in Ayrshire. They are not big affairs but they've done well enough.'

Rose could see by his and Adeline's clothes that they were wealthy, and she was not surprised they were involved in the coal mining industry as they appeared to be acquainted with William.

'About five years ago, a man came to work for me. Before long, he was courting my daughter, Adeline. Well, she fell head over heels in love with him and they married a year later at the wee kirk in our village. That man's name was William Mitchell.'

Rose wondered why the man was telling her this story. It had no relevance to her whatsoever, but to be polite, she let him continue.

'One night, William Mitchell vanished,' he said. 'He left his wife and wee laddie, emptied their bank account and disappeared into thin air.'

'I'm very sorry to hear that, Mr Campbell,' said Rose sincerely.

'It's taken me a while to track down the scoundrel,' said Mr Campbell, 'but my perseverance has finally paid off, and I have found him at last.'

Rose raised her eyebrows.

'This may come as a shock to you,' he said, 'but I believe our William Mitchell and your William Ashworth are one and the same man.'

Rose stood up, shaking her head, her eyes wide as she looked at the gentleman and his daughter.

'You think my husband is William Mitchell,' she said. 'The man who abandoned your daughter and grandson.'

'I'm almost certain of it,' said Mr Campbell. 'The man in this wedding photo is a very good likeness.'

'No, he can't be,' said Rose, shaking her head again, unable to process the information. 'I'm sure there's been a terrible mistake. William has been away for a few days but I'm expecting him home shortly. We'll soon sort this out.'

Rose took her seat again. The young woman opposite her had remained silent throughout the conversation, apart from the earlier inappropriate outburst of laughter. She must have been dreadfully hurt when her husband left her and their son, thought Rose.

She looked at Adeline more closely. She was short and slightly plump. Her mid-brown hair was tied back under a pretty hat, her nose was a little large and slightly hooked, and her dark eyes were small and brooding. In reality, she was quite plain, and Rose couldn't imagine that her William would have married this woman. Mr Campbell must be mistaken.

Rose flinched at the sound of the front door opening.

'I'm home!' shouted William. 'It was an incredible match, Rose. I must tell you all about it over dinner.'

Rose heard William remove his hat and coat and put them on the coat stand in the hall. A few seconds later, he walked into the breakfast room, and his face turned pale as he looked wildly from Mr Campbell to Adeline, cursing under his breath. Rose wondered if he might flee from the house.

'William,' said Mr Campbell, rising to his feet. 'It's been a long time.'

Rose was surprised that neither of the men held out their hands in greeting if they were acquainted.

William shook his head slowly and sighed, and he then surprised Rose when he sat down at the table, his shoulders slumped. She tried to catch his eye to work out what was happening, but he avoided her eye contact.

What was going on?

Clearly, William knew both Mr Campbell and Adeline, which implied Mr Campbell's tale was true.

Who was this man she had married?

'You're a difficult man to track down, William,' said Mr Campbell, retaking his seat. 'I've been searching for you ever since you deserted our Adeline and Billy. The poor lad was distraught when his father disappeared without a word, and Adeline was embarrassed beyond words when you left and took her money. It proved what everybody had been thinking—that you'd only married her for her money.'

'I'm very sorry,' said William, facing Adeline. 'But in my defence, I knew your father would take care of you both.'

'Aye, and he has,' she said sharply. 'But it wasn't his place to after we were wed. You were my husband and it was your responsibility to take care of me and our wean. What you did to me and our Billy, walking out on us like that, was...was disgraceful and you know it!'

Adeline's bottom lip quivered as though she was fighting to hold back tears, and Rose felt sorry for the woman.

William nodded sheepishly.

'Now that we have found you, I must inform you that my daughter will be filing for a divorce,' said Mr Campbell. 'She wants her name removed from yours—permanently.'

Rose watched the proceedings as if she wasn't there. It felt like she was a participant in a bizarre dream. Everything Mr Campbell had said about William had been absolutely true. William had not denied the accusation or tried to defend himself in any way whatsoever.

William had been married to Adeline before he married her. She couldn't understand how the man had had the cheek to lie to Reverend Hardy and say that he was single and free to marry her when he was already committed to a woman who had borne his child. She swallowed loudly.

Mrs Newton held Rose's hand, and Rose was grateful for the support. It reminded her that she must stay strong while she was in company.

'I imagine this young lady has something to say to you, too,' said Mr Campbell, looking at Rose, and all eyes turned towards her.

Rose cleared her throat.

'I believed everything you told me, William,' she said. 'I had no reason to doubt your word and I married you in good faith. Ever since then, I have regretted that decision. As your wife, you have made my life a misery. I've hated every minute that I've spent under your roof.'

William's face turned paler at her words, knowing they were true.

'You beat me,' said Rose, 'and you never apologised or showed regret for it.'

'Stop right there!' said William. 'You can't fire accusations at me without proof.'

'Yes, he did beat her,' said Mrs Newton firmly. 'I saw the evidence for myself. He might have carried on and killed her if he hadn't been stopped. This wasn't just a few cuts and bruises, you understand, Mr Campbell. This young woman suffered broken bones at his hand.'

Mr Campbell's face turned red, and he said, 'It appears you may have several court hearings to attend, William. Divorce, bigamy and possibly assault. There is at least one witness who can corroborate her story. If your marriage to this woman had been legally binding, she would not be able to bring charges against you, but as it isn't, she can have you charged for assault if she wishes to do so.'

'Rose doesn't have money for solicitors and such like,' said William. 'She's a miner's daughter.'

'I will pay for her counsel, you swine!' said Mr Campbell.

'Thank you very much, Mr Campbell,' said Rose. 'That's very generous of you.'

'It's no trouble at all, my dear,' he said. 'This man has treated you abominably. It's the least I can do.'

Then, Mr Campbell faced William and said, 'When we're finished with you, William Mitchell, you'll be ruined. You'll more than likely end up in gaol. Mrs Newton, perhaps you could fetch the constable and we'll make a start right away. There's no better time than the present.'

As Mrs Newton left the room, everything became too much for Rose, and she felt as though she was floating as she slid into unconsciousness.

When she came round, she was lying on the sofa in the drawing room with Doctor Fawcett's tall, lean figure standing over her, holding something foul-smelling under her nose.

Slowly, she sat up, feeling dazed.

'Are you alright, Rose?' asked William. 'You gave us all a fright. I brought the doctor over to check on you.'

Rose nodded.

'Fainting is not uncommon when women are in a delicate condition,' said the doctor.

Everyone in the room looked horrified by his words.

'Didn't you know your wife was with child, Mr Ashworth?' asked the doctor.

'No,' he said. 'Rose has not told me she's pregnant.'

Rose dropped her head into her hands. She hadn't known she was pregnant but guessed she should have. Her courses had never been regular, and it was not uncommon for her to go two months without a bleed, but she had been feeling a little unwell lately and had skipped breakfast on a few occasions.

Silent tears streamed down Rose's cheeks. The reality of her situation was beginning to sink in. She was not married to William and never had been. William was going to prison. She had no money or job and nowhere to live. And she was going to have William's baby. Could things get any worse?

'I know it will be difficult for you,' said Mr Campbell. 'But don't you worry about the child's upkeep. I'll make provisions for that.'

Rose was so choked up that she couldn't respond to his generous offer.

Chapter 43

Tow Law, County Durham
March, 1882

The news that she was carrying William's baby had utterly shaken Rose, and she was glad when Mrs Newton returned to the house.

Mrs Newton introduced the constable to Mr Campbell. The men shook hands and sat on the sofa, and Mr Campbell explained why Mrs Newton had invited him to the house.

Seeing Rose's distress, Mrs Newton sat down beside her, handed her a handkerchief and put an arm protectively around her shoulders.

'Rose needs a minute,' said Mrs Newton. 'Will you excuse us, please?'

'Certainly,' said Mr Campbell. 'Take all the time you need.'

Mrs Newton helped Rose to her feet and took her upstairs to her bedroom.

Once she was away from William and the visitors, Rose burst out crying.

'What's got into you, Rose?' asked Mrs Newton, bewildered. 'Before I went to fetch the constable, you were so brave, standing up to William the way you did, and when I get back, your colour's all gone, and you're crying.'

'I'm pregnant,' Rose managed to say between sobs. 'With William's baby.'

'Oh, no!' said Mrs Newton, stepping back. 'Not now that you're rid of him and you're free to live your life with your young man. Why did this have to happen? Life can be so unfair, Rose. God help you, you poor thing.'

Rose sat on the edge of the bed, contemplating what had taken place that afternoon. It was a lot to take in. Then she thought about how she had suffered as William's wife, and intense anger at his deception and treatment of her threatened to overcome her. He had tricked her, used her, and abused her, but she would suffer no more at William's hand. It felt like a huge weight had been lifted from her. She was finally free of him. Everything else paled into insignificance compared to that.

'Are you ready to face the constable's questions now?' asked Mrs Newton.

'Aye, I am.'

The ladies entered the drawing room downstairs, and Rose was composed as she sat in an armchair.

'I've had a word with this gentleman,' said the policeman, nodding towards Mr Campbell, 'and he's told me what's been going on here and I'm very sorry to hear it, miss.'

'Thank you,' said Rose.

'I'm Police Constable Walker,' he said, holding out his hand in greeting. 'I don't think I've had the pleasure...'

'Mrs Ashworth. No, Miss Lawson,' she replied, shaking his

hand. 'Please call me Rose.'

'Right then, Rose, I've got a few questions for you, if you don't mind,' said the constable. 'When and where were you and William Mitchell married?'

'I knew him as William Ashworth,' said Rose. 'We were married at St. Philips and St. James Church in Tow Law on the twenty-fourth of June.'

'Before the wedding, did he ever tell you that he had been married before?'

'No,' said Rose firmly. 'I had no idea that he was already married.'

The constable glared at William, who seemed to shrink into his seat and looked more like a scolded schoolboy than the mine manager he was. He really was a coward. Why hadn't she noticed that before? He had used a spade against Daniel and hired men to attack him, yet he had used his fists and boots on her, a woman who couldn't defend herself.

'There is no doubt in my mind after speaking with Mr Campbell and yourself that William is a bigamist,' said Police Constable Walker, 'and he will be arrested for it, but first, I need to ask you about the assaults Mr Campbell mentioned.'

Rose nodded her assent.

'Why didn't you report William for assault at the time it happened?' asked the constable. 'We could have seen the damage he'd inflicted for ourselves then.'

'Because I believed I was his wife,' said Rose. 'What would the police have done about a man hitting his wife?'

'Ah! Fair enough,' said the constable, looking ill at ease. 'Have you sustained any injuries from these assaults?'

'Yes,' said Rose. 'I had broken ribs, a broken nose, and cuts and bruises.'

Mrs Newton reached out, took Rose's hand and said, 'I saw the injuries for myself. She was in a right state. I reckon he would have killed her if another fella hadn't stepped in and put a stop to it.'

'Another fella? Who is this fella?' asked the policeman. 'Would he be willing to testify in court?'

'Daniel Kelly,' said Rose. 'He doesn't live around here any more.'

'Do you know where he can be contacted?' asked the constable.

Rose hung her head and said, 'Sorry, I don't know where he is.'

'That's a shame,' said the policeman, 'but with your word and that of your housekeeper, I think that should be enough to get a conviction.'

'There is somebody else who saw how badly injured I was,' said Rose. 'His name is Jimmy McNally. He tended my wounds. He lives in Tow Law.'

'The boxer! Very good, Rose,' said the constable. 'I'll have a chat with him. If he's willing to give evidence in court, we'll have a better chance of getting a conviction.'

'I hope he will,' said Rose, staring fiercely at William.

'You let that young boxer tend your wounds?' asked William. 'My God! That's so indecent I don't know where to start.'

'He wouldn't have needed to if you hadn't caused those wounds in the first place,' said Rose sharply, no longer afraid of him.

'William Mitchell, if that is your real name,' said the policeman, 'I am arresting you for committing bigamy and for the serious assault of Miss Rose Lawson.'

The constable read William his rights and then accompanied

him out of the house.

Rose sighed loudly when the door closed behind them.

'That is our mission done,' said Mr Campbell. 'I'm so sorry that William deceived you into marriage and mistreated you. In some respects, it is unfortunate that you are carrying his child, but a life is a life, and it must be God's will. No doubt He has his reasons.'

'Thank you, Mr Campbell,' said Rose.

'Will you be alright?' he asked. 'I mean financially.'

'I don't have any money,' said Rose. 'William wouldn't let me work. He doesn't give me housekeeping money or an allowance. He controls the bank account and pays the bills himself.'

Mr Campbell shook his head and said, 'Why doesn't that surprise me? He must have a small fortune stashed away. He took my daughter's money when he left Scotland and I expect he is in receipt of a good salary from the mine here.'

Mr Campbell took several bank notes from his inside jacket pocket and gave them to Rose.

'Treat this as a gift,' he said. 'I only wish there was more I could do.'

'Thank you,' said Rose. 'You revealed the truth and freed me from an unhappy marriage, Mr Campbell, and William will get what he deserves for what he's done to Adeline and me. I'm very grateful to you.'

Mr Campbell and Adeline said their farewells and left the house.

'Now,' said Mrs Newton, getting to her feet. 'I don't know about you, but I need a cup of tea.'

When she was alone, Rose smiled. She was rid of William at last. Then, she remembered the baby she was carrying in her womb. She would never be rid of William if she gave birth to his child, and the smile disappeared from her face.

Mrs Newton brought in a tea tray and a plate of ginger biscuits.

'Here,' she said, handing Rose a cup and saucer, 'drink this and get something to eat. You've hardly eaten anything today. Ginger is good for nausea.'

Rose sipped at the hot drink and nibbled at a biscuit. Discovering she was hungry, she finished it and picked up another.

'You can't stay here, dear,' said Mrs Newton. 'William will come back when the constable is finished questioning him. Do you think your parents would take you in?'

Rose almost choked on her tea.

'My family have had nothing to do with me since I came back to Tow Law,' said Rose. 'They'd take in a stranger before they'd take me in.'

'Well, in that case, you will come and live with me,' said Mrs Newton. 'My husband has passed, as you know, and my sons have moved away, so I live by myself now. You might not realise it, Rose, but I've come to think of you as a daughter over these past few months and it would be a pleasure to have you stay with me.'

Rose's eyes filled with tears as she hugged the older woman.

'Thank you,' she said. 'That's very kind of you.'

44

Chapter 44

Tow Law, County Durham
March, 1882

Rose took her clothes and a few belongings from Laburnum House and closed the door behind her without any regrets. Although the house and the gardens were beautiful, and she had admired them once, the place was full of bad memories now.

Mrs Newton walked alongside Rose as they carried her things to her home on Weardale Street. They followed two shepherds and their collie dogs along the road, driving a flock of sheep to Mr Vickers's new mart on Castle Bank.

Mrs Newton's house was at the end of a short terraced row. It had one room downstairs, one upstairs and a small backyard with a coal house and ash closet. Inside, the house was clean and tidy and furnished with good-quality pieces. Multi-coloured crocheted cushions adorned the chairs and sofa. Rose thought it looked homely and knew at once that she would be comfortable there.

The fire had been banked earlier that morning, and Mrs Newton took the poker from the companion set by the hearth and brought the fire back to life by lifting the coals to let the air get underneath. Orange flames soon warmed the room.

'You can have the room upstairs,' said Mrs Newton. 'I prefer to sleep down here by the fire these days. Take your things up and get settled in. There's plenty of room in the cupboard to hang your dresses up.'

Rose opened the door at the bottom of the staircase and climbed the wooden steps. The room she entered had a double bed, a cupboard built into the wall, and a dressing table with a large mirror and a chair. She looked out of the window, which had a lovely view of Weardale; the high hills were still capped with snow. All was quiet except for a few children playing in the lane in front of the house.

Rose wondered if her child might play out there one day. She touched her lower tummy and felt a slight bulge. She didn't know how long she had been pregnant or when the baby was due, but she'd often heard her mother say to her sisters, 'They'll come when they're ready.'

She missed her mother. She wished they were on better terms because she could use some of her common-sense advice; she had no doubt her mother would know the best way to handle the situation, but since she had upset her parents by leaving William, running away with Daniel and missing her sister's funeral, there was little hope of a reconciliation between them.

Rose would have loved to see her parents' faces when they discovered how horribly wrong everything had turned out with William, the man they approved of as her husband, but she couldn't gloat. Nobody could have predicted what happened.

William had fooled them all, her more than anybody.

Looking back at the time she'd spent as his wife, at his beck and call day and night, Rose felt miserable and even more so because he had left her with a child in her belly. Through no fault of her own, before very long, she would be an unmarried mother with an illegitimate child to bring up herself.

'Come down when you're ready,' shouted Mrs Newton. 'I've made an omelette for tea.'

Although she didn't have much of an appetite, Rose ate downstairs at Mrs Newton's table, grateful for her friendship and generosity.

'What will you do for work when William moves out of the house?' asked Rose.

'I won't be going back to work for Mr Ashworth, or whatever he's called, but when he moves out, I'll go to the house and offer my services to the new people. In the meantime, we'll be alright. I have some savings put away so don't you worry about that.'

'You can have this,' said Rose, handing Mrs Newton the bank notes Mr Campbell had given her.

'No, I can't,' replied Mrs Newton, passing them back. 'You'll need that for you and the baby.'

Reluctantly, Rose took back the money.

'I should look for a job,' she said decisively.

'Not in your condition, Rose,' said Mrs Newton. 'And after what's happened, people won't know what to think. Why not let things settle down for a bit?'

'I can't sit here all day and live off your charity,' said Rose. 'I'll have a walk up the street in the morning and see if I can find some work, even if it's just for a few months to tide us over.'

Mrs Newton smiled sadly at Rose and said, 'Well, if you're sure that's what you want to do.'

The following morning, Rose set off from the house, fighting a bitterly cold wind but with high hopes of finding a suitable vacancy that would bring some money into the house while Mrs Newton was unemployed. Her first call was at Mr Merritt's bakery, where she had worked before she married William.

She stepped inside the shop, adjusted her hat, which had blown askew, and asked the woman behind the counter if she could speak with the baker.

He came into the shop and greeted her coolly.

'Good morning, Mr Merritt,' she said with a cheery smile. 'I'm looking for work and wondered if you might have something for me. As you know, I'm a hard worker and reliable, and I can clean, bake and serve. I'll do anything you need me to.'

'You left me in the lurch when you got married. You didn't give me any notice at all,' said Mr Merritt sharply. 'Anyway, your husband didn't seem too keen on you working here. What's changed?'

Rose looked down at her feet, wondering if she should tell him the truth and decided she would. The news about William and their false marriage would spread soon enough.

'It turns out that my husband, as you put it, was already married when he married me. I found out yesterday.'

'By God! So, Mr Ashworth is a bigamist,' said Mr Merritt with a chuckle. 'Well, I never. And he had the nerve to show you up for running off with that Irish fella like you did. By! Who'd have thought it?'

'I certainly didn't,' said Rose sternly, thinking it was hardly a laughing matter. 'But now that I'm not his wife, I need to find work.'

'Look, I'm sorry, Rose. I took on another young lady when you left. Annie here,' he said, nodding towards the woman behind the counter who was cleaning the shelves, pretending not to eavesdrop on their conversation. 'I can't afford to take anyone else on just now. Business has been slow since the ironworks closed.'

He smiled weakly and returned to his bakery.

Rose tried the newsagents next, and then several general dealers, an off-licence, a sweet shop, a couple of grocers, and even her brother-in-law's butcher shop, but the owners all turned her down.

On her way back up the street, she stopped at the dress-maker's shop, glad to be out of the wind for another minute or two.

'Good morning, Mrs Collins,' she said, with less enthusiasm than she'd had earlier in the day. 'I wondered if you might need some help in the shop.'

'I'm sorry, Mrs Ashworth,' said the dressmaker. 'I work alone. I always have done.'

Rose was disappointed that there wasn't a job for her, but she thanked the lady for her time. As she opened the door to leave, she asked, 'The red dress that was in your window last year, was it sold?'

'Yes, a young man bought it for a relative of his,' said the dressmaker. 'You know, that dress would have looked lovely on you. It's a shame your husband couldn't see that.'

Rose nodded sadly and left the shop, so preoccupied with the dress that she almost collided with Jimmy McNally outside on the street.

'Steady on there, Rose,' he said, holding her by the arms to stop her from toppling over.

'I'm sorry,' said Rose, stepping back when she regained her balance. 'I don't know what I was thinking, barging out of the door like that without looking where I was going.'

'No harm done,' he said.

Rose smiled. As she didn't see Jimmy often, she thought she should make the most of this opportunity.

'I just wondered, Jimmy, do you have an address for Daniel?' she asked. 'Or do you know where he is?'

Jimmy's eyes narrowed. 'Now, why would you be wanting that information, Rose?'

'Things have changed,' she said in a low voice. 'Yesterday, I found out that William is a bigamist. He was married before he came here. Before he married me. That means I'm not his wife. I wish to God I'd known that when Daniel took me to Yorkshire. I would never have come back here.'

Jimmy let out a low whistle.

'I'm sorry, but I can't help you, Rose,' he said, shaking his head. 'I wish I could, really I do. Daniel hasn't written to me since he left and I have absolutely no idea where he is. I would tell you if I did. He'd be thrilled to bits to hear your news.'

Rose could see by Jimmy's eyes that he was telling the truth.

'If you hear from him,' said Rose. 'Please tell him what I've said.'

'I will.' Looking down at her belly, he said, 'I see you're expecting.'

'Is it that obvious?' asked Rose, shocked that he could tell. Her hand moved to her bump.

'Maybe not to most people, not yet anyway, but I notice things like that,' he said. 'Is it our Daniel's?'

'Unfortunately not,' said Rose sadly.

'Are you sure?' asked Jimmy. 'It's not long since you and

he—'

'It's impossible,' said Rose, shaking her head. 'We never...'

'Good God, Rose. I'm so sorry. I just assumed...' Jimmy touched her arm in support. 'I wish I knew where our Daniel was, for both your sakes. He'd take care of you and the baby. He thinks the world of you, you know that.'

'And I think the world of him,' she said as she wrapped her shawl tighter around her body.

'I should warn you that you might get a visit from the police,' said Rose. 'I've charged William with assault. I gave them your name as a witness to my injuries.'

'That's fine, Rose,' said Jimmy. 'I'll do whatever I can to help.'

Rose walked back to Mrs Newton's house feeling deflated. What a morning! Not only had she failed to secure a job, but all hope of finding Daniel had gone, too. If his cousin didn't know where he was, nobody would.

She would have travelled anywhere in the world to find him, but she had no idea where to begin her search. He might still be somewhere in England, he could have returned home to Ireland or he might have boarded one of many ships leaving England for far-flung lands.

Rose wiped away the tears from her cheeks before entering Mrs Newton's house.

45

Chapter 45

Tow Law, County Durham
March, 1882

William spent the whole evening at the police house in Tow Law, answering questions about his marriages and the assaults on Rose. The clerk wrote down everything he told the constable, who had warned him to be careful because anything he said could be used in court.

Walking home, he thought about Scotland and his marriage to Adeline. By travelling to England the previous year and using a false surname, William thought he had escaped his past life. He'd endured a miserable existence with his ugly but wealthy wife. Yes, that was why he'd set his sights on her, for her money. The gossip at the time of their marriage had been correct.

As a young lad from an impoverished background in Glasgow, he'd yearned for money and status, but he hadn't particularly wanted the woman who had given him those things. Not only was Adeline displeasing to look at, she was as dull as dishwater, not that he'd had much experience with dish-water, but whenever they had gone out together, he had been embarrassed to have her by his side and introduce her as his wife. Finally, when he could stand it no longer, he took her money and ran away in the dead of night, and his only regret had been leaving his son. He missed the wee lad.

Since he'd left Scotland, William had been careful not to have his photograph taken. He bolted from the field when he realised a photographer was at the football match to take team pictures. Rose's parents had taken him by surprise on his wedding day, inviting the photographer to the house to take a wedding photograph. Although he hadn't been overjoyed, William couldn't see much harm in it as the picture would never leave their home.

He hadn't been thinking clearly when he'd given the photo-graph to the newspaper editor while Rose was missing. When it was printed showing both Rose and himself, William knew there was a chance that somebody might recognise him, and it appeared he had been right. Someone had seen him and given the article to Adeline or her father, leading them straight to his door.

When he returned to Laburnum House, the place was empty. Rose had taken her clothes and gone. What had he expected? She would hardly stay with him now that she knew they weren't legally married, especially after how he'd treated her. There was nothing he could do about that now. Briefly, he wondered where she might be. He was sure her parents wouldn't have taken her in after she'd embarrassed them by leaving her middle-class husband and running off with an Irishman.

William had always been fond of women with blonde hair

and delicate features, and he'd been attracted to Rose the first time he saw her at the kirk. He would miss his dear Rose—in his bed, especially.

He regretted beating her. He had known she was a coal miner's daughter when he'd tricked her into marriage. It wasn't her fault that she was an uneducated and illiterate young woman with little knowledge of etiquette, but still, that had annoyed him somewhat, reminding him of his childhood and the world he had left behind.

Controlling his temper had always been a problem. Adeline put up with it and hadn't spoken to anyone about what went on between their four walls in Muirkirk, but she had never riled him as much as Rose did. Adeline had been brought up as a lady and acted like one.

When he'd seen Rose in the arms of the Irishman in the back garden that afternoon, he'd lost his temper and taken out his anger and frustration on them both.

Mrs Newton had voiced his own thoughts earlier that day when she'd said he might have killed Rose if he hadn't been stopped. Once again, William wondered if Kelly hadn't come to Rose's rescue if he would have gone that far. In a blind rage, he didn't know what he was doing. He might have killed her; he would never know for sure.

William wondered if he should disappear again and resurface in a distant town with another surname. It had worked once before, and if he hadn't been stupid enough to give their wedding photograph to the editor of a newspaper, his secret would never have been discovered.

Rose would have lived with him as his wife and done everything he wanted for the rest of his life, which would have been perfect. But now she was lost to him forever. Even when the divorce from Adeline was finalised, he could never persuade Rose to marry him again, not after what he'd done.

If he disappeared, now that the police and the courts were involved, it wouldn't just be a scorned wife and her father searching for him wherever he went; the authorities would be looking for him, too. He knew he wouldn't get away with it for a second time.

William entered the drawing room and poured himself a large glass of brandy, savouring the rich, mellow flavour and enjoying its calming effect on him, wondering how long he would be forced to go without it when he was imprisoned. The constable had said he'd face the magistrate soon and that the case would be heard at the Summer Assizes held in Durham in July, where the judge would decide his sentence. Until then, he was a free man. He expected he'd be sent to prison; the question in his mind was for how long.

The Weardale Iron and Coal Company would not allow him to continue working there when the directors learned that he had been charged with several crimes, and he knew he would be asked to vacate the house immediately.

Too much had occurred that day for him to think clearly. The shock of seeing Adeline and her father again, being interrogated by the constable, and discovering Rose was pregnant was too much. He wondered if it was his child she carried or the Irishman's.

He poured another glass, thinking he'd sleep on his problems and decide what to do in the morning. After several more glasses, he stumbled to bed.

When the morning came, William's head was fuzzy, and he wondered how much brandy he'd had the night before.

He reached across the bed for Rose's soft, warm body, but

her side of the bed was cold and empty. Had she got up already?

He rapidly got dressed and went downstairs. Mrs. Newton was not in the kitchen making breakfast, and she was nowhere to be found.

Then, slowly, William recalled the previous day's events and sighed loudly. Rose had gone, and it appeared Mrs Newton had left his employment.

In the kitchen, he cut a slice of bread from yesterday's loaf, spread it thickly with butter and jam, and poured himself a glass of milk. That would have to do for his breakfast.

After eating, he put on his coat and hat, saddled his horse, and rode to the mine. There, he wrote a letter of resignation, addressed it to the company secretary, and left the office with no intention of returning. He was disappointed things had turned out this way because he had enjoyed his job at the mine immensely, and also the salary and status that came with it. Everyone in the town had acknowledged his presence and called him sir; he loved it.

On the way home, he wondered about renting a small house. He needed somewhere to stay for a few months until his case went to trial, and there were plenty of empty properties in the town since the ironworks closed. Most of the previous occupants had accepted jobs in Tudhoe and taken their families there, some had decided to stay and find work elsewhere, and he'd set a few of them on at Black Prince.

Thinking about it, he decided Tow Law was probably not the best place to stay while he awaited trial. He didn't want to face the wrath of Rose's parents when they found out that not only had he deceived and defiled their daughter but beaten her, too, and it would be awkward if he encountered Rose.

The men who had worked for him at the pit wouldn't take

too kindly to the fact that he was a bigamist; a bigamist who had beaten his *wife*, a local woman. As loyal as they were to one another, he wondered if they might mete out their own form of justice. The prospect of being beaten to a pulp by the men who had once respected him filled him with fear.

No, it would be better to leave Tow Law. He'd look for a house or lodgings somewhere else, perhaps in Durham city, as that was where the trial would be held. Fortunately, he had plenty of money in the bank, so he didn't need to search for a job in the meantime.

He rode to the mart on Castle Bank and dismounted.

'I would like to sell my horse and his tack,' said William.

The auctioneer appraised his horse and gave him an estimate of its value.

'Can I leave him here until the next sale?' asked William.

'Yes, of course, sir.'

William gave the auctioneer details of the bank account where the payment should be deposited and then walked the rest of the way home.

At Laburnum House, he packed his belongings into a trunk. He then went to the conservatory and admired how much his orange tree had grown since he'd bought it. He saw tiny buds on the grapevine, a promise of green leaves and luscious fruit later in the year. Sadly, he closed the door on them and walked out of the house, carrying everything he owned.

William was free, a man of independent means, with no job, property, or family to tie him down, yet he had never felt more trapped.

46

Chapter 46

Tow Law, County Durham
May, 1882

Rose tossed and turned all night. The room was hot and humid, and the baby growing inside her was unsettled. When she slept, her dreams were of Daniel, and it felt wonderful to be held in his strong arms, gazing into his smiling blue eyes and kissing his tender lips. She longed to hear his voice again, telling her how much he loved her and wanted her.

When she woke in her bed alone, she felt utterly bereft. She missed Daniel now more than ever.

There was nothing to stop them from being together any more—apart from the fact she didn't know where he was or how to get in touch with him. She thought there must be a way and desperately wondered who he might have spoken to before he left Tow Law. She worked herself up into a frenzy. She had to know where he was. She had to find him.

It was still very early. From the faint glow at the window, Rose guessed the sun would rise soon, so it wasn't yet five o'clock.

She dressed quickly and quietly, not wanting to disturb Mrs Newton, who was sleeping downstairs. Then, she crept down the wooden staircase, avoiding the step that creaked and went outside into the still, warm air.

Nobody was on the High Street as she marched up the road to Mrs McKenna's house on her mission to find out where Daniel had gone. Jimmy didn't know, but Daniel might have said something to Mrs McKenna or one of the other lodgers. It was unlikely, she knew, but even if there was a slim chance, she had to know.

Rose rapped at the door. There were no lights on in the house nor any movement inside. She knocked louder, hoping Mrs McKenna or one of her sons who slept in the front room might hear. Still, nobody answered the door.

'Mrs McKenna!' she shouted, banging on the door with both hands.

Next door, the bedroom window opened, and her mother's face appeared.

'Rose!' she said. 'What the hell are you doing knocking on *her* door at this time in the morning?'

'Go back to bed, Mother,' said Rose. She couldn't deal with one of her mother's inquisitions when so much was at stake.

'Don't you tell me what to do, young madam,' said Jane. 'Not when it was you who woke us up. It's disgraceful you running around the town at this ungodly hour chasing that bloody Irishman like a bitch in heat. That's what you're there for, isn't it? Eh?'

Rose wanted to die on the spot with shame. Other windows and doors along the street had opened, and some of their neighbours had heard her mother's damning words. But everything she'd said was true.

Mrs McKenna opened the door, took Rose's arm and pulled her inside the house.

'My God, what a mouth she has on her,' said Mrs McKenna. 'I'm sorry you were on the other end of it. It's usually me. I've heard it so often now, it's water off a duck's back. Come on in and sit down. I'll make a pot of tea.'

Rose wandered to a chair, sat down and watched Mrs McKenna fill the kettle with water and hang it over the fire to boil. Her two sons still were still sleeping on the alcove bed their mother had recently vacated.

'You're very quiet,' said Mrs McKenna. 'You mustn't let her upset you, not when you're in your condition.'

Rose's hand went to her belly.

'How far on are you?' asked Mrs McKenna.

'I don't know,' said Rose.

'I'd guess you're about seven months looking at the size of you,' said Mrs McKenna with an experienced eye. 'Not much longer to go.'

She put a teaspoonful of tea leaves into the pot, poured the boiling water from the kettle over them and replaced the lid.

They heard footsteps upstairs. A man walked down the stairs and went out the back door to use the netty.

Mrs McKenna poured the tea and handed Rose a cup.

'They'll all be down wanting breakfast soon,' she said. 'I'm thinking you'd better tell me what you've come here for this morning while you've got the chance.'

'I need to find Daniel Kelly,' said Rose, thinking her statement confirmed her mother's suspicions. 'I wondered if he might have said something to you or one of the men staying here about where he was going. I already asked Jimmy, and he doesn't know where he went.'

'He never said anything to me, love,' said Mrs McKenna, 'and if he didn't tell Jimmy, I can't imagine he told anyone else because those two were as thick as thieves, but you're welcome to ask the fellas when they come down. I'd better get started on breakfast.'

Rose sat quietly sipping her tea as Mrs McKenna fried bacon and eggs for her lodgers and then cut thick slices of bread from a loaf she must have made the previous evening.

Jimmy came downstairs first, and his surprise at seeing Rose was evident.

'What are you doing here?' he asked.

'She wants to find Daniel,' said Mrs McKenna. 'She thought somebody here might know where he went.'

'I've still not heard from him,' said Jimmy. 'I'm sorry, I've no idea where he is.'

When asked if they knew Daniel's whereabouts, the other three lodgers looked at her blankly and shook their heads.

'I'm sorry, love,' said Mrs McKenna after the men left for work. 'Is the bairn his?'

Rose swallowed loudly, and her voice broke when she said, 'No, but I wish it was.'

Mrs McKenna came to her and wrapped her arms around her.

'I'm sorry, Rose,' she said. 'I hope you find him.'

Rose sobbed loudly. She knew that was the end of her short-lived search for Daniel. She had made a fool of herself and nobody could tell her where he had gone.

47

Chapter 47

Tow Law, County Durham
July, 1882

Rose put on her shift and a loose-fitting dress with a buttoned front. The light material flowed over her enormous bump. She ran her hands over it, felt her baby moving inside her, and smiled. Then, she fastened her hair into a neat bun and went downstairs carrying her hat.

'You look very smart,' said Mrs Newton. 'Let me help you with that.'

When she'd securely pinned Rose's hat in place, Mrs Newton said, 'Come on, dear. We don't want to be late.'

The ladies left the house and strolled to the end of the street, where a carrier waited for them. The young man helped them to climb onto his cart.

Rose found the journey to the station at Waterhouses uncomfortable. It was early in the day, but already, it was warm, and there was no breeze to cool her down. Her baby kicked and thumped the whole way. Her stomach churned with nerves, she presumed, and she felt queasy as the cart lurched over the bumpy roads.

She wasn't entirely sure what would happen at the courthouse; she'd never been to one before. Constable Walker had told her she should answer the judge's questions truthfully and honestly in front of everyone present, which filled her with fear. How many people would be there? What might the judge ask her?

Rose was grateful that Mrs Newton was accompanying her as she didn't think she would have had the courage to go alone. She was still very annoyed that William had conned her into a fake marriage and treated her so badly, but at least she had found out the truth and didn't have to spend the rest of her life with him.

Today, he would get the punishment he deserved. Rose had mixed feelings about that. Her words would influence the judge's decision, and despite what William had done to hurt her, that was a heavy weight to bear.

The cartman pulled up his horse outside the station and helped the ladies climb down. They thanked him. Mrs Newton paid him for his services and then bought two tickets to Durham at the ticket office. The train journey wasn't long, and soon the ladies were walking through the city of Durham, from the station to the courthouse.

Rose and Mrs Newton climbed up the steps to a large pair of wooden doors, and they entered the austere stone building. A man in a black suit asked their names and the purpose of their visit and ushered them to their seats at the front of the courtroom.

When Mr Campbell and Adeline arrived a few minutes later, Mr Campbell inclined his head at Rose and Mrs Newton, and

Rose was pleased to see a friendly face in the unfamiliar surroundings.

The courtroom fell silent in anticipation of the judge's arrival. Edward Armstrong-Harrison entered shortly afterwards wearing long black robes and a grey wig. He climbed the steps to a raised platform at the front of the room and stood by an oversized, ornate chair.

Rose thought his outfit looked quite comical, but she didn't laugh or smile.

Everybody stood up when the judge appeared and waited for him to be seated before they sat down again. Rose copied what everyone else did, assuming they knew the correct way to behave.

'Good morning,' said the judge, his voice loud and clear, filling the room. 'Bring in the accused and swear him in, please.'

William was led to the dock by a policeman. He was neatly dressed and looked every bit the respectable man he had always portrayed himself to be, but there was a pallor to his skin that Rose hadn't seen before, and she almost felt sorry for him. He wiped his brow with a handkerchief, which he returned to his pocket before putting his hand on the Bible and swearing to tell the truth, and then he turned to face the judge.

'Mr William Mitchell, you are on trial here today because you are accused of the felonies of bigamy and serious assault,' said the judge. 'In the first instance, we will examine the charge of bigamy against you. How do you plead?'

'Not guilty, Your Honour,' said William, sounding sincere.

'In that case, we will hear what Mrs Adeline Mitchell and Miss Rose Lawson have to say on the matter, and then you will be given the opportunity to defend yourself. Do you understand?'

'Yes, Your Honour,' said William.

The judge asked Adeline to stand up and swear on the Bible that she would tell the truth and to confirm that Mr William Mitchell was the man she had married, which she did.

'Please tell the court how you and Mr Mitchell met,' said the judge.

'William came to work at one of my father's coal mines in Ayrshire,' said Adeline. 'The mine is close to our house in Muirkirk. I saw him on several occasions at the mine office when I visited my father and a few times when he passed our garden. He would chat to me and flatter me when my family was out of earshot. Even though he was just a clerk at that time, I thought he was handsome and charming. Eventually, I succumbed to his advances and consented to him courting me.'

'Thank you, Mrs Mitchell,' said the judge. 'Now, please tell us about your marriage to Mr Mitchell.'

'As is proper, William asked my father for my hand in marriage,' said Adeline. 'My father agreed because he could see William was an ambitious young man and believed he had the aptitude to be a capable manager in years to come. He never spoke to William about this, but he envisaged that William would take over his mining business when he retired. Anyway, William and I were married in the village church by the Reverend Fergus Buchanan almost a year to the day after we met. Our son was born eleven months later. I named him William after his father, and he's known as Billy.'

'Am I correct in thinking you only have the one child, Mrs Mitchell?' asked the judge.

'Yes, that's right,' said Adeline sourly. 'If my husband had stayed with me, I expect there would have been more.'

'I understand your husband walked out on you and your son,' said the judge. 'Please tell us exactly what happened. Did you have a disagreement beforehand?'

'No, Your Honour,' said Adeline. 'There was nothing un-usual happened in the days and weeks leading up to his disappearance. He went to work as normal and came home and ate dinner with us. Then, one morning, I got up and saw his clothes were gone. I went to my father's house and told him what had happened. My father went out on his horse to look for him. William wasn't at the mine, and nobody in the village had seen him that morning. My father was, quite rightly, concerned that William had abandoned me and our Billy. He went to the bank in Cumnock and discovered William had taken all but a few shillings from our bank account. Most of it was my money that my parents gave me on our wedding day.'

'How much money did Mr Mitchell take from your joint bank account?' asked the judge.

'One hundred and six pounds,' she replied. 'One hundred pounds of that was my parents' wedding gift. The six pounds was what he had managed to save.'

'The fact that the money was given to you and that you view it as yours is irrelevant in the eyes of the law, Mrs Mitchell. As I'm sure you are aware, what was yours became your husband's when you married him, so I will say for the record that no theft has taken place. Thank you, Mrs Mitchell. You may sit down,' said the judge. 'Can we swear in Miss Lawson, please?'

Rose's voice faltered as she swore on the Bible in front of everyone that she would tell the truth, the whole truth and nothing but the truth. She had never spoken in front of so many people before and felt uncomfortable being studied by so many pairs of eyes.

She thought Adeline had done ever so well to tell her story clearly, which spurred her on to do the same, although she dreaded having to say anything of a personal nature in front of strangers.

'Miss Lawson,' said the judge. 'Please could you confirm that Mr William Mitchell, who is standing in the dock today, is the man you married, believing him to be Mr William Ashworth?'

'Yes, sir, he is,' said Rose.

'Please tell the court how you came to meet Mr Mitchell and about your wedding,' he prompted.

'I first saw William at the church in Tow Law,' she said. 'My father told me his name was William Ashworth and that he was the new boss at Black Prince Colliery, where my father works. I had no reason to suspect anything different. The first time William spoke to me was when he came into the bakery where I worked, and I saw him a few times after that. We hadn't spent much time together before he came to my parent's house and asked if he could marry me. This came as quite a shock as he hadn't said anything to me about getting married before then. My mother and father were over the moon that a mine manager wanted to marry me. I'm a just coal miner's daughter. I'm not a wealthy lady like Mrs Mitchell. Anyway, my father gave his permission. William got a marriage licence and made the arrangements. It all happened very quickly. We were married soon afterwards at the church in Tow Law. It was on a Friday. The twenty-fourth of June.'

'Did Mr Mitchell ever say or hint at the fact that he'd been married before?' asked the judge.

'No, sir,' said Rose.

'Did he ever say or hint at the fact that he had another family living elsewhere?'

'No, sir. I knew nothing about his past before he came to Tow Law except that he was from Scotland,' said Rose. 'He never talked about his family.'

'I see. Thank you, Miss Lawson. Please be seated,' said the judge. Turning his attention to William, he said, 'Mr Mitchell, you have heard what the two ladies said. Do you have anything you wish to add?'

'No, Your Honour,' said William.

'Alright,' said the judge. 'Would you care to change your plea to the charge of bigamy?'

'Yes, Your Honour,' said William, looking sheepish. 'Guilty, Your Honour.'

There was a slight pause in proceedings while the judge shuffled some papers. Then he said, 'I have listened to the testimonies from both Mrs Adeline Mitchell and Miss Rose Lawson, and I have seen the marriage registers from both parishes and the entries undoubtedly prove that these two marriages did take place as they say, albeit with the groom using a different surname. However, it is clear to me that the two signatures were made by the same hand. Mr Mitchell, you have changed your plea to guilty and I believe this to be true. Therefore, the jury does not need to give a verdict in this case. All that remains for me to do is to pass sentence.'

The judge paused again, taking a sip of water, before saying, 'The felony of bigamy is a serious crime that offends against both the secular and spiritual authorities, and as such it has carried the penalty of death for many, many years.'

Rose heard a collective gasp in the courtroom. Her heart pounded in her chest. She had expected William to go to prison for what he'd done, not to be hanged. She would never have agreed to speak out against him in court if she had known the outcome might lead to his death.

'Mr Mitchell abandoned his wife and child in Scotland,' continued the judge, 'and then using a false identity, he deceived a young woman into marrying him, and I can see that this woman is currently with child. My ruling in this case is that Mr Mitchell is to be detained in Her Majesty's Gaol in Durham for four years. I also rule that one hundred pounds from his assets should be returned to Mrs Mitchell and the remainder of his assets should be divided equally between Mrs Mitchell and Miss Lawson to help with the upbringing of their respective children.'

'But sir!' exclaimed William. 'I have good reason to doubt that I am the father of Rose's unborn child.'

'Silence in court!' shouted the judge, his voice echoing around the room. 'You will speak only when asked to speak. Do you understand, Mr Mitchell?'

William nodded.

'I have made my decision and it stands.'

Rose was relieved that the judge had not questioned her about the father of her baby. She didn't want to speak about her relationship with Daniel Kelly in public; it would be so embarrassing. She was grateful that the judge had provided for her child, too. After finding it impossible to get a job, she needed all the help she could get, and she would give some of the money to Mrs Newton for letting her stay in her home.

Rose thought four years in prison seemed to be a fitting sentence for William's crime, more so than being hanged, at least. Although she had grown to hate and fear William, she would not have wanted his death on her conscience.

48

Chapter 48

Durham City
July, 1882

'The next case also relates to William Mitchell,' said the judge, 'so anyone involved in this case should remain in the courtroom. Everyone else may leave now if they wish to do so.'

Rose looked at Mr Campbell and Adeline, expecting them to leave at this point in the proceedings, but they remained in their seats. A few people left the room, and Rose spotted Jimmy McNally coming in and sitting near the back.

'Mr Mitchell,' said the judge, 'you have also been charged with serious assault against Miss Rose Lawson, who was living with you as your wife at the time. How do you plead to the charge of serious assault?'

'Not guilty, Your Honour,' said William, his head high and his eyes looking directly at the judge.

Rose realised what a convincing liar he was. It was no wonder he had fooled her and her family. He could have been a professional actor.

'As before,' said the judge, 'we will hear the evidence from Miss Lawson and the other witnesses, and then you will have an opportunity to speak if you wish.'

Turning to Rose, he said, 'Miss Lawson, remember that you are still under oath. Please tell the court about the first time Mr Mitchell assaulted you, with the reason you think he attacked you and the injuries that you sustained from the assault.'

Rose looked at William. He didn't look like a violent man, and she feared the judge might not believe what she was about to say. She cleared her throat before speaking.

'The first time William raised his hand to me was when he came home from work one day and I didn't have his dinner ready. He was angry. He slapped my face, and I fell and hit my head against the wall. After that, I was frightened to upset him again.'

'And the next occasion...' prompted the judge.

'The next time was much worse,' said Rose. 'William came home from work and saw me hugging a friend in the garden. He dragged me into the house by my hair and punched me in the face, the chest and the belly. I shouted for my friend to help me and I remember falling to the ground and being kicked. Then, I don't remember anything else. William broke my nose and my ribs that day, and I had cuts and bruises all over my body.'

'Was that the last time Mr Mitchell assaulted you?' asked the judge.

'No, sir,' said Rose. 'William made up a set of rules and I didn't agree with them.'

'Out of interest, what were these rules?' asked the judge.

'He paid someone to chaperone me whenever he was out of the house and to report back to him. He made me do all the housework and gardening at his large house and forbade the chaperone from helping me. He wouldn't give me any allowance or housekeeping money and insisted on paying the shopkeepers himself. And there were more...of a personal nature, sir.'

The judge raised his eyebrows and said, 'What happened when you disagreed with these rules being imposed by Mr Mitchell?'

'I was sitting on a chair in the drawing room at the time. He punched me in the chest so hard that the chair fell backwards and I hit my head on the floor, hard enough to cut it.'

'Thank you, Miss Lawson. Please take your seat,' said the judge. 'Do we have Mr James McNally in the courtroom?'

Jimmy stood up and raised his hand.

After Jimmy had been sworn in, the judge said, 'Mr McNally, I believe you witnessed the extent of Miss Lawson's injuries after the second and most brutal attack by Mr Mitchell.'

'Aye, Your Honour, I did,' said Jimmy. 'Rose was unconscious when my cousin carried her out of the house and away from Mr Ashworth...sorry, I mean Mr Mitchell. He asked me to treat her injuries.'

'Are you a doctor, Mr McNally?' asked the judge.

'No, Your Honour. I'm a boxer. I've had a lot of practice fixing people up after fights.'

'I see,' said the judge. 'Please continue.'

'When I first saw Rose that evening, I wanted to cry, I did,' said Jimmy. 'She had bruises all over her body from her head to her feet. She had several minor cuts as well—on the bridge of her nose, her arm and her shin. Her ribs caused her the most pain. I'd say that two of them were broken, and her nose was broken as well. No woman should have to suffer like that at the hands of a man.'

'Thank you, Mr McNally,' said the judge. 'You may be seated.'

Jimmy sat down and smiled reassuringly at Rose.

'Mrs Mitchell,' said the judge, turning to Adeline. 'I believe you have something you would like to say on this matter.'

'Yes, Your Honour,' said Adeline, rising to her feet. 'I lived with William Mitchell as his wife for four years. In that time, I saw his temper surface many times and he hit me on several occasions. I have no doubt that what Miss Lawson has told the court is true.'

'Thank you, Mrs Mitchell, you may be seated.' Turning to William, the judge asked, 'Have you anything to say in your defence, Mr Mitchell?'

'Who doesn't get upset when there's no dinner ready for them after a hard day's work?' William asked the court, and a few men laughed loudly.

'Silence!' shouted the judge. 'Is that all, Mr Mitchell?'

'Rose was seeing another man when she was living under my roof. I caught them together in the garden,' said William. 'Daniel Kelly was not her friend as she claims, he was her lover. Again, I ask you, what man wouldn't lose control at seeing his woman in the arms of another man?'

Murmurs could be heard from the people present.

'Rose left me and ran away with her lover last year,' continued William. 'For all I know, it could have been him that put that baby in her belly.'

'Miss Lawson,' said the judge. 'This is the second time that Mr Mitchell has expressed doubts that he is the father of your unborn child. Please tell the court who is the father of the child you are carrying, and remember that you are still under oath.'

'Yes, sir,' said Rose, standing up again. 'It's definitely William's baby.'

'How can you be so sure?' asked the judge. 'Mr Mitchell claims you ran away with another man, Daniel Kelly, your lover.'

Blushing furiously, Rose wanted the floor to open up and swallow her. Lowering her head, she mumbled a reply.

'Miss Lawson, speak up!' said the judge. 'I did not hear your answer, nor did anyone else in this courtroom. Tell us, did you or did you not have sexual intercourse with Daniel Kelly when you ran away together?'

'No, I didn't!' said Rose, looking directly at the judge. 'William is the father. He's the only man I've ever...ever lain with.'

William looked astonished at her words.

'And what about the man he claims you ran away with?' asked the judge.

'Daniel Kelly was my neighbour when I lived with my parents. He walked past our house on his way home from work, and sometimes he stopped for a chat. When William saw us together in the garden, he got so angry that he picked up a spade and hit Daniel's head with it. There was so much blood, I thought he'd killed him.' Rose paused and cleared her throat. 'Daniel was unconscious when William dragged me into the house. He must have come round and heard William beating me and my cries for help. When he came inside, he found me lying unconscious on the floor. He carried me to a safe place where he got his cousin, Jimmy McNally, to treat both our injuries. We did go away together, to Yorkshire, to get away from William, but we never...lay together.'

'How long were you and Mr Kelly together in Yorkshire, Miss

Lawson?' asked the judge.

Rose blushed furiously at the question.

'Please answer the question, Miss Lawson,' he prompted.

'We were in Yorkshire for a month,' she confessed.

She noticed the looks of surprise on the faces of those in the courtroom.

'A month is a significant length of time,' said the judge. 'Where did you stay while you were in Yorkshire?'

'Daniel got a job at a coal mine in a little village called Denaby Main,' said Rose. 'We stayed in a colliery house there.'

'To obtain colliery housing, Mr Kelly must have lied about your relationship. He must have told the manager there that you were his wife, did he not?'

'Yes, sir, he did.' Rose hung her head, knowing how bad that sounded.

'It's hard to imagine that a mature man and a mature woman who care for one another enough to run away together and live in the same house pretending to be man and wife for a whole month did not have sexual relations during that time.'

'But it's true, sir,' said Rose. 'Every word I've told you is true. I was so badly hurt. Daniel took me away from Tow Law to keep me safe until I recovered. Mrs Newton, here, was a witness to it all. She saw the injuries that both me and Daniel had after William attacked us.'

'Mrs Newton, is that true?' asked the judge.

Mrs Newton rose and said, 'Yes, Your Honour. As I said in the statement I gave to the police constable, I saw Rose and Daniel the day after it happened. I helped Rose change her clothes before she left the town and packed a bag for her. She was in a lot of pain from the broken ribs, and her nose was broken as well. She was in a terrible state, Your Honour, with cuts and bruises all over her body, just like she said. Daniel had a cut on his head an' all. It must have been over three inches long, and it had been stitched. I'm pleased Daniel took Rose away. If you ask me, I reckon he stopped William from killing her that day.'

'Indeed!' said the judge, raising his eyebrows. 'Please take a seat, Mrs Newton. It appears that the accused is lucky that Mr Daniel Kelly did not inform the police of his injuries or there may have been a second charge of serious assault against him today.'

Rose, who had remained standing during Mrs Newton's short testimony, said, 'That wasn't the worst assault on Daniel, sir. William paid some miners to attack Daniel when he came back from Yorkshire. Daniel was unconscious for nearly a week and he was paralysed for well over a month!'

'I understand your concern for Mr Kelly,' said the judge, 'but the accused is not on trial for assaulting Mr Kelly today, he's on trial for assaulting you. Please sit down, Miss Lawson.'

Mrs Newton took Rose's hand and squeezed it tightly.

'Mr Mitchell, you pleaded not guilty to the charge of assault,' said the judge. 'After hearing the evidence against you, I wonder if you might like to change your plea.'

'Guilty, Your Honour, but on every occasion I was provoked,' said William defiantly.

'I think you're a man who is easily provoked, Mr Mitchell,' said the judge. 'You deceived this young woman into believing she was your wife, and then you repeatedly assaulted her, and on one occasion that assault was very serious indeed. From the testimonies that the court has heard, it appears Mrs Newton and Mr Kelly were both concerned for Miss Lawson's safety while she was living under your roof.'

The judge rearranged some of his papers, and Rose realised he did this to look busy while considering the case.

'Serious assault is the act of violently inflicting bodily injury on another person, and you are certainly guilty of that crime,' he said. 'You are a dangerous man with an uncontrollable temper. I hereby sentence you to four years imprisonment to run consecutively with your previous sentence. William Mitchell, you will spend the next eight years in Her Majesty's Gaol at Durham. From what I have heard, you are very lucky that Mr Daniel Kelly is not standing in this courtroom accusing you of assault because, from the constable's notes and Miss Lawson's testimony, it appears he suffered extensive and debilitating injuries because of you, and you would be facing a much longer prison sentence. But, alas, I can not take the crimes committed against him into account at this time as unfortunately, he is not present in this courtroom.'

Rose looked at William, who appeared shocked by the judge's harsh words.

William hadn't expected the judge to learn of his attack on Daniel. He sighed loudly and shook his head. He had admitted his guilt, and now he had to come to terms with the punishment. Eight years in a prison cell. He hated confined spaces; it would be hell on earth.

Rose thought she would feel relieved after the trial ended and William had received his sentence, but instead, she felt sad. She wished she had never met William, and none of this would have happened. Rose placed her hand over her large bump. She had resented carrying his child at first, but as the baby had grown inside her, her feelings towards him or her had changed. It wasn't the baby's fault that she had fallen pregnant to a conman.

'Come on, Rose,' said Mrs Newton. 'Let's get you home.'

Chapter 49

Tow Law, County Durham
July, 1882

Sam and Jane Lawson walked to Mrs Newton's house, where they'd heard their daughter was staying. Sam hesitated slightly at the door before knocking loudly.

'Good afternoon,' said Mrs Newton when she opened it, immediately recognising the couple as Rose's parents, who she'd met on Rose's wedding day.

'We've come to see our Rose,' said Sam. 'We heard about what happened with William and the trial. Well, everybody has, haven't they? It's the talk of the town. Anyway, we just wanted to know if she's alright.'

'Just give us a minute,' said Mrs Newton, closing the door and turning to Rose, who was sitting by the window sewing baby clothes. 'Your parents are here. Do you want to see them?'

Rose shook her head and said, 'I don't know.'

'It's up to you, dear,' said Mrs Newton. 'I know they haven't treated you very well lately, but they are your family.'

'I suppose I should hear what they've come to say,' said Rose. 'Let them in, please.'

Mrs Newton opened the door and invited the couple into the house. They sat on a two-seater sofa, moving the cushions around to get comfortable, and then looked at their heavily pregnant daughter.

'My goodness!' said her mother. 'I knew you were expecting, but I didn't realise you were so far on.'

'That's not what we came to talk about, Jane,' said her father, rolling his eyes at his wife. Turning back to Rose, he said, 'We'd like you to know how sorry we are about what William did to you—lying about who he was and marrying you under false pretences, like that. He pulled the wool over our eyes, an' all. It's despicable behaviour for a man in a management position. And...and I'm sorry to hear that he beat you...' Sam swallowed loudly and said through gritted teeth, 'If I could get my hands on him right this minute, I'd give him a taste of his own medicine.'

'Thank you,' said Rose, knowing her father spoke from his heart.

'I know we've not been around for you recently,' he said, 'but if there's ever anything you need, come to us, please. We've lost one daughter already. We don't want to lose another.' He sniffed loudly. 'And if anyone treats you like that again, promise me you'll come and tell me.'

Rose nodded, moved by her father's words. Momentarily, she wondered if her parents had forgiven her for running away with Daniel.

'Me and you don't see eye to eye on a lot of things,' said her mother. 'We never have done. I'll not change my mind about the Irish, you can be sure of that, so as long as you stay away from him, we'll be willing to help you if we're able.'

That was as good as Rose could expect from her mother, and she thanked her, too. Her mother was too set in her ways to change.

But Rose knew if Daniel walked through the door now, she wouldn't hesitate to leave everything behind, including her family, to be with him again.

'I heard you did alright out of it,' said her mother. 'How much of William's money did you get?'

'That's none of your business, Jane,' said Sam firmly.

'It said in the paper that you got three pounds,' she said and watched for her daughter's reaction.

'The judge awarded me half of William's savings. I got five pounds to help bring up the baby,' said Rose.

'With five whole pounds in savings, a lot of men would be willing to take you on, even with another man's baby,' said Jane. 'You should think seriously about it. That bairn will have a hard life if it's brought up without a father.'

Rose, who was used to holding her tongue after living with William, nodded. She'd learned it was the easiest thing to do when she disagreed with people and wanted to avoid further discussion or trouble.

As the Lawsons appeared to have sorted out their differences, Mrs Newton offered Sam and Jane a cup of tea, but they politely declined.

'We'd better be going. We don't want to impose,' said Sam. Then, he added, 'Thank you very much for looking after our Rose. We had no idea what was going on in that household. It's shameful.'

'Take care of yourself, Rose,' said her mother, getting to her feet, 'and send us word when the baby comes. It's dropped, so it won't be long now.'

Rose watched her parents leave with mixed emotions. It was good that they wanted to make amends now that they knew William had been lying and mistreating her, but she couldn't help thinking that her relationship with them would never be the same as it had been before William came into their lives.

Her parents had made no reference to her baby being illegitimate, but how could they when they believed her and William to be married just as much as she had? What an awful situation he had left her in. She recalled Mr Campbell's words when he said God must have his reason for bringing this child into the world and hoped he was right.

Two days later, Rose's baby was born after a long labour—a big, healthy girl weighing eight pounds and ten ounces, who announced her arrival with a loud cry.

'Look at her,' said Mrs Newton when the midwife placed the infant in her mother's arms, 'she has fair hair like yours.'

Rose smiled down at the little bundle wrapped in a cot sheet, relieved that her labour had finally ended and that she and her baby had survived the ordeal. Tears blurred her vision as she thought about Daisy, who had not been so lucky.

'You've done very well, dear,' said Mrs Newton. 'There's no need to cry. Let's get this little lass fed and then you can get some rest. You're exhausted.'

Rose unbuttoned her nightdress and held her baby to her breast, and soon, the infant suckled heartily. Within a few minutes, the contented baby was asleep.

'Now then, don't you worry about a thing,' said Mrs Newton, lifting the baby from its mother's arms. 'I'll look after her until you wake up and you'll feel a lot better then, I promise.'

Mrs Newton sat in a chair by Rose's bed, rocking the child in her arms and singing to her quietly.

Rose had never felt so tired, and she was lulled into a deep sleep by Mrs Newton's song. When she woke several hours later, she was ravenously hungry and tried to get out of bed to get some food, but her legs buckled underneath her, and she fell to the floor.

'What are you doing up?' asked Mrs Newton, who had dozed off in the chair after putting the baby into her crib. She stood up, helped Rose to her feet, and propped her up in bed.

'I was hungry,' said Rose. 'I was going to get something to eat.'

'When you've just had a bairn, you need to stay in bed and rest, at least for a couple of days,' explained Mrs Newton. 'Some new mothers take to their bed for a few weeks or even a month, it takes that much out of them. Now, you stay here and I'll bring up a tray for you. What would you like?'

'Bread and butter...and some cheese...and a piece of cake if there's any left.'

Mrs Newton laughed and said, 'It's good to see you've got an appetite.' She went downstairs to fetch Rose a glass of milk and some food.

Rose peered across at the crib in the corner of the room, knowing the baby sleeping peacefully in it would change her life completely. There had been so many changes in her life recently that she craved stability. She wondered if she would ever find it.

A few days later, Rose felt much stronger and went downstairs carrying her baby.

Mrs Newton poured a cup of tea, sat opposite Rose, who was nursing the infant, and said, 'Have you decided what you're going to call her yet?'

'Hmm. I don't know,' said Rose. 'I've known you for ages, I live in your house and I don't know what your first name is.'

Mrs Newton let out a small chuckle. 'Well, I've been called nothing but Mrs Newton for so long now, it feels strange to say it. My Christian name is Lydia. I was named after an aunt on my mother's side of the family. I never knew her, of course, she died before I was born.'

'Lydia,' said Rose. 'I like that. I'll call her Lydia after you.'

With glassy eyes, Mrs Newton said, 'I would be honoured, thank you.'

Chapter 50

Nottinghamshire
July, 1883

After leaving Tow Law, Daniel moved around the country, doing various seasonal farm jobs. He moved from one farm to another to sow and reap crops, weed fields, lamb ewes, shear sheep, and make hay. He could turn his hand to anything that needed to be done.

Being a transient worker suited Daniel perfectly. He needed time to recover his mind and body and to regain his fitness. After meeting Rose and falling head over heels in love with her, and everything that had happened afterwards, he didn't want to get attached to anyone again—it hurt too much. Leaving Rose with William had been the hardest thing he'd ever done.

Working outdoors in the fresh air was the perfect therapy. Daniel led a simple life, working hard for his keep, and that's how he liked it.

He hadn't contacted his cousin Jimmy at Tow Law or his family in Ireland to tell them where he was or what he was doing. Nobody needed to know. And with no news from them, he had nothing to worry about.

Still, Rose was forever on his mind. There wasn't a day or a night that he didn't think about her. He wondered how she was keeping and what she was doing and prayed that her husband was treating her more kindly.

Daniel envied William Ashworth for having Rose as his wife more than he could put into words. That was all he wanted for himself—for Rose to be his wife. Nothing else mattered. His feelings towards her had never changed from the moment they'd met. He loved her when they were neighbours chatting over the garden wall, and he loved her still, although she was many miles away.

Daniel had just arrived at a farm near Nottingham with eleven other workers who had been employed to cut the grass for hay. The farmer showed them to the barn where he kept the tools, to the circular stone in the farmyard where they would sharpen the implements at the end of the day and then led the way to the first field.

Daniel picked up a scythe and followed the group. The men spread out across the field and began cutting the knee-high grass. There was not a cloud in the sky. By noon, the heat from the sun was almost unbearable. Daniel was sweating with exertion; his damp shirt stuck to his body, so he removed it and hung it over the field wall.

The farmer's wife brought jugs of ginger beer to the gate, and her daughter carried a tray of meat pasties, one for each of the workers. The men downed their tools and went to the gateway for their meal. Daniel noticed the women looking at the scars on his body, and he returned to grab his shirt and put it back on to cover them. Men never seemed to notice the marks from the severe beating he'd suffered, but women couldn't hide their looks of sympathy, and he hated that.

Bitterness flooded his veins. He had taken a dislike to a few people over the years, but he had never hated anyone until he met William Ashworth. He would never forgive William for what he'd done to Rose and himself. He was an evil man, yet nobody could see it. He hid it well under his tailored clothing and his air of authority that bordered on arrogance.

The men returned to work, and Daniel took out his anger and frustrations on the grass with his scythe. They had another short break in the mid-afternoon and then continued working until six o'clock in the evening. When they finished for the day, the exhausted men drifted back to the farmyard and sharpened their tools in readiness for the following day.

A couple of tables had appeared in the barn for the labourer's evening meal. Afterwards, they would bunk down on the remains of the previous year's hay for the night. It was the standard accommodation for itinerant farm workers.

That night, Daniel enjoyed a meal of boiled potatoes and chicken stew. When the farmer's wife returned to the barn to clear away the dishes, she carried a bundle of papers.

'If any of you read,' she said, 'I've brought some old newspapers and periodicals over. They might help to pass the time.'

A couple of the men stepped up to browse through the pile and took something to read. One of them sat next to Daniel and opened the newspaper he held. When the man turned the page, Daniel glanced at the paper and spotted a photograph of William Ashworth.

'Hey!' he said to the man, pointing at the photograph. 'I know this man. Can you tell me what it says about him, please?'

'I'll read it to you, if you want,' said the man. 'The story is from last year. It's dated July, 1882.'

Daniel nodded quickly, anxious to know why William's photograph was in the paper.

The man read the newspaper article in full:

'William Mitchell Esquire, aged twenty-nine years, originally from Scotland but lately a resident of Tow Law in this county, was found guilty at the Durham Assizes yesterday of the felonies of Bigamy and Serious Assault. Assuming the name of William Ashworth, Mitchell married the unsuspecting Miss Rose Lawson of Charlton Street, Tow Law last year when he was already married to Mrs Adeline Mitchell, née Campbell, from Muirkirk in Ayrshire, hereby committing Bigamy. Miss Rose Lawson was also the victim of Serious Assault at the hand of the said Mitchell, but as she believed she was his wife at the time, she did not inform the constable about his mistreatment or press charges against him. However, once she discovered that her marriage was not legally binding, she accused Mitchell of the crime. Mitchell was sentenced to four years imprisonment for the charge of Bigamy in the first instance and another four years for the charge of Serious Assault in the second. Mitchell will be incarcerated in Durham Gaol for a total of eight years for his devious and brutal crimes. Whilst sentencing the said Mitchell, Edward Armstrong-Harrison J.P., who presided in this case, declared that Mitchell should repay his wife, Mrs Adeline Mitchell, the sum of one hundred pounds that he had taken when he deserted her and their young son, and that his remaining savings amounting to the sum of six pounds should be split equally between his wife, Mrs Adeline Mitchell, and his victim, Miss Rose Lawson, the young woman he duped into marrying him and later assaulted on several occasions.'

Daniel raised his hand to his head and tried to take in what he had heard. He couldn't believe it. Rose was not married to William. She had never been. William had conned her into marriage and beaten her. He had witnessed that for himself, and he cringed when he remembered seeing her battered body when she'd removed her dress in the barn.

Considering their marriage was a sham, how had William had the nerve to track Rose down when she'd escaped to Yorkshire and reclaim her as his wife?

Then, when Daniel had followed them home and tried to speak to Rose, he'd almost been killed for it. At times, when he'd been laid in his bed for weeks on end afterwards, unable to move, he wished William's men had killed him because if he were dead, he would no longer miss Rose. And if they had killed him, William might have been hanged for his murder.

When Daniel finally recovered from his injuries and the terrifying paralysis, he abandoned Rose. Against his better judgment and his heart, he left her with William. He'd no reason at that time to doubt that William and Rose were man and wife; he'd seen them at the church after the wedding with his own eyes, and he hadn't suspected a thing.

Rose was single now—or at least she had been twelve months ago when the newspaper printed the story. Had she waited for him? Or had she given up on him returning for her and settled for another man?

He'd seen how her family shunned her when she returned from Yorkshire and didn't think she would receive any help from them. Where was she? How had she managed for the past year? Was she alone?

'You look miles away. Are you alright?' asked the man who had read the story to Daniel.

'Aye, I am, thank you,' said Daniel, 'but I can't stay here any longer.'

'Where are you going?' asked the man.

'Back to where I belong,' said Daniel with an enigmatic smile.

He went outside, knocked at the farmhouse door and asked to see the farmer. The middle-aged man came outside, smoking his pipe, and said, 'What is it?'

'I'm sorry to disturb you,' said Daniel. 'I've had news from home, and I need to go back.'

'But you've just been here the one day,' said the farmer, surprised to hear that Daniel wanted to leave so soon.

'I'm sorry,' said Daniel, 'but I need to leave right away.'

'Young men today,' said the farmer under his breath. 'I'll pay you what you're due and then you can be on your way.'

'Thank you,' said Daniel.

The farmer went indoors and returned shortly afterwards with some coins, which he handed Daniel.

'I'm going to Nottingham first thing in the morning,' said the farmer. 'I've got some vegetables to take to the market. I can give you a lift to the station if you want.'

'Thanks very much,' said Daniel. 'I'll be up at dawn.'

Daniel hardly slept that night. His mind went over and over everything he had learned from the newspaper article, and his overactive imagination invented all sorts of scenarios of what might have become of Rose since the trial. He pictured her destitute, dressed in rags and living in a workhouse, married to a widowed miner and looking after a dozen of his children, and getting on a train to leave Tow Law with no intention of ever returning. But if she left her home town, where would she go?

He had to return to Tow Law in the hope of finding her there, but he feared she might have moved on. With the three pounds awarded by the court, she could have travelled anywhere.

He tried to think logically. Rose had unwittingly been living in sin with William during their sham marriage. She was the victim in this case. Is that how the people of Tow Law would view the situation? Would they accept her back into their community after what had happened, or would they shun her, as her parents had?

After a disrupted night's sleep, Daniel rose before daybreak and watched the sunrise paint the sky the most beautiful shade of orange as he waited in the yard. The farmer left the house and nodded for Daniel to follow him. They went to another barn, and the farmer opened the double doors to reveal a large cart laden with farm produce. Then, he went to the stables and led out a large draught horse. Daniel helped harness the animal and attach it to the cart, and then they were on their way.

Daniel appreciated the ride to Nottingham, as it would have taken him hours to walk there. The farmer stopped the cart outside the station, and Daniel jumped down. He thanked the farmer and bought a ticket for the next train travelling north.

51

Chapter 51

Tow Law, County Durham
July, 1883

Four train journeys later, Daniel exited the carriage and stepped onto the platform at Tow Law Station in the late afternoon. He looked around, hoping to catch a glimpse of Rose in the town, but she was nowhere to be seen.

He walked briskly to Laburnum House, wondering if there was a chance she might still be there. He knocked at the door, and a young maid opened it.

'Does Miss Rose Lawson live here?' asked Daniel.

'No, sir,' she said. 'This is Mr and Mrs Jennings' house.'

'Do you know where Rose moved to when she left here?' he asked.

'I'm sorry, sir, I don't know anyone called Rose. I came here from Cramlington with Mr and Mrs Jennings last year.'

'Thank you,' said Daniel, turning away and wondering where to look next.

He decided to try her parents' house on Charlton Street. Ten minutes later, he knocked at the door, which Rose's mother answered. He had never liked Mrs Lawson and wished he'd thought to wait a while until her father returned from work. He seemed like a decent sort of fellow.

'I'm looking for Rose,' said Daniel. 'Is she here?'

'No, she's not!' said Jane. 'She's not been welcome under my roof since you had the bloody cheek to run off with her.'

'Do you know where she is?' he asked patiently. 'It's important that I see her.'

'If I did, I wouldn't tell the likes of you!' said Jane, slamming the door in his face.

He was not surprised by Mrs Lawson's reaction, but he was disappointed that he'd not found Rose or discovered where she was.

He wondered if Jimmy might still lodge with Mrs McKenna, and he knocked on the next door.

'Daniel!' said Mrs McKenna. 'What a surprise! Come on in, won't you? I've just made a fresh cup of tea. Will you have one?'

'Yes, please,' said Daniel, suddenly feeling thirsty and hungry. He had been so concerned with returning to Tow Law and finding Rose that he'd had nothing to eat that day.

Mrs McKenna brought another cup and saucer to the table in the front room and poured him a cup, then she brought an old battered biscuit tin, took off the lid, and he gladly took a slice of freshly baked cake from it.

It felt so good to be in a house that felt like a home. He hadn't seen Mrs McKenna since he'd left over a year and a half ago, yet she had welcomed him back like one of her own family.

'Your Jimmy will be pleased to see you,' she said. 'He's been worried sick about you.'

'I should have written to him,' said Daniel, thinking that if he had bothered to stay in touch with his cousin, he would have learned about Rose's sham marriage and William's prison sentence much sooner. 'Is Jimmy still staying here?'

'No, he's got himself a house now—and a wife!'

'He's married?' asked Daniel, shocked at the news.

'Aye, it was a few months ago,' said Mrs McKenna. 'They're living on the High Street, in the rooms above the pharmacy.'

Daniel finished the tea and the cake, thanked Mrs McKenna, and went to his cousin's house. A small woman with dark brown hair and delicate features opened the door. He introduced himself and discovered that she was Catherine, Jimmy's wife. She invited him in to wait for Jimmy, who she expected would be back from work soon.

About five minutes later, Jimmy came through the door, black with coal dust. He took a step back when he saw Daniel rise from a chair.

'Daniel!' he said, grinning. 'It's good to see you.'

He hugged his cousin firmly.

'Jimmy!' said Catherine. 'Stop that! You'll dirty his clothes.'

Jimmy released Daniel from his vice-like grip.

'Where have you been? What have you been doing? Why have you come back?' asked Jimmy, throwing questions at him in rapid succession like punches.

'One question at a time,' said Daniel, laughing.

'I'll tell you what,' said Jimmy. 'I'll have a wash, we'll have a bite to eat, and then you can tell me over a pint at O'Riley's.'

'That sounds like a good plan,' said Daniel, patting his cousin on his shoulder. There had been many changes in their lives since they'd last seen each other.

Jimmy washed, changed his clothes, and returned to the

front room carrying a package wrapped in paper and fastened with string. 'This is for you,' he said, handing it to Daniel.

Daniel took it, thanked his cousin and placed it in his travel bag.

Catherine served them a hearty meal of minced beef and dumplings with mashed potatoes. Daniel's stomach growled when she carried the plates to the table, and Jimmy told him to tuck in.

When they finished the meal, Daniel picked up his bag.

'What are you doing?' asked Jimmy. 'You'll be staying here with us tonight, and for as long as you need to, so put that down.'

'Thanks, Jimmy,' said Daniel, placing the bag in the corner of the room.

At O'Riley's, Jimmy told Daniel all about Catherine and their marriage. Then Daniel filled Jimmy in with what he'd been doing since he left Tow Law and finished by telling him about the newspaper article he'd seen the night before.

'Aye, that was a bad business. Hard to believe, really,' said Jimmy, shaking his head. 'I went to the court as a witness.'

'Do you know where Rose is now?' asked Daniel.

'Aye, I do,' said Jimmy, raising his eyebrows.

'Are you going to tell me?' asked Daniel.

'Is it worth another pint?' asked Jimmy mischievously.

'It's worth a hell of a lot more than that, and you know it,' said Daniel sternly.

'Sorry, Daniel, I was just teasing,' said Jimmy. 'Rose is staying with Mrs Newton, her old housekeeper. They live on Weardale Street. Her house is the last one at the end of the row.'

'Thank you, Jimmy,' said Daniel, getting to his feet.

'You're not going there now, are you?' asked his cousin.

'Aye, I am,' said Daniel. 'I'm not wasting another minute.'

'Good luck to you, then!' said Jimmy, raising his glass.

Daniel half walked and half ran to the row of cottages on the edge of the town, and when he reached it, he paused for a minute and looked around. Weardale Street was a quaint row of stone-built houses. They weren't back-to-back houses like some streets in the mining town. A narrow lane ran in front of the row, edged with long grass and meadow flowers. The aspect was pleasant and quiet, and the views were spectacular.

So, this was where Rose had been for the last year, living with the kind lady who had helped them to escape. Tentatively, he walked to the last house and knocked at the door.

Rose stood on the threshold, her eyes wide.

'Daniel?' she whispered in disbelief.

'Hello, Rose,' he said. 'Aye, it's me. I came as soon as I heard what happened.'

'Daniel,' she said again before rushing into his arms and clinging to him. He held her firmly, never wanting to let go of her again.

They stood together for several minutes before she released her hold, took a step back and said, 'You'd better come in.'

He followed her into the front room, sat beside her on a small settee, and took her hands in his. He gently kissed her lips. They jumped apart when they heard footsteps coming down the stairs, and then Mrs Newton opened the door and entered the room.

'She took a while to settle,' said Mrs Newton, 'but she's asleep now.'

When she saw Daniel, her face showed her surprise.

'Mr Kelly,' she said. 'We weren't expecting you.'

'I'm sorry for coming without letting you know,' said Daniel. 'I just found out about everything that happened last night and wanted to get here as soon as I could.'

'I'll take a book upstairs and sit with the bairn for a bit,' said Mrs Newton. 'I'm sure you two have a lot to talk about.'

When she left, Daniel looked quizzically at Rose.

'A bairn?' he asked. 'Is she yours?'

Knowing that Daniel might not want her when he knew she had another man's child, Rose looked down and said, 'Aye, she's mine.'

When he said nothing, she looked up into his eyes, which looked lost.

'And William's,' he said bitterly. 'I could throttle him for what he's done to you.'

'William is in Durham Gaol and he'll be there for another seven years. He can't do anything to hurt me—or you.'

'Did you ever feel anything for him?' asked Daniel, wondering why he'd asked the question when he dreaded to hear the answer.

'No!' said Rose. 'My heart was yours long before I met William.'

'When I declared my love for you, you turned your back on me,' he said, looking pained. 'We have the same obstacles to face now that we did back then when you told me we couldn't be together.'

'No, Daniel. They're not the same obstacles,' said Rose, shaking her head. 'I don't care what my mother thinks any more, or anyone else for that matter, and I would convert to any religion on the planet right now if it meant I could spend the rest of my life with you.'

Taking her hands in his, he said, 'I had a lot of time to think on the way here. Neither of us needs to change our religion.'

'I'm sorry, Daniel, but I can't live with you if we're not married,' said Rose. 'I know I did before, but I've got a daughter to think about now.'

'I wasn't suggesting that we live in sin, Rose,' said Daniel. 'What I meant was that we could go to Gretna Green and get married there. They don't care if people are Catholic or Protestant—they'll marry any couple who love each other and want to get wed.'

Tears of joy filled Rose's eyes as she asked, 'When can we go?'

52

Chapter 52

Tow Law, County Durham
July, 1883

When Daniel left the house that evening, Rose hugged herself and grinned. She had never felt so happy.

'I thought I heard the door latch,' said Mrs Newton, standing at the bottom of the stairs. 'Has he gone?'

'Aye,' said Rose, still smiling. 'He's coming back first thing in the morning.'

'Oh!' said Mrs Newton. 'Did everything go alright?'

'Better than alright,' said Rose. 'Much better. Tomorrow, we're going to Gretna Green and we're going to get married.'

'Congratulations!' said Mrs Newton, hugging Rose. 'He was always a better match for you than that other one.'

'William was the easy option at the time,' said Rose, sitting on the sofa, reflecting on the past. 'Even then, it was Daniel I loved. I don't know why I didn't fight for him. I should have. I guess it was mainly because of my mother. I saw how she severed all ties with Hannah McKenna, who is her Goddaughter because she married a Catholic man, and with them living next door to each other, I lived with that feud for years.'

'You should always follow your heart in life,' said Mrs Newton, who sat down beside her, 'even if it's not the easiest path.'

'I wish I'd had you to advise me back then,' said Rose, smiling fondly at the older lady.

'You can leave Lydia here with me for a few days if you want,' said Mrs Newton, 'so you and Daniel can have some time to yourselves.'

'Thank you,' said Rose. 'That's very thoughtful.'

'I thank God for sending you and Lydia to me,' said Mrs Newton. 'I was a bitter old woman dwelling on my past. My husband, I told you about. My eldest son went to Middles-brough to work at the ironworks there. I heard he's married and has some children. I don't know how many. My youngest son moved to Newcastle and got a job at the lead works up there. I don't know if he has a family or not. I haven't seen or heard from either of them since they left. I was a sad and lonely old woman until you came into my life.'

'We won't leave you,' said Rose, with a tear in her eye. 'I promise.'

Rose seemed to have gained a parent figure exactly when she needed one, and Mrs Newton had gained a daughter.

'Get up to bed before you set me off,' said Mrs Newton, pushing Rose playfully. 'Goodnight, dear.'

The following day, Daniel was up early. He washed quickly, grabbed his bag and left Jimmy's flat at first light. He couldn't wait to see Rose again. Soon, they would be man and wife, and he vowed never to leave her again. While they had been apart, he realised that being separated from her was worse than death.

Mrs Newton opened the door to him and invited him into the house, and seconds later, Rose came downstairs carrying her daughter.

'Daniel,' she said, 'this is Lydia.'

'I'm pleased to make your acquaintance, Miss Lydia,' said Daniel formally with a bow, and then took her small hand and kissed it.

Lydia giggled at his antics.

'I think you've made a good first impression,' said Rose, laughing. 'Mrs Newton has offered to look after her while we're away.'

'That's very kind,' said Daniel.

'You are sure about this, aren't you?' asked Rose. 'It's not just me that you're taking on now, it's Lydia as well.'

'I've never been more certain about anything in my life,' said Daniel seriously.

'Come on then,' said Rose, smiling up at him. 'Let's go!'

Rose handed her child to Mrs Newton and said farewell to them both. She joined Daniel at the door, and they walked hand in hand to the railway station, receiving more than a few surprised looks from people they passed on the way.

They travelled by rail to the tiny village of Gretna Green, just north of the Scottish border, changing trains at several stations. For the whole journey, they chatted, catching up on everything they had missed while apart and learning more about each other.

When they arrived, they went to the blacksmith's shop to arrange their wedding. Much to their delight, they were told it could take place the following morning.

They found a small inn, where Daniel booked a room for the night and ordered food for them to eat in their room. The meal was beef pie with peas and gravy. It tasted good, but neither had much appetite, even though they had eaten little during the journey to Scotland.

Daniel had a glass of ale with his meal, and Rose had a glass of wine. They sat by the low fire, sipping their drinks.

'I know you won't officially be my wife until tomorrow, Rose,' said Daniel, his eyes dark and his voice low, 'but would you mind if I shared your bed tonight?'

'I'd be upset if you didn't,' said Rose, standing up, wrapping her arms around Daniel's body and looking up into his eyes. 'We've waited so long to be together, I don't want to wait another minute.'

Daniel lowered his head and kissed her lovingly. Then, he helped her to undress and carried her to the double bed in the centre of the room, where they made love for the first time.

Hours later, Rose lay in Daniel's arms, ecstatically happy. Spending the night with Daniel had been far better than she'd imagined. More than anything, she wanted to be his wife and spend the rest of her days with him. Daniel completed her.

The following morning, the couple had breakfast at the inn and returned to their room to prepare for the wedding ceremony.

Daniel took a package from his travel bag and said, 'This is for you, Rose.'

Wondering what was in the parcel, Rose untied the string and unwrapped the paper to reveal a red satin dress—the same dress she had admired in the shop window. She gasped in delight as she unfolded it and held it up in front of her.

'You were the young man who bought it?' she asked. 'But

how could you afford it?'

'Our Jimmy bought it for me,' said Daniel. 'That night, when I went for him to tend your wounds, I gave him my winnings from his fights and asked him to buy it. I hoped that one day I'd be able to give it to you.'

'Thank you so much, Daniel,' she said sincerely, delighted to hear that he'd been so sure they would have a future together that he'd bought her the dress. 'It's a wonderful gift.'

Rose couldn't believe the dress she'd longed to wear so many times was actually hers. She was grinning from ear to ear.

'I hated myself for crushing your dreams back then,' he said. 'I wanted to prove to you that dreams can come true.'

Rose placed the dress over the back of a chair and wrapped her arms around Daniel.

'I didn't need the dress to know that,' she said, kissing his lips. 'Having you here with me is enough.'

They held each other tightly.

'Come on. It's time to get dressed,' said Daniel, smiling at her. 'We have a wedding to go to.'

THE END

Author's Historical Notes

Tow Law (tow is pronounced to rhyme with cow) is a small town on a hilltop in County Durham. Today, Tow Law is very different from the industrial town it used to be in the late nineteenth century.

Originally a landscape dotted with small farms, the town began to develop when the Weardale Iron Company built its ironworks there in 1845. Iron ore was brought by rail from Weardale, and the coking coal to fire the furnaces was mined in and around Tow Law. A year later, the company changed its name to the Weardale Iron and Coal Company.

Many mines were sunk in the area because the coal seams were close to the surface. Black Prince Colliery opened in 1849, employing up to seven hundred and fifty men and boys at its height, and closed in 1933. Work at the Inkerman Colliery began later, in 1873. The pit was named after the Battle of Inkerman, which took place during the Crimean War, for which the Weardale Iron and Coal Company supplied the cannonballs. The mine closed in 1969.

The population at Tow Law peaked at five thousand in 1881. The Weardale Iron and Coal Company's ironworks closed in 1882, and around one thousand people moved to the village of Tudhoe, near Spennymoor, where the company owned another large ironworks. The sudden loss of a fifth of the population must have had a dramatic impact on the town.

The closure of this ironworks was not the end of ironworking at Tow Law. Bond's Foundry, which opened in 1868, fared much better and continued working into the twenty-first century.

Until the middle of the nineteenth century, the southern part of Tow Law was in the ancient parish of Wolsingham, and the northern part was in the parish of Satley. The Anglican church dedicated to St. Philip and St. James opened in Tow Law in 1867. A temporary Roman Catholic church known as St. Thomas's was built in the 1860s, but as the Catholic church at Wolsingham was also called St. Thomas's, the name was changed to St. Joseph's in 1872 to avoid confusion. The current Roman Catholic Church of St. Joseph's opened in 1876. There was also a Presbyterian Church, a Wesleyan Methodist Chapel and a Primitive Methodist Chapel in the town.

The National School was established in Tow Law in 1849, but education was not compulsory for children aged from five to ten years in England until 1880. Many children would not have attended school and would have been unable to read and write. The Roman Catholic School was opened in 1870, with nine Sisters of Mercy from the convent of St. Joseph as teachers.

Several years ago, Chris Lloyd wrote in *The Northern Echo* that Tow Law had "a reputation for being uncouth, a gamblers' den of iniquity". In a town where men worked long hours in dangerous conditions, there were many public houses in which to spend their free time socialising and drinking alcohol. Planned and unplanned fights would have been a regular occurrence on the streets of Tow Law, and betting would have been commonplace.

Football plays a small part in my novel, but it has been important to the people of Tow Law since at least the 1880s.

The vicar of St. Philip and St. James Church was the team captain in 1881. In 1890, the Tow Law Football Club was formed and still plays as Tow Law Town Football Club in the Northern League.

Tow Law is renowned for its inclement weather. Situated on a hill over one thousand feet above sea level, Tow Law is exposed to the elements. It is frequently windy, and at the time of writing, several wind farms surround the town. In past winters, severe snowfalls resulted in drifts reaching the roofs of two-storey houses. Perhaps the worst winter was in 1947 when the town was cut off for over six weeks. Even now, the road at Tow Law is usually the first section of the A68 to be closed in winter due to drifting snow.

Margaret Manchester
    September, 2024

About the Author

Best-selling author Margaret Manchester was born in Weardale, County Durham, England. She developed a strong interest in family and local history from a young age. She discovered many of her ancestors had lived and worked in the area for centuries, either as miners, smelters, or farmers.

Margaret studied local history and archaeology at the University of Durham and was awarded a Master's in Archaeology. She then taught archaeology, local history and genealogy.

Margaret still lives in County Durham with her husband. In addition to writing, she is the director of an award-winning family business, and she enjoys spending time in her garden, with her dogs, and cooking.

You can connect with me on:

- https://www.margaretmanchester.com
- https://twitter.com/m_r_manchester
- https://www.facebook.com/margaretmanchesterauthor
- https://www.instagram.com/margaret_manchester

Also by Margaret Manchester

The Lead Miner's Daughter (Weardale Series, Book 1)
Historical Family Saga Novel

Amazon #1 International Bestseller

Northern England, 1872. Mary Watson, a lead miner's daughter, leaves her childhood home to work at Springbank Farm. She soon meets a handsome neighbour, Joe Milburn, and becomes infatuated with him, but is he the right man for her?

Mary's story is woven into a background of rural life and crime in the remote valley of Weardale. Not one but two murders shock the small community.

Find yourself in the farmhouse kitchen with the Peart family, walking on the wide-open fells, seeking shelter underground and solving crimes with PC Emerson as this intriguing story unfolds.

Will the culprits be brought to justice? And will Mary find true love?

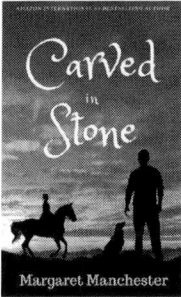

Carved in Stone (Weardale Series, Book 2)
Historical Family Saga Novel

Amazon #1 UK Bestseller

Northern England, 1881. Sent away during her brother's trial, Phyllis Forster returns home after a seven-year absence to find the Weardale people have turned against the Forster family and she desperately wants to win back their respect. Can trust and harmony be restored in this rural community?

At twenty-eight years of age, she has almost given up hope of love and marriage and throws herself into the management of the family estate until two very different men come into her life.

Ben, troubled by the past and full of anger and distrust, is a shepherd who shuns the company of others until his new boss arrives at Burnside Hall.

Timothy, the new vicar, is preoccupied with the ancient past, but he takes a keen interest in Phyllis.

Will she settle for just a husband? Or will she defy convention and follow her heart?

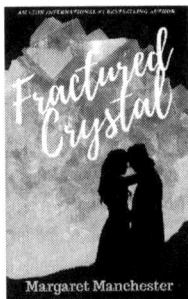

Fractured Crystal (Weardale Series, Book 3)
Historical Family Saga Novel

Northern England, 1895. Josie Milburn meets Elliott Dawson, a man who shares her interest in collecting crystals. Defying an age-old superstition, Elliott takes Josie into a lead mine, an action that sets off a sequence of dramatic events, beginning with a miner's death the same day.

Elliott and Josie face a series of trials involving tragic loss and the unveiling of family secrets, which change their lives and fortunes in ways that they could never have imagined.

Will these traumatic circumstances bind them together or break them apart?

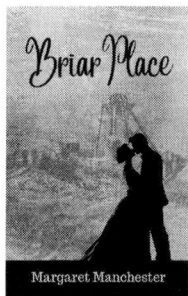

Briar Place (Weardale Series, Prequel)
Historical Family Saga Novel

Amazon #1 UK Bestseller

Northern England, 1849. A dispute between the lead miners and Mr Sopwith brings about a strike with disastrous consequences. Loyalties are tested, blacklegs punished and families divided.

At Briar Place, the Dixon and Lowery families were friends and neighbours, but not any more. Jack and Bella are caught in their feud. Will their relationship end in heartbreak or can love conquer all?

When the repercussions of the strike finally come to an end, seventeen-year-old Lizzie Lowery is left to pick up the pieces.

A compelling family saga set during the historic miners' strike at Allenheads in 1849.

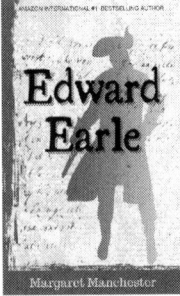

Edward Earle

Historical Novel

The Story of an 18th-century Orphan Boy.

Northern England, 1757. When tragedy befalls him, Edward Earle spends five years in a Sunderland orphanage, where he befriends Tommy Bell. As a young man, Edward vows to spend his life helping orphans, but he needs money for his mission, and he and Tommy turn to a life of crime to fund it. His only regret is that his chosen path leads him away from the woman he loves.

Edward is hurt by the betrayal that led to his capture and spends his time in Durham Gaol reflecting on the past. Facing the death penalty for highway robbery, he prays for a second chance.

Can Edward escape the hangman's noose, put right his wrongs, and find what he truly wants?

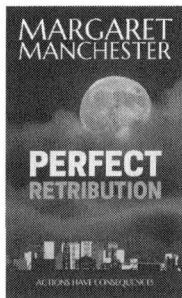

Perfect Retribution

Contemporary Psychological Suspense Thriller

Actions Have Consequences

Dan Howard posts a scathing review of a local business. When the owners refuse to pay compensation, Dan launches a vindictive online campaign to ruin their reputation. What he doesn't realise is that his actions have real-world effects.

James Webster, a quiet shop assistant caught in the crossfire, sees his life unravel as the attack escalates. Pushed to the edge, James begins to plot revenge—methodical, personal, and chillingly precise.

As their lives collide, a spiral of obsession and retribution unfolds. How far will James go? And at what cost?

Killhope Man

Non Fiction: Investigation of a Historical Mystery

In 1921, a body was found in a peat bog on an English moor, sparking a romantic legend of a fallen Jacobite soldier. Almost a century later, local archaeologist and author, Margaret Manchester, embarks on a meticulous investigation to unravel the truth. By dismantling myths and re-examining every clue—from clothing buttons to the shape of the coffin—she pieces together a compelling new identity for the mysterious Killhope Man, revealing his story.

Printed in Dunstable, United Kingdom

72546010R00172